WHEN THE DEVIL HOLDS
THE CANDLE

Karin Fossum made her literary debut in Norway in 1974. The author of poetry, short stories and one non-crime novel, it is with her Inspector Sejer mysteries that Fossum has won the greatest acclaim. Awarded the Glass Key for the best Nordic crime novel, *Don't Look Back* was the first to be translated into English, followed by *He Who Fears the Wolf*. The Sejer mysteries are currently published in sixteen languages.

ALSO BY KARIN FOSSUM

Karin Fossum

WHEN THE DEVIL HOLDS THE CANDLE

Translated from the
Norwegian by Felicity David

VINTAGE BOOKS
London

Published by Vintage 2005

6 8 10 9 7

Copyright © J.W. Cappelens Forlag, A.S. 1998
English translation copyright © Felicity David 2004

Karin Fossum has asserted her right under the Copyright,
Designs and Patents Act 1988 to be identified as the author
of this work

Originally published with the title *Djevelen holder lyset*
By J.W. Cappelens Forlag, A.S., Oslo, 1998

First published in Great Britain in 2004 by
The Harvill Press

Vintage
Random House, 20 Vauxhall Bridge Road,
London SW1V 2SA

www.vintage-books.co.uk

Addresses for companies within The Random House Group Limited
can be found at:
www.randomhouse.co.uk/offices.htm

The Random House Group Limited Reg. No. 954009

A CIP catalogue record for this book is available
from the British Library

This edition has been published with the financial assistance
of NORLA

ISBN 9780099461128

The Random House Group Limited supports The Forest Stewardship
Council (FSC), the leading international forest certification orginisation
All our titles that are printed on Greenpeace approved FSC certified paper
carry the FSC logo. Our paper procurement policy can be found at:
www.rbooks.co.uk/environment

Typeset by SX Composing DTP, Rayleigh, Essex
Printed and bound in Great Britain by
Cox & Wyman Ltd, Reading, Berkshire

With thanks to Terje Ringstad and Tor Buxrud

If you had never existed, you wouldn't have read this.

And it wouldn't have made any difference. And when you no longer exist, it will be as if you had never read this. It makes no difference. But now, as you are reading, something happens: it eats up a few seconds of your time, like a tiny gnawing animal, furry with letters, blocking the path between you and your next minute. You will never get it back.

Undisturbed, it chews on the micro-organisms of time. It never gets its fill.

Nor do you.

– Tor Ulven

CHAPTER 1

The courthouse. September 4, 4 p.m.

Jacob Skarre glanced at his watch. His shift was over. He slipped a book out of his inside jacket pocket and read the poem on the first page. It's like playing Virtual Reality, he thought. Poof! – and you're in a different landscape. The door to the corridor stood open, and suddenly he was aware that someone was watching him. Whoever it was was just beyond what he could see with his excellent peripheral vision. A vibration, light as a feather, barely perceptible, finally reached him. He closed his book.

"Can I help you?"

This woman didn't move, just stood there staring at him with an odd expression. Skarre looked at her tense face and thought that she seemed familiar. She was no longer young, maybe about 60, wearing a coat and dark boots. A scarf around her neck. Enough of the pattern was discernible under her chin. The design seemed a sharp contrast to what she most likely possessed in the way of speed and elegance: racehorses with jockeys in colourful silks against a dark blue background. She had a wide, heavy face that was elongated by a prominent chin. Her eyebrows were dark and had grown almost together. She was clutching a handbag against her stomach. But most noticeable of all was her gaze. In that pale face her eyes were blazing. They fixed him with a tremendous force and he could not escape them. Then he remembered who she was. What an odd coincidence, he thought, and waited in suspense. He sat there as if riveted by the probing silence. Any moment now she was going to say something momentous.

"It has to do with a missing person," was what she said.

Her voice was rough. A rusty tool creaking into motion after a long repose. Behind her white forehead burned a fire. Skarre could see the flickering glow in her irises. He was trying not to make assumptions, but obviously she was in some way possessed. Gradually it came to him what sort of person he was dealing with. In his mind he rehearsed the day's reports, but he could not recall whether any patients had been listed as missing from the psychiatric institutes in the district. She was breathing hard, as if it had cost her immeasurable effort to come here. But she had made up her mind, and at last had been driven by something. Skarre wondered how she had made it past the reception area and Mrs Brenningen's eagle eye, coming straight to his office without anyone stopping her.

"Who is it that's missing?" he asked in a friendly voice.

She kept staring at him. He met her gaze with the same force to see if she would flinch. Her expression turned to one of confusion.

"I know where he is."

Skarre was startled. "So you know where he is? He's not missing, then?"

"He probably won't live much longer," she said. Her thin lips began to quiver.

"Who are we talking about?" Skarre said. And then, because he guessed who it might be. "Do you mean your husband?"

"Yes. My husband."

She nodded resolutely. Stood there, straight-backed and unmoving, her handbag still pressed to her stomach. Skarre leaned back in his chair.

"Your husband is sick, and you're worried about him. Is he old?"

It was an inappropriate question. Life is life, as long as a person is alive and means something, maybe everything, to another being. He regretted the question and picked up his pen from the desk, twirling it between his fingers.

"He's almost like a child," she said sadly.

He was surprised at her response. What was she really talking about? The man was sick, possibly dying. And senile, it occurred to him. Regressing to his

3

childhood. At the same time Skarre had a strange feeling that she was trying to tell him something else. Her coat was threadbare at the lapels, and the middle button had been sewn on rather badly, creating a fold in the fabric. Why am I noticing these things? he thought.

"Do you live far from here?" He glanced at his watch. Perhaps she could afford a taxi.

She straightened her shoulders. "Prins Oscars gate 17." She enunciated the street name with crisp consonants. "I didn't mean to bother you," she said.

Skarre stood up. "Do you need help getting home?"

She was still staring into his eyes. As if there was in them something that she wanted to take away with her. A glow, a memory of something very much alive, which the young officer was. Skarre had a weird sensation, the sort of thing that happens only rarely, when the body reacts on impulse. He lowered his gaze and saw that the short blond hairs on his arms were standing on end. At the same moment the woman turned slowly around and walked to the door. She took short, awkward steps, as if she were trying to hide something. He went back to his chair. It was 4.03 p.m. For his amusement, he scribbled a few notes on his pad.

"A woman of about 60 arrives at the office at 4 p.m. She seems confused. Says her husband is missing, that he doesn't have long to live. Wearing a brown coat

4

with a blue scarf at her neck. Brown handbag, black boots. Possibly mentally disturbed. Left after a few minutes. Refused offer of help to get home."

He sat there, turning her visit over in his mind. Probably she was just a lost soul; there were so many of them nowadays. After a while he folded the piece of paper and stuck it into his shirt pocket. The incident didn't belong in his daily report.

*

HAS ANYONE SEEN ANDREAS? That was the headline in the town's largest newspaper, set in bold type. That's the way newspapers express themselves, using an informal tone to address us directly, as if we were on first-name terms and have known each other a long time. We're supposed to break down the barriers of formality and use a straightforward, youthful tone, in this fresh, onward-storming society. So even though very few people actually knew him or used his first name, let's just cut right to the chase and ask: Has anyone seen Andreas?

And the picture of him. A nice-looking boy of 18, with a thin face and unruly hair. I say "nice-looking", I'm generous enough to admit that. So handsome that things came easily to him. He strutted around with that handsome face of his and took things for granted. It's a familiar pattern, but it does no-one any good to look like that. Handsome in a timeless, classic sense. A charming boy. It costs me a bit to use that word, but all the same . . . charming.

On the afternoon of September 1, he left his house on Cappelens gate. He said nothing about where he was off to. Where are you going? Out. That's the kind of answer you give at that age. A sort of infinite guardedness. You think you're somebody so exceptional. And his mother didn't have the sense to press him. Maybe she used his obstinacy as food for her martyrdom. Her son was in the process of leaving her, and she hated that fact. But it's really a matter of respect. She ought to have raised the boy so that it would be unthinkable for him not to reply in a polite and precise manner. I'm going out, well, with someone. We're thinking of going into town. I'll be home before midnight. Surely that's not too much to ask, is it? But she had failed, as have so many others. That's what happens when you invest all of your energy in yourself, your own life, your own sorrow. I know what I'm talking about. And the sorrow was going to get worse. He never came home.

Yes, I've seen Andreas. I can see him whenever I like. A lot of people are going to be surprised when he's finally found. And of course they'll speculate, they'll guess, and write up reports, and carry on discussions and fill numerous files. Everyone with his own theory. And all wrong, of course. People howl with many voices. In the midst of that din I've lived in silence for almost 60 years. My name is Irma. At last I'm the one who's doing the talking. I won't take much time, and I'm not saying that I have a monopoly on the truth. But what you're reading now is my version.

A childhood memory comes back to me. I can summon it up whenever I like. I'm standing in the porch with one hand on the door knob. It's quiet inside, but I know that they're there. Yet there's not a sound to be heard. I open the door very quietly and walk into the kitchen. Mother is standing at the counter, lifting the skin from a boiled mackerel. I can still recreate the smell in my nose, a cloying, unpleasant odour. She shifts her heavy body a little, indicating vaguely that she has noticed my presence. Father is busy over by the window. He's pressing putty into the cracks in the frame to keep the draught out. It's an old house. The putty is white and soft like clay, with a dry, chalk-like smell. My two sisters are sitting at the kitchen table, both busy with books and papers. I remember that pale, almost nauseating light when the sun cast its yellow rays into the green kitchen. I'm maybe six years old. Instinctively I'm scared of making any noise. I stand there, all alone, and stare at them. They're all busy with something. I feel very useless, almost in the way, as if I'd been born too late. I often thought I might have been an accident that they were unable to stop. There are two years between my sisters. I came along eight years later. What could have made my mother want another child after such a long time? But the idea that I might have been an unloved obligation makes me miserable. I've had it for so long, it's a well-worn idea.

This memory is so real that I can feel the hem of my dress tickling my knee. I'm standing in the yellowish-green light and noticing how alone I am. No-one says hello. I'm the youngest. Not doing anything important. I don't mean that my father should have stopped what he was doing, maybe lifted me up and tossed me in the air. I was too heavy for him. He had rheumatism, and I was big and chubby, with bones like a horse. That's what mother used to say. Like a horse. It was just Irma who had come in. Nothing to make a fuss about. Their heads turning imperceptibly, in case it was someone important, and then discovering that it was only Irma. We were here first, their looks said.

Their indifference took my breath away. I had the same feeling as when I persuaded Mother to tell me about when I was born. And she shrugged, but admitted that it had happened in the middle of the night, during a terrible storm. Thunder and a fierce wind. It made me happy to think that I had arrived in the world with a crash and a roar. But then she added, with a dry laugh, that the whole thing was over in a matter of minutes. You slid right out like a kitten, she said, and my good feeling drained away.

I waited, my knees locked, my feet planted on the floor. I'd been gone for quite a while, after all. Anything could have happened. We lived near the sea, didn't we? Ships from other countries regularly docked in the harbour. Sailors swarmed through the streets, staring at anyone over the age of ten. Well, I was six, but I was as sturdy as a horse, as I mentioned. Or I could have been lying with a broken leg or arm on the pavement near Gartnerhall, where we often played on the flat roof. Later, three Alsatians stood guard up there, but before that happened we used to play on the roof there, and I might have fallen over the edge. Or I could have been crushed under the wheels of a big lorry. Sometimes they have 20 tyres, and not even my big bones would survive that. But they were never worried. Not about things like that. About other things, yes. If I was holding an apple, had someone given it to me? I hadn't pinched it, had I? No? Well, did I thank them nicely? Had they asked me to say hello to my mother and father?

My brain was churning over to think up some kind of task. Some way that I could make my way into the companionship that I felt they shared. Not

9

that they turned me away, just that they didn't invite me in. I'll tell you one thing: those four people shared an aura. It was strong and clear, and reddish-brown, and it hardly flickered at all, the way it does for the rest of us. It was wrapped around them as tightly as a barrel hoop, and I was on the outside, enveloped in a colourless fog. The solution was to do something! The person who is doing something cannot be overlooked, but I couldn't think of anything. I didn't have any homework because this was before I had started school. That's why I just stood there, staring. At the boiled mackerel, at all the books lying around. At Father, who was working carefully and quietly. If only he would have given me a piece of that white putty! To roll between my fingers.

For a paralysing second I was struck by something that I think is important; important in order to explain both to myself and to you, who are reading this, how it could happen. The whole thing with Andreas. I suddenly became aware of the tremendous set of rules governing that room. In the silence, in the hands that were working, in the closed faces. A set of rules I had to submit to and follow to the letter. I was still standing in the silence of the kitchen, I felt that set of rules descend on me like a cage from the ceiling. And it struck me with enormous force: within that set of rules I was invulnerable! Within that clear framework of diligence and propriety, no-one could touch me. The concept of "within" meant the possibility of being around people without anyone looking askance, without offending anybody, and at the same time feeling a sense of peace because you were like everyone else. You thought the same way. But in my mind I saw a narrow street with high walls. It was to be my life. And a terrible sadness overwhelmed me. Until that moment I might have believed in Freedom, the way children do; they believe that anything is possible. But I made a decision, even though I was so young and might not have understood it all. I obeyed a primeval instinct for survival. I didn't want to be alone. I'd rather be like them and follow the rules. But something departed at that instant – it rose up and flew off and it vanished for ever. That's why I remember the moment so clearly. There in the kitchen, in the yellow-green light, at the age of six, I lost my freedom.

That silent, well-mannered child. In Christmas and birthday pictures I'm sitting on my mother's knee and looking at the camera with a pious smile. Now I have an iron jaw that shoots pain up into my temples. How could things have ended up this way? No doubt there are many different reasons, and some of it can be put down to pure coincidence, the fact that our paths crossed on one particular evening. But what about the actual crime? The impulse itself, where does that come from? When does murder occur? In such and such a place, at such and such a moment in time? In this case I can share the blame with circumstance. The fact that he stepped into my path, that he was the sort of person he was. Because with him I was no longer Irma. I was Irma with Andreas. And that was not the same as Irma with Ingemar. Or Irma with Runi. Chemistry, you know. Each time a new formula is created. Irma and Andreas destroyed each other. Is that true? Does it emerge over a period of years? Does the crime lie dormant in the body's individual coding? Is the murder a result of a long, inevitable process? Of necessity, I have to view my life in the light of the horrible thing that happened, and I have to view that horrible thing in the light of what has been my life. Which is what everyone around me will do. They'll look in my past life for something that could explain whatever part of it can be explained. The rest will be left to float in a grey sea of theories.

But to get back to the past: I was standing there, in the silence of the kitchen. My wordless presence made the silence shrill. It had felt so beautiful, but now they couldn't stand it any more. Mother turned around and crossed the room. She bent down and sniffed at my hair.

"Your hair needs washing," she said. "It smells."

For a moment I considered going to fetch my art supplies. I could smell the oily scent of the pastels I liked to use. But I left the kitchen, went out to the garden, over the fence, past the abandoned smithy and into the woods. Among the spruce trees there was a pleasant, grey-green darkness. I was wearing brown sandals, and on the dry path I came across an ant hill. I poked at it with a twig, gleeful at the chaos I was able to create, a catastrophe in that well-ordered society that might take weeks to repair. The desire to destroy! The feeling of joyous power as I scraped inside that ant hill with the twig. It felt good. I looked around for something to feed them. A dead mouse, something like that. Then I could have stood there and watched while they devoured it. They would have dropped everything and forgotten about the catastrophe; having something to devour would come first, I was sure of that. But I didn't find anything, so I kept on walking. I came to a derelict farmhouse, sat down on the front steps, and thought about the story of the people who once lived there. Gustav and Inger and their twelve children. Uno, Sekunda, Trevor, Firmin, Femmer, Sexus, Syver, Otto, Nils, Tidemann, Ellef and Tollef. It was incomprehensible, nevertheless true: none of them is now alive.

Yes. The God that I don't believe in knows that

I've seen Andreas. I think back to that terrifying moment when I felt it coming, the desire to destroy him. At the same instant I saw my own face reflected in a windowpane. And I remember the feeling, a sweet pressure, like warm oil running through my body. The certainty that this was evil. My face in the bluish glass. The hideous, evil person you become when the Devil holds the candle.

14

CHAPTER 2

September 1.

A boy was walking through the streets alone. He was wearing jeans and a Nike jacket, black with an olive green yoke and a red-and-white swoosh on the back. They were expecting him home by 6 p.m. He might make it. A faint glow from a hazy sky hovered over the town. The wind was picking up. It was September and perhaps a bit melancholy, but that's not what he was thinking. Up until now life had been good.

The boy was about seven, thin and nice-looking. He was walking along with his hands in his pockets. In one pocket there was a bag of sweets. He had been walking for 15 minutes and had begun to sweat inside his jacket.

He raised a hand to wipe his forehead. His skin was the colour of coffee. His hair was thick and curly and black, and his eyes flashed in his dark face.

Then, behind him, a car turned into the street. In the car were two men, peering out of the windows.

They both felt that right now life was very boring. This town wasn't exactly brimming with surprises. It just sat there, split in half by a grey river, content with its mediocrity. The car was a green Golf. The owner went by the nickname of Zipp. He was named for the sound of a zip opening in the fly of a tight pair of jeans, or more specifically, one being opened with trembling fingers and blazing cheeks. His real name was Sivert Skorpe. Zipp had blond, wiry hair, and his young face always had an inquisitive expression. Bordering on sheep-like, some might say, though he usually had luck with the ladies. He wasn't bad-looking, and besides, he was gentle, playful and simple. Not entirely without depth, but he never turned his thoughts inward, and that's why he lived his life oblivious to what existed deep inside. His companion looked like a faun, or something else from a fairy tale. He didn't try to compete. He seemed to have set himself above the chase, as if the girls should come to him, or something like that. Zipp could never understand it. He was driving at a leisurely pace. Both were silently hoping for the same thing, that something would happen. Then they caught sight of the boy.

"Stop!" said the passenger.

"What the hell. Why?" Zipp grunted and stepped on the brake. He didn't like trouble.

"I just want to have a little chat."

"Shit, Andreas. He's just a kid."

"A little black kid! I'm bored."

He wound down the window.

"You're not going to find any money on that brat. And it's money we need. I'm as thirsty as hell."

The car drew up beside the boy. He cast them a glance and then looked away. It wasn't good to look people in the eye. Or dogs. Instead he fixed his gaze on his shoes and didn't slow his pace.

"Hey, Pops!"

A young man with reddish-brown curls was staring at him from the car window. Should he answer? The man was grown-up. The car was following him.

"Helluva a nice jacket you've got." The man nodded with admiration. "And it's a Nike! Your dad must make good money, right?"

"My grandfather gave it to me," the boy muttered.

"If you were a size bigger, I'd swipe it from you," the man said, laughing. "But it'd be a bit tight on me."

The boy didn't reply, just kept his eyes firmly fixed on the tips of his shoes.

"I'm only kidding," the man went on. "Just wanted to ask for directions. To the bowling alley."

The boy risked a glance. "It's over there. You can see the sign," he told him.

"Oh, yeah. I was only kidding, as I said."

He gave a low, ingratiating laugh and stuck his head all the way out of the window.

"Want a lift home?"

The boy shook his head vigorously. He could see a doorway up ahead.

"I live over there," he lied.

"Is that right?" The man was laughing hard. "What's your name?"

The boy didn't answer. He had said his name often enough to know what the reaction would be.

"Is it a secret?"

"No."

"Well, then what is it, boy!"

"Matteus," he whispered.

Dead silence. The man in the car looked at his companion.

"What the hell," he shouted. "That's really cool! Is it really Matteus? The Gospels and all that shit?"

He clucked his tongue. "Where are you from?"

Smiling, he looked at the black curls and brown cheeks. For a moment there was a flash of yearning in his eyes that the boy couldn't possibly see.

"Right over there," he said, pointing.

"No, I mean what country are you from? You're adopted, aren't you?"

"Give it up, Andreas," said Zipp with a groan. "Leave him be."

"Somalia," the boy said.

"Why didn't they give you a Norwegian name like other children that are adopted? Not that it matters." He tossed his head. "I feel a little faint every time I meet black or Chinese children named Petter and Kåre. Shit, it's really starting to get to me."

He laughed out loud, revealing a row of sharp, white teeth. Matteus pressed his lips together. His name was Matteus when they found him, the people he called his mother and father, at an orphanage in Mogadishu. They didn't want to change it, but sometimes he wished that they had. Now he just stared at the doorway up ahead, clutching his bag of sweets in a brown fist and casting a glance at the car. Then he turned and took a few steps up the gravel path towards the house that wasn't his at all. He saw a rack holding rubbish bins. He slipped behind them and crouched down. A nauseating, rotting smell came from the rubbish. The car accelerated away and disappeared. When he thought they were out of sight, he crawled out and continued on his way. He was walking faster now. His heart, which had been pounding, began to calm down. The incident had made his stomach churn, giving him a vague presentiment of what awaited him in his future. A car was coming down the street. For an awful moment he thought they might have turned around and come back. They realised that he didn't live there, and they had come to get him! His heart was pounding hard again as he heard the car approach. It stopped on the other side of the street.

"Hey, Matteus! You off out again? You sure do get around, Pops!"

Matteus ran. The men laughed and the engine started up. The car disappeared, headed into town. It was 6.15 when he reached his front door.

Zipp and Andreas supposed that they knew each other pretty well. In fact, they were aware of little, insignificant things, such as one another's likes and dislikes, and something about how they functioned in the world. Apart from that, they were both too preoccupied with themselves to look to the other for anything new. Zipp knew that Andreas' preferred brand of beer had a blue cap. That he liked The Doors and didn't like mustard on his sausages. And that no girl was ever good enough for him. This was something that Zipp couldn't understand. The girls were always looking him over. Andreas is too good-looking, thought Zipp. His looks had given him an indolent, sauntering demeanour that occasionally irritated Zipp. There was something intractable about Andreas, something invulnerable and sluggish that almost made you want to hit him, or stick out your leg to see him lose his balance. If that was even possible. Furthermore, Zipp knew where Andreas lived and worked. He had been up to his room and visited his workplace, at the Cash & Carry. He worked among racks of tins of paint, bread knives and Teflon frying pans. It was a place for old ladies. Andreas was the only guy who worked there.

Andreas knew that Zipp's father had died years ago, but he couldn't remember what his name was or why he had died. He also knew that Zipp was unemployed and was always bumming money from him. He liked having company and he owned a car. The car had, of course, belonged to his father. His mother didn't know how to drive, but she did pay for the petrol. Zipp's mother did shift work at some kind of home and was almost never around. She was either at work or asleep. In Zipp's basement they had a little room, a place where they could hang out when they were broke. It was pleasant to stick with the familiar. Zipp was predictable, and Andreas liked that. And last, but not least, being friends with Zipp felt safe.

They didn't have much to offer one another, yet they still hung out together. Anything was better than solitude. If Zipp ever suggested including a third or a fourth person, Andreas would talk him out of it, saying that it would just complicate things. Besides, they didn't have room for women in the car, which was a good argument. They fell out a few times, but none ever developed into a fight. They agreed on most things and usually it was Andreas who managed to turn any conflict to his advantage. He did it so effortlessly that Zipp never even noticed. They had crossed a few boundaries. Insignificant things: once in a kiosk where they had stolen some cartons of cigarettes and money; another time when they stole a car. The Golf had a dead battery, and the idea of trudging through the streets like a couple of schoolboys didn't appeal to them. But they didn't drive far. Basically they were quite cowardly. They never resorted to violence, and they had never owned a gun between them, although Andreas had a knife that was given to him as a confirmation present. Sometimes it hung from his belt, hidden under his shirt. The knife made Zipp uncomfortable. Sometimes they drank too much, and the knife would swing like a pendulum on Andrea's narrow hips, readily accessible. Not that Andreas set out to provoke anyone, or let himself be provoked by others. He had just the opposite effect on people. They felt good in his company, they would relax and sit staring into his pale blue eyes. But when Andreas drank, he changed. A restlessness would come over him, and the lazy boy would develop an almost feverish agitation. His thin fingers couldn't keep still; they were in constant motion, plucking at everything. Zipp was always amazed by this. He, on the other hand, would become dull and sleepy if he drank too much.

Andreas was actually quite remarkable. He was more like a mood, as if he weren't entirely present. He didn't belch when he got drunk. He didn't cough, and he didn't hiccup. Everything around him was quiet. And he didn't have any particular kind of smell. Zipp used Hugo Boss aftershave when he could afford it, or he would steal a bottle from the Cash & Carry if he was feeling confident. Andreas never used aftershave. He always looked the same; his hair never got greasy, he was always clean, but not too clean. If Zipp happened to wake him up on a Sunday morning, and he appeared in the doorway wearing his bathrobe, he never looked tired. His eyes were wide open. His hair was always the same length. His shoes never looked worn out. It was strange.

Right now Andreas was waiting for his wages. Between them they were worth the princely total of 60 kroner. Not even enough for two beers.

"What are you thinking about?" Andreas said out of the blue.

Zipp grimaced, "I'm thinking about Anita."

"Shit, is she really worth thinking about?"

"What do you mean?" Zipp looked sullen.

"The girl's as dead as a doornail."

"You can say that again." Zipp had to look out of the window to hide his face. "How much buckshot is there in one cartridge?" he said tonelessly.

"Depends. Why do you ask?"

"I'm thinking about her face. How it looked afterwards. Anita was so pretty."

Andreas shrugged. "If you stand close enough, the shot comes out like one huge bullet. By the way, I talked to Roger. He said her nose was sticking out and her whole jaw was wide open. One of her eyes was gone." He took a drag on his cigarette. "And Anders," he said, "he was standing right behind Anita when the shot was fired. The top of his skull was totally perforated."

Zipp sat in silence, painting the picture in his mind. There was no end to the details. His brain was stuffed with images from films, X-rated, wide-screen and with digital sound effects.

"Fucking hell."

Andreas rolled his eyes. "Why are you carrying on like this? It's not like she was your sister. That's life, Zipp. 'All these moments will be lost in time, like tears in rain.'"

Andreas was quoting Roy Batty. But Zipp was still thinking about Anita. He thought about her laugh, her voice and her scent. He remembered the tiny green gemstone in her nose. Everything blasted to smithereens.

"Well, you know I've been in the sack with Anita. It's weird to think about it," he said in a low voice.

"Is there a single jam jar in the whole town that you haven't dipped your wick in?"

"Ha, ha. Not many." He snorted up the snot running from his nose. "The Devil must have got into Robert," he muttered. "I know Robert. Something must have made him go crazy."

"Okay, so that's what we'll say. He was possessed. But not by the Devil."

"No?"

"Good Lord, man. He was dead drunk! He was possessed by alcohol. His brain was pickled. Blotto, unpredictable and insane! There's your Devil."

"I think I'm going on the wagon," said Zipp gloomily. This made Andreas burst out laughing because the idea was preposterous. Then the moment passed, the mood lifted, and Zipp erased the bloody image from his mind. For a while they drove in silence.

"Were you with the Woman yesterday?" Out of the corner of his eye Zipp glanced at Andreas' thigh in the light-coloured slacks.

"Yes, I was," he replied. Zipp heard the smile in his voice, and the warning not to ask anything more. Not that it was a secret. He had plainly told

Zipp that they were sleeping together. Or had he? Maybe he was just pulling his leg. Andreas was so secretive, so difficult to work out.

"I can't understand why you bother," laughed Zipp.

"A few extra kroner," said Andreas curtly. His voice didn't sound annoyed, but there was a wariness to his tone. "You're always so thirsty."

And then he added, with great pathos: "I'm doing it for us, Zipp."

Zipp tried to listen for everything he wasn't saying. Andreas was modelling for an artist. She painted him in the nude. Zipp tried to imagine what pose he took, whether he was lying on a sofa or sitting on a chair, or maybe standing up in some impossible position. He hadn't dared to ask. But Zipp was curious. The thought of taking off his clothes in front of a woman and letting her look at him while he stood there, passive, made him uncomfortable. Of course they had sex afterwards. According to Andreas. But the feeling, thought Zipp, of having to stand there, motionless, while the Woman examined his body in every detail. Not that he was shy of it. He wasn't fat or too small, or anything like that. But to be observed like that, by a woman.

"Isn't that damned painting ever going to be finished? You've been going there for months."

Zipp inhaled more smoke. Without under-standing why, he sensed that he had approached somewhere dangerous. At the same time he felt compelled to go on. It occurred to him that he had never seen Andreas get angry. He was always calm, soft-spoken and reassuringly the same. For eleven years he had been the same.

"It takes a year to make a good painting," Andreas said firmly, as if he were instructing a child. He twisted the ends of his scarf. They matched his shirt.

"A whole fucking year? Well, then you've got a whole lot of shit ahead of you."

Zipp flicked the ash from his cigarette out of the window. "Just think if she gets famous and they hang the painting up so that God and everybody else can see it. In the bank, for example. Or at the Saga cinema. Shit, that would really do me in."

Zipp put the car in neutral. Andreas patiently watched the red light.

"No-one will recognise me," he said, his voice calm.

"No? Is it one of those Picasso things with both ears on the same side of the head?"

Andreas uttered a weary laugh at his friend's boundless ignorance.

"It's going to be a good painting," was all he said.

"How old is this chick, anyway?"

Andreas winked. "Old enough to know more tricks than any of the schoolgirls you hang out with."

This was the kind of remark that Zipp loved. Anything that referred to his performance in bed, of which he had the highest regard. Oh yes!

"You whoring pig," he sneered. "Is it possible for a choirboy like you to learn any tricks?"

That was when Andreas turned to face him, just as the light went green. He looked Zipp up and down, from his bristly hair that refused to lie flat, to his turned-up nose and the cleft in his chin, to his plump thighs and the ridiculous tight jeans he always wore. Stretch to fit. But the small head and powerful torso reminded Andreas of what Zipp really was. A stud. He started sweating. Andreas sat there, assessing him, his body, every last detail. And he rejected it! Zipp wouldn't have a chance with the Woman.

Zipp regretted having started this conversation. This is how it always ended up. He would try, but he never got anywhere. If only he had some damn money for a beer! Surreptitiously he studied his companion. Andreas had style. He wore wide-legged trousers and baggy shirts. Nothing gaudy. Moccasins on his feet, never running shoes. In the summer he rolled up his sleeves and unbuttoned his shirt. But always loose clothing, light-coloured and lightweight. His clothes seemed to flutter about him, making him look slimmer and lankier even than he was. Zipp squeezed the exact same number of kilos, 63, into tight jeans and T-shirts that fit him like a second skin. Above them he wore a leather jacket. It was short-waisted and wide in the shoulders, but somehow it didn't give him the athletic look he was after. Instead it gave him a puffed-up look. This surprised him, because he wasn't overweight. He was slightly bowlegged and he had a ponytail, but his appearance was pretty ordinary. He envied Andreas his style and elegance, but he couldn't emulate it. The effect wouldn't be the same. Not that he was unlucky with the ladies. But even in that department Andreas had overtaken him. He ignored them. Except for the Woman. And Zipp still didn't know how old she was. Thirty? Or more? Forty, or fifty even? Zipp had an aunt who was 50. The thought gave him the creeps. A 50-year-old woman. With children and stuff like that. How did women look – down there – after they'd squeezed out a brood of children? They had to look different from girls.

"Does she have any children?" the question slipped out.

"Quite a few," Andreas said, nodding. "Four or five."

"Shit, there must be plenty of room inside a bitch like that, huh?"

Andreas rolled up the window, and a sour little smile appeared on his face.

"I've seen things you wouldn't believe."

"What's that supposed to mean?"

"They're much, much deeper, Zipp."

High above the town, with a view of the river, stood an imposing house from the early twentieth century. In need of repair here and there, but the green panelling was still holding up to all kinds of weather. This was where the artist Anna Fehn lived.

One evening in early summer she was wandering around in the town square, observing people. She had a trained eye. Most people aren't especially attractive, she thought. Most of them are a random selection of genes from the two sets which served as the basis for their existence. Long arms and legs from the father, tiny hands and feet from the mother. Almost no-one comprises a harmonious whole. Almost no-one makes an impression. Yet she knew that it wasn't a matter of heavy or light, rough or fine, but how they carried themselves, how they moved. With a consciousness of who they were, and with pride as the dominant force, or squeezed into a nature, a form, they refused to acknowledge. But then she caught sight of Andreas. At an outdoor café with someone. Her first thought was that he looked bored. Life wasn't enough for him. There was something important that he had yet to find. Not original – the same was true of most people. But he wasn't sitting there with the usual gaping expression, forever turning his head to look at girls, or preoccupied with whether anyone might be looking at him. He sat there in utter peace, with his long legs stretched out under the table. Anna took in the leather shoes on the pavement, the cotton shirt against his pale skin. His hair moved very faintly; his slender fingers were wrapped around his glass. He was practically lying in his chair, which was tilted on to its back legs. To be able to sit like that, perfectly balanced, at risk of toppling over and banging his head on the concrete, and yet he looked so relaxed. So uninterested. So impregnable. It made an impression on her. She looked at his companion. They seemed an unlikely pair. Both of them had downed the best part of a pint, but they weren't yet drunk. Otherwise they looked like most young people their age. Didn't belong to any specific group, not headbangers or punks, but just ordinary boys of around 20 years old. Yet Andreas had a lazy elegance about him and a splendid head of hair reaching to his shoulders. She tried to define the colour. If she mixed carmine, burnt sienna, and a light ochre, and then added some ivory nuances, she might come close.

Anna moved nearer. If she divided his face up

31

into sections, the way artists do – the forehead, cheeks, eyes, jaw – it struck her that he wasn't strikingly handsome in the classic sense. His eyes were set a little too deep, his nose was long and narrow and crooked and at the tip it bent down towards his mouth, which was a bit too small, but evenly shaped and nice-looking. His chin was narrow and jutted out. Over his left eyebrow he had a birthmark, exactly on his hairline. Yet, taken together, his features made a strong impression. Impossible to ignore. He was thin, long-limbed and well-defined, in spite of his young age. She played with the idea of how he would look naked. There was something about young boys that disappeared as they crossed the boundary to become grown men. That moment when their bodies hesitated, just before that last step towards adult gravity. He was at that point right now. His skin had a sheen to it that reminded her of cream. He was either a university student or a young man in his poorly paid first job. Undoubtedly he needed money. For a moment she turned her back to him and stared at a lit-up window, at a dress that she couldn't afford. No, be honest, it's too short for you! She laughed at herself and then turned back. She didn't want to approach him as long as his friend was there, in case it might embarrass him. So she waited patiently. Sooner or later one of them would need to find the toilet below the square. While she waited, she placed him in the pose she instinctively thought would show him at his best. That lazy, casual expression was also a pose, a form of protection that he used. His friend hadn't seen through him. He looked younger, and maybe a little less shrewd. And then, abruptly, he got up and disappeared. Anna Fehn took quick action. She walked to the table and leaned towards him.

"I'm a painter, and I'm always looking for models. If you're interested in earning a few kroner, call me at this number. My name is Anna."

She held out her card. He wasn't startled, just looked back at her with a certain curiosity. And then he took her card, and stuck it in the pocket of his baggy shirt, which was unbuttoned. She caught a glimpse of his boyish chest.

"Just to be clear," she added, "I'm talking about posing in the nude."

. He nodded. He understood. That very evening he called her from a pay phone. She thought he must live at home and didn't want to involve anyone else. He was at her door the next evening. He undressed without embarrassment, but cast a quick glance at her, said he'd never done this before. Businesslike, she explained to him what to do, but she allowed herself to show a maternal warmth. She would have liked to show something else, but she was old enough to be his mother, for heaven's sake. On that first evening she made only a rough sketch, and assured herself that he could hold the pose for a reasonable length of time, without discomfort. He put his clothes on and left. After that he came back every week at the same time.

They didn't really get to know each other. Andreas never talked about himself, and he wasn't interested in knowing anything about her. He had no plans or desires for the future. Now and then he talked about his friend Zipp. Or occasionally, about a film that he liked. Or about music. Nothing else.

The impulse came unexpectedly. She was not prepared, she had never planned it. Dreamed about it, maybe, but who wouldn't? One evening, as she worked, he seemed to fall into a reverie. He was no longer holding the pose, and his gaze was lost in one of the big paintings on the wall. Something of the tension in his body dissolved. She wanted to point this out, but changed her mind. For a long time she was able to study him unobserved. She held her breath and stood still with the brush in her hand. She knew he wasn't thinking about her; she would have sensed it if he was. She walked over to him. He pulled himself together, moved back into his original position. But she had seen him, caught him unawares. He didn't like that. She wanted to tell him that it didn't matter. She gave him a quick smile and patted his cheek. But when she felt his skin under her hand, she couldn't stop. He had high cheekbones that were beautiful and prominent beneath his white skin. He did not turn away. He stood still and allowed her to caress him. The sharp light, which came from a lamp to the left, was meant for her work. She could see every pore of his skin, as well as the thin veins in his temples. And his eyelids, like tissue paper. His skin smelled like skin, his hair like hair. He acquiesced and let her have what she wanted. Her body had been asleep for a long time. She was overwhelmed by everything that awakened, that trickled and flowed. She wanted to surrender, to make love as if it were a matter of life and death, to shriek and scratch, but she controlled herself. She didn't want to frighten him away. Afterwards, when he left the house, she came to her senses. He lacked fire. She had thought that there would be a flood of passion, because he was so young. It must be there somewhere. But she never found it. Yet they continued. Every time she had finished her work, they would go to bed. He never took the initiative, she was always the one who did that. May this painting never be done! she thought. Without feeling any shame. They were both grown-ups. Deep inside she hoped that he bragged about it to others.

CHAPTER 3

I sell curtains and bed linens and fabric in a very respectable shop. I'm home each day by 5 p.m. The rest of the evening I spend indoors, pottering around. Almost no-one ever comes here, once in a while my friend, or perhaps my son. Ingemar. I listen politely to whatever he says. He never asks me to visit or anything like that, it's too difficult for us. The visits are more like an obligation, when we check up on each other. Make sure that everything is all right. It's nice to be able to say at work now and then that Ingemar was here for coffee yesterday. So reliable and proper. Socialising, spending time with other people, noticing their smell, or the certainty that they notice my smell, is more than I can bear. I go shopping at regular intervals and buy what I need. Never more than that. Sometimes I go to the library, where I borrow biographies. Or I look through the newspapers. It doesn't cost anything, you know. I go there right before closing time, when it's quiet and there's never a queue at the check-out desk. The librarian is a man. He looks sad. What a burden it must be to have to read everything.

I don't talk to my neighbours. If they say hello over the fence, I say hello back, but keep walking. I'm not unhappy, but I'm not happy either. I don't know anyone who is. A doctor that I see once a year says that I'm as healthy as a horse. He says this in a stern, admonishing way, and I know what he's getting at, but he can't possibly understand. I don't feel like explaining. He's not being malicious or pretentious, he just sits there and looks at me. Wants to offer me something, but he doesn't really have the strength for it.

People are so different. It's easier to love things, or tasks, or animals maybe, but they smell and they leave hair everywhere, or something even worse. I spend the evenings tidying up the house. I wash and put things away and wipe and dust. Everything is clean. Finally I splash some bleach in all the drains. It kills bacteria and removes odours. Behind the house I have a beautiful garden and a small gazebo. If I sit outside in the summer I put up a windbreak made of canvas. If anyone were to stand behind the hedge and look in, they wouldn't be able to see me. Not that I'm sitting there wearing nothing but my underwear; that would never occur to me. But I like this enclosed space. I've never bothered anybody. Never made big demands or behaved unreasonably.

I don't cheat on my taxes, I don't shoplift, I pay all my bills a day or two before they're due. On Saturday evenings I sometimes drink a little wine, but never too much. I watch television. Read the newspapers. I know what's happening out in the streets and in Algeria and Rwanda. I sleep well, I rarely dream, and I'm not afraid of dying. In fact, I often wish I would die. Die suddenly, while I'm sitting in the red chair, without being aware of it. Next to the window, with the sun on my face. The last thing I felt would be a faint warmth. How sad it will be when I'm not here any more!

In short, I fulfil my obligations. What's wrong with obligations? Aren't they what hold society together? Every night when I go to bed, I can cross off one more day. That's a relief. I'm not ashamed. When I wake up in the morning, I'm always amazed that I'm still here. But I think that's great, and I do what I'm supposed to do. You mustn't think that I'm unhappy or anything; I'm doing fine. Or was. Until the incident with Andreas happened.

I was 16 when I left the yellow house. All the rules had closed around me like a cage. I didn't let anyone in. Behind the bars, I constructed a life, a state in which I could survive, one consisting of order and regulation, discipline and control. My parents regarded me with doubt and relief. There was something clearly legible in their eyes. Don't blame us, they said, if anything goes wrong. They didn't wave when I left. They wanted above all things to be left in peace. I never acquired a faith in God, either. There's more between heaven and earth, my mother would say, with her back turned. They passed on to me what they had learned themselves, the best way to make it through life. So I left, with the rules as a weight on my shoulders, and from behind the cage bars I observed the world. Everyone around me was vacillating and without purpose and disgustingly impulsive. Human beings have a tendency to just drift along, and that makes me nervous.

I have a friend. Did I mention that? Runi. She rarely visits me. Usually it is I who goes to visit her, and that's what I prefer. A guest in my house makes me feel like a prisoner. I can't get up and leave when I want to. She talks a lot and has all sorts of worries. No more than I do, but I'm not as eager to talk about them. Except for now, to you. Runi's a beautiful woman; in appearance, I mean. Modern without going over the top. She knows she's attractive. That's important to her. Most of the time she's gentle and talkative and lively. But she cackles wickedly about everything that's troublesome, and sometimes she's a downright nuisance. It wears me out. Occasionally there are things that I'd like to tell Runi, but I don't. Like when I use her toilet. I go into the tiny room, lift up my skirt and pee. Wipe myself thoroughly. Wash my hands. It costs me nothing. I can't tell this to Runi, because she wouldn't understand. You wouldn't either. Of course she's charming, but she lacks any connection with herself and with the ground she walks on. She never thinks things through. When something happens, she's never prepared. That childish attitude, thinking that nothing will ever harm her, where does she get that from? She's an adult now. And a terrible liar.

One time – well, I have to confess it was in a fit of drunkenness – I was sitting in her living room, eating cake. With icing and green gumdrops on top. She started talking about how vigorously she always did the Friday cleaning, and how much her back hurt afterwards. I had my own thoughts on the subject. I could smell the dust in the room. I have a very keen sense of smell. When she went out to the kitchen to get something, I grabbed a gumdrop from the cake and tossed it under the sofa. And then I waited. At first for a week, but then I put my heart and soul into it and waited another week. And then, to really test fate, I waited one week more. Then I paid her a visit. When she went to the bathroom, I bent down and found the gumdrop. It wasn't green any more, and it was furry. I never confronted her with the furry gumdrop; I'm not a mean sort of person. I try to offer her something, since we're friends, for God's sake. And what is a friend? Someone to spend time with, without too much discomfort? Because I don't really care for her that much. If she died I'd be extremely upset, but at the same time a lot would be over and done with. Grieve for her? That's not how I'd feel. It's good to be done with things.

She encourages me to go out, sometimes to a restaurant, or to the theatre. It takes an effort for me to do that. To sit there in a crowd of people, so close that you can hear what they're saying, is very stressful. One time we went to Hanna's Kitchen because it was Runi's birthday. That was a long time ago. We were sitting at a table right next to two young women, well, young compared to us, but definitely adults. They were howling and carrying on, giggling like a couple of teenagers. And they drank too much and got very drunk. I realised after a while that they were actually two streetwalkers. I'm no fool. Some of their conversation can't be repeated, it was so vile. And having them so close like that. Unable to get away! Runi makes all the arrangements if we're going to do something together. Sometimes I feel quite moved, when I hear her voice on the phone, when she asks me if I'd like to come along, and her anxiety that I might say no. She doesn't have anyone else. Life isn't easy for anybody.

If I'm ever brought before a court, they'll probably declare me guilty by reason of insanity. But I'm not. I remember everything, so I should be held accountable, shouldn't I? And you can see that my thoughts are coherent and orderly, can't you? That I'm a normal human being and not mentally deficient? I'm sure of that.

I've pulled a plastic tarpaulin over the body. I don't plan on moving him. How could I manage that? He weighs a ton, so the most I could have done would be to lug him into a corner. I've hung an old potato sack over the window. A bare bulb hangs from the ceiling. He's lying on his back with his arms at his side. He's no longer handsome. As I've said so often, physical beauty is a fragile gift. I myself have little to lose. I'm know that I'm ugly. No-one has ever said as much out loud, but I can see it in people's eyes when I meet their gaze: the dead look they give me. "Why can't you fix yourself up?" Runi asks me, annoyed. It scares her that I don't fight back. Let the young people be sleek in peace, is what I think now. Like Andreas, he's young and sleek. Well, not any more. My thoughts are with him. It's not that he's been forgotten or anything. He'll never be forgotten. But as for myself, I'm not so certain.

CHAPTER 4

Andreas smoked Craven A cigarettes. Not Prince or Marlboro, like other people. Every time he was out of cigs he'd go to a kiosk, lean forward and say: "Craven". And they would nod behind the counter and search the shelves. Not many people bought that brand. He sought attention wherever he went, but as soon as he got it, he rejected it. Zipp knew that he himself was not fussy, and had no specific preferences whatsoever. He couldn't really tell the difference, anyway, between a Prince and a Marlboro. Or between Coke and Pepsi. He had to look at the name on the label. He wondered if other people were lying, or whether they were actually more canny than he was. Maybe Andreas was lying. He wasn't altogether trustworthy. Something was lacking. He could never say: "One time last year" or "last Saturday" or "dammit, Zipp, guess what happened yesterday!" He never talked about anything in the past. Only about the present moment, or what was to come. And it wasn't because what had happened in the past was too awful to talk about; that wasn't it. And Zipp ought to know. They'd been hanging out together for eleven years. But had he ever heard Andreas say: "Do you remember that time?" No, that would never happen.

"In 2019," said Andreas, "we'll be 39 years old. Have you ever thought about that?"

Zipp shrugged. No, he hadn't, and he didn't feel like doing the arithmetic, but it was probably about right. Almost 40.

"What about it?"

Andreas studied the pavement ahead. "By then human beings will have colonised several of the planets. All the animals will be extinct. The air will be lethally polluted, and the first replicants will be living among us without our knowing."

"You've been watching too many videos," Zipp said. "We need money, man!"

Andreas read aloud what it said on a poster on a wall: "Saga Sun Trips. Clean air, crystal clear water. I know," he said. "Drive over to Furulund."

He issued the order in a gentle manner, as if Zipp were a long way his junior. It did not occur to him that he might be contradicted, at least not with any seriousness.

"Furulund? Why there?"

"It's quiet out there."

"But what about the money, Andreas!"

"Just so," he said calmly.

Zipp made a U-turn, and Andreas pulled a comb out of his pocket. He started combing his unruly hair.

"Out to get the ladies?" Zipp teased. "Someone younger for a change?"

Andreas struggled with his curls. "Shut up and drive."

Zipp drove the Golf as fast as it would go, past Dynamite Industries and along the fjord. Andreas remained alert. After five minutes he told Zipp to slow down. A cyclist was coming in the other direction, a man on a racing bike. He had a touring rucksack on his back, he was wearing a helmet and cycling gloves, and he was moving at quite a speed. Andreas dismissed the man and stared through the windscreen. They were approaching a public park, which consisted of a decent swimming area, tables and benches and several large permanent barbeques which were always in use during the summer.

"Turn right," Andreas said.

"There's just a lousy kiosk down there, and it's closed for the autumn," Zipp objected.

"There are people here," Andreas said. "It's a tourist area. If we're lucky, we'll find an old lady with a handbag."

Zipp manoeuvred the car cautiously down towards the sea.

"Slowly. We're strangers here, we're looking for something."

"Looking for what?"

Andreas shook his head in disbelief.

"We're going to stop someone and ask for directions."

"Who?"

"Whoever turns up," he said with a groan. His friend's simple-mindedness was unbearable.

"What a shitload of trouble it is to live in a society that charges 40 kroner for a pint. If it's going to be any fun tonight, we're going to need at least a thousand," Zipp said.

The ocean poured in over the shore. Greyish-green, foaming, and ice-cold. They came to an old dilapidated clubhouse. Outside it, pieces of broken patio furniture had been piled into a heap, a midsummer bonfire that would never be lit. The summer had been very dry. They turned into the car park and surveyed the area. In the distance they saw a figure plodding along the shoreline. Andreas opened the glove compartment and took out a cap. He pulled it down over his forehead and tucked his curls underneath. Zipp grinned when he read the words on the blue fabric.

"'Holy Riders. On the Road for Jesus.' Shit, you're bad, Andreas!"

A strong wind was blowing. Andreas stuck one foot outside the car.

"A woman," he said. "With a pram. Excellent."

"Why?"

"Women get so helpless when they're pushing a pram."

He turned to look at Zipp. "Just think what's inside."

"What exactly are you planning to do?"

Zipp was nervous. He couldn't very well object; they were friends, did everything together. But he often thought that one day they would cross a boundary too far. Andreas had his knife in his belt, under his shirt.

"First we have to see if she's got a handbag with her. If she lives nearby, she probably left it at home. Otherwise women always carry a handbag."

They waited as the figure came closer slowly. She was pushing the pram along the beach, and the wheels were sinking into the soft sand. She was very tall, with a scarf round her head and a light-coloured coat which flapped in the wind.

"She must be two metres tall!" said Zipp, who was 1.70 himself.

"Doesn't matter. Girls don't have much in the way of muscles."

The woman caught sight of the car. She leaned down to pat what lay inside the pram. They could see part of a blue quilt. Andreas strained his eyes.

"I see her handbag," he whispered. "It's on top of the blanket. That's great!"

"Why?"

"It's more difficult when they carry their handbags over their shoulders." He sat for a moment, squinting under the peak of his cap, going over his plan of attack. It wasn't a time for threats or violence, but for pure cunning.

"You stay here. Keep the engine running. Find something in the glove compartment. Pretend that you're sitting here looking at a map or something. I'll get out and ask for directions – to somewhere. The football field. I'll snatch the handbag and hightail it back."

"She'll get our registration number!"

"They usually don't. They get too damned scared."

Andreas got out and approached the woman. She took stock of him and slowed her pace, casting an uneasy glance at the car.

Women are strange, thought Andreas. It's as if they can smell that something is up. Or maybe they just look at things in a different way from men. Because they have more enemies, maybe that's it. To be a woman and have to be on guard all the time, what a fucking strain that must be! She had actually started in the direction of the car park, but then she would have to pass the car. Suddenly she turned the pram around and set off in the opposite direction. The manoeuvre was pitifully obvious. He wondered where the idea came from. Whether on account of the foaming sea, because her path was blocked on one side, or maybe because of the child, the responsibility for someone other than herself. And because they were male. A sudden fear. In addition, the wind was fierce and the waves were slamming hard against the shore. No-one would hear her if she yelled. Andreas stopped, shook his head and stared after her. She turned around, wary. He reacted fast and made a helpless gesture with his hands. The light was white and harsh, making his face shine. She started up a path that rose steeply along a ridge above the sea. Possibly a way out. Zipp sat in the car and waited. He followed Andreas with his eyes, Andreas followed the woman. She quickened her pace, but then she heard his voice behind her and again she turned around. In spite of everything, most people found it difficult to ignore someone who was calling out in a friendly manner. And surely he couldn't be dangerous or anything like that! What a ridiculous idea! She had merely taken precautions, withdrawn from a potential danger. The baby in the pram had shown her so clearly how dangerous the world was. She hardly slept at night; when she fell asleep the child was erased from her consciousness, and she couldn't allow that to happen.

"Excuse me!"

Andreas called out in a paper-thin voice. The yellow shirt flapped around his slender midriff. His right hand held the shirt over his knife. He looked like a very tall kid of confirmation age. Zipp, still in the car, saw the woman stop at last. It didn't seem right to choose her, not a woman with a little baby. There was something about the way that she was clutching the handle of the pram that frightened him. A sense of desperation in those white hands tight around the handle. It wasn't because of the handbag, but because of the little bundle under the blue blanket. He realised that something might happen, that she was unpredictable because of the baby. He put the brake on and got out. He did this even though Andreas had told him to stay in the car.

Andreas was almost level with her. He stopped a short distance away so as not to seem threatening. And he had an air about him that was hard to resist. Zipp could see in her eyes that she had read what it said on his cap, that she had noticed the little white cross and the words underneath. Her shoulders relaxed. She even ran her hand over her scarf, almost coquettishly, and looked at him with a smile. Andreas opened his mouth and said something. The woman replied and started pointing, past the car park and up towards the road. Zipp stared at the pram and caught sight of the handbag.

A nylon bag, black and red. Andreas moved a few steps nearer as he looked the other way. He was backing up towards the handbag. Zipp kept walking.

Then Andreas noticed him, and for a moment he looked confused. They were high up on the path now. There was no beach below, just a bare slope descending to the water that ended in piles of sharp rocks. Andreas made his move. He leaned and grabbed the handbag, then ran hell for leather back towards the car. The woman screamed. In desperation she tried to make sense of the new situation, the fact that they had duped her, after all, just when she had decided that they were decent boys with good intentions. Something took hold of her, a violent rage, or maybe it was a sense of impotence. She kicked on the brake of the pram out of pure reflex, and started running.

"Get in the car!" Andreas shouted.

But Zipp stood stock still. They came running towards him, but he didn't move because he could see the pram starting to roll down the slope towards the water. She hadn't set the brake properly! Paralysed, he watched the little blue plush pram tip over the edge. He screamed as he ran like crazy and almost collided with Andreas. But the woman stopped in her tracks. She finally realised what was happening. She whirled around and saw Zipp leap over the edge and vanish. And then she gave a piercing shriek and started to run. Andreas stopped where he was and stared in astonishment. The handbag slipped out of his hands. In the distance he heard the roar of the waves, the sound of heavy swells that almost knocked him over. He heard several faint screams before Zipp's blond head appeared over the edge. His face was red with agitation.

"Run, for God's sake, run!"

"What about the baby!" shouted Andreas. He grabbed the handbag and ran after Zipp.

"The pram stopped against a stone and tipped over! The baby fell out! Oh, fucking hell!"

They threw themselves into the car and drove out of the car park with a screech of tyres. Neither of them dared to look back. But they could still hear the roar of the waves, a loud thundering that rose and fell.

"Shit! The baby was screaming its head off!"

"Calm down, it went fine."

"Fine? That baby could have drowned!"

"He didn't drown!"

"But he definitely hurt himself. Shit, you should have heard him screaming!"

"It would have been worse if he didn't."

"Jesus Christ."

"Cut out the Jesus crap!"

The Golf roared along the road, sending up a

shower of gravel and careening wildly. An ugly grinding sound came from the gearbox. Andreas had to hold on to the door handle. He tore off his cap and stuffed it into his pocket. His curls came tumbling out.

"She saw both of us. She saw the car. Do you have the handbag?"

Zipp was stammering.

"Do you think I'm an amateur?"

"We'll have the police at the door by tonight."

"No, we won't. She's too preoccupied with the baby. She'll forget about everything else."

"Are you out of your mind?" shrieked Zipp, as he struggled to hold the steering wheel in his trembling hands.

"I know what women are like. She'll be thanking God because the baby survived and she'll realise how unimportant the money is. Mothers have a whole new set of values in life. So shut up and drive!"

He bent over the bag and rummaged inside it. Pulled out a baby bottle.

"The milk's warm," he said in surprise. After that he took out a dummy, a mosquito net for the pram and a purse. He tore it open. "Her name's Gina," he said.

"Is there any money?" asked Zipp in confusion.

"A few hundred-kroner notes. Four. Shit, Zipp,

let me tell you, I'm a genius of cunning and strength! According to the Tyrell Corporation. Nexus 6 fighting model!"

*

My mother was not really a mother, but rather a kind of corrective entity. That's why I'm a well-behaved girl. I say "yes, please" and "no, thank you". I have a firm handshake. Look people in the eye. Remember names. Remember little things, what people like and don't like, notice how attractively they blush. I'm not so dangerous. I take good care of myself, I do not lack for anything. It's no sacrifice. A person can argue his way through life and insist on having his own way or someone else having theirs, and live a life of pain. Why should I do that? Nothing is important to me, or not important enough. I don't mind standing at the end of the line, I'm a patient person. If others are in a hurry, I let them go ahead of me. It amuses me. I laugh at them when they're not looking. Laugh at their life-or-death expressions. It's only on bad days that I cry. But I don't have many bad days. Or didn't.

Sometimes I do cry, almost astonished at the crack that opens without warning. When I look at pictures from poor countries. Children with flies on their lips, toothless old people with no flesh on their bones, scabs and sores, with no water; they look at me reproachfully. Maybe part of the blame is mine.

Somebody is to blame. But I've never done anything about it.

I'm glad that Henry disappeared. I saw it coming. Saw his expression when I got undressed at night. Not disgust, just a terrible embarrassment, and I didn't help him. That wasn't my job. Henry was supposed to help me. That's what the doctor said, let your husband help you. But he couldn't do it. It's easier to live alone. And this way he won't have to deal with everything that happens. That's good. My son Ingemar never mentions his name. I tell him that he doesn't have to, only that he has to try to understand. He doesn't love me, I realise that. He doesn't hate me either, I've never thought that he did, but the only life I know I've dumped on to his shoulders. He's a decent person too. Works for the Pricing Commission. He doesn't owe any money, and he doesn't drink. I don't know exactly what he does at his job, maybe he decides what things should cost. Everybody complains about the price of everything, and everybody's salary is too low. "Let's go on strike!" they all shout. "We're not going to stand for it any more, we've been passed over, we're not appreciated, the others have got something, why shouldn't we!" No-one ever grows up these days. Everywhere I go I see whining children. Runi, for example, she whines a lot.

Once in a while I wish that Ingemar would come

over and we could go into town together. Arm in arm. Irma Funder walking along the street with her grown-up son. He's not tall or handsome, but quite nice-looking. He gets his heavy face from me, and it suits him. He's extremely serious. The kind of person who has thought things through. It's true that he doesn't have any great ambitions, but he fulfils his obligations, and he never complains. Walking through town with Ingemar. We go to a café. He pays and carries our tray to the table. Pulls out my chair. But he never comes. It's been a long time since he came to see me. If I suggested it – how about the two of us going into town? – he would look at me in surprise. But now I'm happy as long as he stays away.

The house is old. Henry said it was built on clay. That it was just a matter of time, or enough rain, before it would pull loose and slide away, slip unhindered down the slope and crash into number 15. He was always so worried, Henry. I love this house. I know every nook and cranny, the contents of every drawer. Each step on the stairs when I leave for work. Left for work. Everything is mine, and old and familiar and always the same. Ingemar once sat here at the table – that was a long time ago – and he'd got it into his head that the house should be painted. Red, Ingemar said. It's white now, with green paintwork. I would get so scared, every time I stepped through the gate. Scared that something huge and red would loom up, and I'd stand there screaming. I'm telling you these snippets of my life because it's important to me that you see that I'm clear-headed, that I remember things, that I'm not crazy. Of course people will judge me. But I prefer to be my own judge. There is no excuse. Nor would I want any. But there is an explanation. Andreas was just a boy. I didn't want him dead. What am I saying? I certainly did want him dead, in that one evil moment. I stood there and thought: Now I'm going to kill him, I have to do it! Was I all alone with that thought? That horrific moment when I destroyed him. I remember a strange light in the room. Where did it come from? Have you ever seen it?

*

The woman moaned and carried on. She was oblivious to everything, to the fact that she was shivering or that the child might get cold because she was standing there holding him. She was all alone with the little bundle with the wet mouth, the thing she loved more than anything else. Sobs! A faint bleating. She could hardly breathe as she listened. He wasn't breathing. She shook him and took a few steps, and finally air filled his lungs. And he started crying again.

She stumbled around among the rocks until the

child calmed down. Carefully took off his hat and found a scrape on his bald head. With one arm she hugged the child to her breast as hard as she dared, with her other hand she struggled to pull the pram up the slope. She slid back, dug her feet hard against the ground to steady herself, gasping in desperation. Finally she reached the top, soaked with sweat. Her arms ached. She put the baby in the pram and spread the quilt over him. One of the wheels was bent and it was difficult to push. Luckily she had her keys in her coat pocket. When she reached home, she lifted the carrying cot out of the frame, put it on the back seat of the car, fastened it with a seat belt and drove to the emergency department. She cursed the two men who had robbed her. Hatred and anger came and went in her body like tongues of fire. May terrible things happen to them! May they crash their car on the way to town, suffer a head injury and be paralysed from the waist down!

The baby was sleeping. Safe and sound. But he had that mark on his head. A tiny scrape. It took her eleven minutes to drive to the hospital. She lifted him out of the carrying cot and took him inside.

A doctor examined the cut. Took off most of the baby's clothes and shone a light into the dark pupils of his eyes. The baby drooled and flailed his arms.

"He looks fine," the doctor said. "You should report the handbag snatching."

"No," she said wearily. "The only thing that's important is my baby."

"What's his name?"

She smiled shyly. "He hasn't been baptised yet. I'll know his name day when I find a name. None of them are good enough," she said proudly. The doctor wrote out a bill since her money had been stolen. It was really just a token amount. Forty kroner.

Then she went home and nursed the baby for a long time. She sat next to his cot, couldn't make herself leave him. Then she changed her mind and carried him to her own bed. Spread the quilt over both of them and turned off the light. Tried to calm down, but couldn't. She didn't believe in God. She had formally withdrawn from the state church. But in the dark, lying under the quilt, she sensed the contours of some kind of purpose. It overwhelmed her. The fact that they did mean something after all, her and the baby, beyond what she meant when she thought clearly about her own life. Something was keeping them company as they lay there together. She felt herself observed. And later, another thought, that someday she would die. Or the boy would. That it might happen suddenly. She placed her hand on his head. It fitted perfectly in the palm of her hand. He didn't move. He was sound asleep.

Zipp and Andreas were busy drinking up her
money. Zipp was hunched over like an old man; it
had all been too much for him. Andreas was rocking
his chair back and forth, silently making his point.
Whoever mentioned the baby first would ruin the
evening. That awful, unexpected event which had
befallen them.

What they had planned was a quick and easy
play, over in a couple of seconds. Wham! Four
hundred kroner. No harm done.

Andreas studied the fan on the ceiling. It was
revolving slowly, and it reminded him of a scene in
a film that he liked. They drank some more,
patiently waiting for the intoxication to spread over
their brows like a cool rag. Life began to look better
as time passed, the girls were prettier, the future
brighter. Zipp wiped the foam from his upper lip.
And then it slipped out.

"What do you think happened to the baby?"

Andreas uttered a huge, world-weary sigh. He set
down his glass without a sound.

"Babies are soft like rubber. The skull hasn't even
grown together, it's elastic."

He met Zipp's frightened eyes. "It's made up of
soft plates that slide over each other under pressure.
Clever, huh?"

"You're making that up!"

Zipp's eyes flickered. Andreas always had an answer, but he could be a shameless liar. At the same time, that's what he wanted. To have an answer at all costs. The woman with the pram had been a bad choice. The beer tasted just as good as always, that wasn't it. But that baby, God damn it, he was just a tiny bundle. Zipp pressed against the edge of the table and tried to steady his heart. He could still see it. That ridiculous blue plush vehicle on its way over the edge. The way it shook and lurched downwards before ramming into a rock, tipping forward and toppling over. The tiny hands flailing helplessly. A deserted kiosk, an abandoned car, shit, that was nothing. But a live human being!

"If anything happened, it'll be in the papers tomorrow."

"Cut it out, Zipp. Just relax!"

Andreas stared up at the fan again. It was revolving in slow motion and did nothing to keep the smoke away. But he liked the way it moved, the steady pace, the big blades like a propellor overhead. The sight made him hum under his breath that song by the The Doors, about never again being able to look into his friend's eyes.

Zipp cleared his throat. "We'll watch a video later. At my house. Okay?"

He gave Andreas an imploring look. He needed to forget the episode by the sea. Three or four pints and an action film. And then to bed. Soon it would be behind them. They would stick to kiosks from now on.

"*Blade Runner*," said Andreas curtly. "If they have it."

"No, not that one. Not again!"

"You don't get it. *Blade Runner* is the best." Andreas was resolute.

"But I've seen it so many times," Zipp complained. "I know what's going to happen."

"Tonight something different will happen," Andreas said. "That film has a life of its own. Layer on top of layer. You can't take it in all at once."

Zipp felt depressed and emptied his glass.

"You have to develop your mind, man. That's what's wrong with you," said Andreas, wiping off the wet ring left by his glass on the table. "You don't realise that time is passing."

Zipp grimaced. Andreas was obsessed with the film *Blade Runner*. He'd seen it a hundred times and could never get enough. He quoted from it at regular intervals. Zipp studied the other guests in the bar. Usually he could manage to attract the attention of some girl, if she wasn't sitting too far away. He would immediately feel a prickling in his crotch. He loved that prickling, it made his blood rush and his head feel giddy. A girl was staring back at him. Andreas followed his gaze and rolled his eyes. A little chick in tight clothes. A striped jumper, too short at the waist, so her midriff was on show. And a tiny little ring in her navel. Her tits poked out like two tennis balls.

"Silicon," Andreas said. "What a fucking bunch of shit girls have under their clothes these days."

"I don't give a damn," Zipp said with a grin. "As long as I get to touch them. You can't tell the real ones from the fake ones, not on young girls like that. What about your Woman?" he went on. "I'll bet she's got breasts that hang down to here. You have no idea what breasts look like on a young girl. It's about time you checked out the situation. She has a friend with her. See, there she comes. Been out to the bathroom to change her panty liner, that's what I reckon. I know girls like her. They get wet if you just look at them."

Andreas regarded the girl's friend with dull eyes. Zipp couldn't see it, but the girl did. The lack of interest in his pale gaze. She turned her back to him, clearly discouraged because she hadn't made an impression.

"They hang around like grouse," Andreas muttered. "They spread their legs before even a shot is fired."

"We're never going to get those ladies to watch *Blade Runner*," Zipp said, sounding worried. "What about *Independence Day*?"

"Over my dead body."

Andreas went over to the bar. Pulled one of Gina's hundred-kroner notes out of his shirt pocket. He didn't so much as glance at the two girls. Come and get us, come and get us! their rounded shoulders begged. Unbelievable! He left a generous tip and carried the glasses back to the table.

"What's so bad about her friend?" asked Zipp.

"Everything," said Andreas. "Up in that head of hers there's only one thing going on."

"Jesus, you're so full of it!"

"There's one tape inside that keeps playing. It's been playing ever since the girl had tits the size of plums. It says: 'Like me, like me, for God's sake, please like me!' And every time that doesn't happen, she's so surprised. It's fucking incredible."

"You're incredible too," Zipp said. "What's the deal with those old bitches you like so much? What does their tape say?"

Andreas took a sip.

"'I like you, I like you.' That's the difference."

They gulped down the ice-cold beer. They had forgotten all about the baby, which was what they had wanted. Later they sat in Zipp's basement room and stared at *Blade Runner*. Andreas was totally infatuated. Zipp was thinking about the girl in the tight jumper.

"That guy there who's folding shapes out of

paper," Zipp said, nodding at the screen. "He's one of the bad guys, right?"

Andreas groaned. "I thought you said you remembered everything?"

"I remember it now. The androids. Replicants. That only live for four years."

"Right, Zipp. So be happy with your allotted time."

Andreas tore off the corner of a magazine lying on the table.

"I can fold a little cock for you."

He leaned closer to the screen. "Now he's ordering a Tsing Tao. Shit, this is good. Salome and the snake."

"I've seen it before," Zipp grumbled.

"The way she dies," said Andreas, waxing emotionally. "It's so fucking beautiful. The way she sails through the glass."

"That's called slow motion. Not especially innovative."

"You don't get it," said Andreas angrily. "Look at her! Wearing only a see-through raincoat. And the blood inside the plastic when the bullets hit – that's pure genius. Salome's death. It's magnificent, plain and simple. And that part's great!" he went on. "'Can the maker repair what he makes?'" He looked at Zipp. "Pressing the eyeballs into the head of a man with your bare thumbs – could you do that?"

Zipp didn't think so. But it occurred to him that Andreas could very possibly be a replicant. Who only livened up at the sight of his own kind. With implanted memories and a built-in emotional response, like Roy Batty. An advanced design from the Tyrell Corporation, "Nexus 6 fighting model". Soon he'd fall victim to reversing cells. And he even wanted to sit through the music of Vangelis during the credits. By then Zipp was on the verge of sleep.

"Wake up," Andreas said, pounding Zipp on the shoulder. "Time to die."

*

I want to be left in peace. The price I pay is that I no longer count, I'm not seen or considered important. Wearing the brown coat I'm not taken seriously. And yet, if people only knew, God forbid, but the worst of all . . .

The doctor tells me that I'm healthy, there's nothing wrong with me. Strong as a horse. That animal keeps plaguing me. I have a brisk gait, move with ease, even though I'm big-boned. Some people would say chubby, but at least I've kept my figure. I'm not tall, which suits me fine because women should be petite. It's strange how different other people are from me. I'm almost invisible, no-one ever notices me. They veer aside if they're heading towards me in the street. But they don't notice who they're skirting around because I'm just a shadow at the corner of their eyes. It doesn't bother me, since I've never known anything else. Oh yes, I have a son. Ingemar. I carried him around when he was little, rocked him and caressed him. Felt almost astonished that he was mine. That he was dependent on me, that he would die if I dropped him. That made Irma blossom. She was needed by another human being. She was life or death! But it didn't last. Nothing lasts. He grew up, passed me by, and looked at my feet when he spoke. Then he moved away. That's how it goes. I'm invisible, so dreadfully ordinary, so terribly different. I know only a few people, I know them better than they know me. They think they know me, but they're wrong. By all reckoning, they're wrong.

Several days passed before they reported Andreas missing in the newspapers. His colleagues at work had come forward to say flattering things about him, as they always do. No-one wants to be embarrassed later, in case he should be found dead. That word hovers between the lines in the paper like toxic bacteria. No-one dares to say it out loud, since it might turn out to be true. Did they think he had committed suicide? No, no, for God's sake, not Andreas. He sauntered through life. He wouldn't leave it of his own free will, and he didn't have any enemies. Yes, it's true that he took chances, innocent kinds of things, the way boys do. A beer or two on a Saturday night. But that's not a crime, surely? We're terribly worried. They pose for the newspaper photographer, loving the spotlight, the fact that they know someone who might have died under mysterious circumstances. If he suddenly shows up, safe and sound, if he'd just been out partying on the Danish ferryboat, what a let down that would be, when it could have been something exciting. I haven't disappointed them.

I've turned off the lights in most of the house. But there's a light on in the bathroom. Soon Andreas will start to decompose. Like a piece of meat that's been left out on the worktop. It changes colour, gets soft and jelly-like, then it starts to smell. At some point the meat becomes poisonous. I'm poisonous now too, perhaps I've started to smell different. I, who am so careful about things like that. I always use soap and deodorant. Wash my hair frequently. And the floors. The windows are shiny. All the door handles are polished and clean. But I myself have become a piece of spoiled meat. I didn't want that to happen.

CHAPTER 5

"Matteus?"

He heard the voice the instant the door slammed. He promptly reached for the bag of sweets in his pocket. Wanted her to notice it and clap her hands.

"Yes," he said in a low voice, rustling the bag. His mother came in from the living room. She pressed his cheek to her breast.

"Did you meet someone on the way home?"

"No, but my jacket was under all the others," he blurted out.

"Grandpa is here."

Matteus rushed into his grandpa's open arms. And then he flew up in the air, flew like the wind, almost up to the ceiling.

"Watch out for your back," Ingrid said to her father.

And then she smiled. After so many years alone, he had at last pulled himself together and grown from 96 centimetres to two metres tall, or so it seemed. Because of a woman.

"You're 17 minutes late," said Sejer, looking at his grandson.

"My jacket was underneath all the others," Matteus repeated.

"I see," said Sejer, smiling. "With all the button-holes tangled up in each other?"

A network of delicate lines appeared on his face as his smile grew. Nothing gave him as much joy as this child with the chocolate-coloured skin. He felt overwhelmed, tender, almost weak in the knees. It was unsettling, considering what life was like and everything that could happen. And that was some-thing about which he knew a great deal. The boy slipped under his arm and grabbed his hands from behind.

"Teach me the police hold!" he begged eagerly.

"I'll give you a police hold," Sejer said, laughing, as he spun the boy around, bundled him up, and carried him to the sofa. "Do you promise to tell the truth, the whole truth, and nothing but the truth?"

Matteus squealed with glee. Ingrid stood leaning against the doorframe, watching them. Sejer looked up. Her back curved in a certain way that reminded him of her mother.

"You forgot about the time because you were having so much fun!" he guessed, looking into the boy's brown eyes. "You forgot your promise to your mother."

"No," shouted Matteus, wriggling on to his stomach.

"You met a stray dog on the street. You sat on the curb to stroke him, while you tried to work out how to get your mother to let you keep him. A scruffy-looking mutt. Am I right?"

"No, no!" he shouted again. He grabbed a pillow and put it over his head.

"You met a gang of bullies, and they wouldn't let you pass."

Silence. Ingrid looked at her father in surprise, and then at her son, who had curled himself up into a ball of corduroy and denim.

"They were sitting in a car."

"Who?"

Ingrid was at his side in an instant.

"Relax," said Sejer swiftly. "He's here, isn't he?"

"What did they do? Tell me!"

"Nothing."

He was talking into the upholstery.

"Don't play games with me!"

"I don't like my name! Matteus is a stupid name!" he shouted, throwing the pillow to the floor. He wasn't crying. He almost never cried. He had soon realised that he was different, that people expected other things from him. That it was best if he moved quietly and didn't make too much noise. With his kind of colouring it was almost too much for them.

"I want to know what they did," said his mother again.

"Ingrid," said her father, "if he doesn't want to tell you, he should be allowed to keep it to himself."

Matteus cleared his throat. "They asked me how to get to the bowling alley. But they knew where it was. Afterwards they came back. They didn't do anything."

He took out the bag of sweets that he had been clutching in his hand, lifted it up to his nose and sniffed at it. It contained sour balls, jelly worms, and marshmallows.

"I'm sorry," said his mother softly. "I was just so worried."

Chief Inspector Konrad Sejer picked up his grandson and sat him on his lap. He buried his face in the boy's curly hair and thought about the years yet to come. Tried his utmost to decipher the shadowy images that lay ahead, far in the future.

"They said I had a cool jacket," said Matteus, grinning.

"What's inside is even cooler," Sejer said. "Walk me to the door. I have to go home."

"No, you don't. I know Kollberg isn't alone."

"I have to go home to Sara."

"Is she going to move in with you? Where am I going to sleep when I come to stay?"

"She's not going to live with me. She lives with

her father, because he's sick. But she comes to see me, and sometimes she stays overnight. If she's there when you come over, you can sleep on the floor. All by yourself. On a foam mattress."

Matteus blinked his eyes in dismay. He stood there holding his grandfather's hand, tugging at it. Ingrid had to turn away to giggle.

"She's not fat, is she? So that there wouldn't be room for all of us?"

"No," Sejer said, "she's not fat."

He patted his daughter rather awkwardly on the arm and went out into the courtyard. Waved to Matteus in the open doorway. He drove slowly towards his apartment building. Later he would remember that, in those few minutes it took him to drive home from his daughter's house, life had seemed so orderly, so predictable and safe. Lonely, perhaps, but he had his dog. A Leonberger that weighed 70 kilos and was lacking in any manners. He was actually ashamed about that. Sara had a dog too. A well-behaved Alsatian. Sejer didn't like surprises. He was used to being always in control. He had almost everything. A good reputation. Respect. And, after many years as a widower, he had Sara. Life was no longer predictable. She was waiting for him now. They had invited Jacob Skarre to dinner. He was a younger officer whom Sejer liked and in an odd way counted as a friend, even though he was old enough to be Skarre's father. But he liked that. Enjoyed being with someone who was still young. And, he had to admit, it was good to have someone who listened, who still had a lot to learn. He had never had a son. Perhaps that was where his fondness for Skarre stemmed from.

He braked gently for a red light. Sara is standing in the kitchen. She's dressed up, but not too much. Probably put on a dress, he thought. She has brushed her long, blonde hair. She's not stressed. Her movements are measured and gentle, like the way I drive my car through town. The nape of her neck. A shiver ran down his spine. Those short, blonde hairs against her smooth skin. Her wide shoulders. She looks at her watch because she's expecting me home, and Jacob could turn up at any moment. The food is ready, but if it's not, that doesn't make her nervous. She's not like other people. She's in control. She's mine. He started humming a tune by Dani Klein – "Don't Break My Heart" – and then he glanced in the rear-view mirror. For a moment he was shocked at how grey his hair was. Sara was so blonde and slender. Oh well. I'm a grown man, thought Konrad Sejer as he pulled in to the garage. He took the stairs, even though he lived on the 13th floor. He was trying to stay in shape, and maybe he'd have time for a shower. He ran up the stairs without getting out of breath. As he pushed down the door handle, he heard his dog making a racket and coming rushing out to greet him. He opened the door a crack and whistled. Once Sejer was inside, the dog stood on his hind legs and pressed him against the wall. Afterwards he was wet all over. Now he definitely needed a shower. The dog sauntered into the living room. Sara called hello.

That's when he noticed the smell. He stood still for a moment, breathing it in. There were several different smells: nutmeg from the kitchen, and melted cheese. Fresh-baked bread from the oven. He could also still smell the dog, who had nearly devoured him. But the other smell! The unfamiliar smell coming from the living room. He took a few steps, peeked into the kitchen. She wasn't there. He kept going, the smell got stronger. Something wasn't right. He stopped. She was sitting on the sofa with her feet propped on the table. Soft music reached his ears from the stereo. Billie Holiday singing "God Bless the Child". She was wearing lipstick and a green dress. Her hair gleamed, blonde and shiny, and he thought: She's beautiful. But that's not it. He glared at her.

"What is it?" she said gently. There was no trace of anxiety in her voice.

"What are you doing?" he stammered.

"Relaxing." She gave him a radiant smile.

"Dinner's ready. Jacob called, said he'd be here shortly."

It smells of hash, thought Sejer. Here, in my own living room. I know that smell, it's not like anything else, I can't be mistaken. He was dumbstruck. He was a mute beast, a fish out of water. The smell was thick in the whole room. He cast a wild glance at the balcony door, went over and opened it. He was so unbelievably surprised, so completely bowled over.

"Konrad," she said. "You look so strange."

He turned to face her. "It's nothing. Just . . . something occurred to me." His voice didn't sound normal. He tried to think. Jacob could be there any second. Sara didn't look stoned, but maybe she would be soon. Jacob would think he condoned it, and he didn't. What on earth should he do? She's a psychiatrist, she works with people who are very sick, many of them destroyed by drugs – heroin and ecstasy – and here she sits, getting stoned. On my sofa. I thought I knew her. But I suppose, after all, I don't. The crease on Sejer's forehead was deeper than it had ever been.

Sara got to her feet. She placed her hands on his chest and stood on her toes. He was still taller than she was.

"You look so worried. Please don't be worried."

The only thing he smelled was the caramel scent

76

of her lipstick. He swallowed hard, and there was an audible gulp in his throat.

Why do I become a child in the arms of this woman? he wondered. And then, out loud, his voice hoarse: "What's that strange smell?"

She laughed slyly. "I put a whole nutmeg in the mousaka by mistake, and I haven't been able to find it."

He stared at his feet. He certainly didn't have time for a shower now. Jacob would be at the door any moment. The fresh September air came streaming into the room. Billie Holiday was singing. He didn't know if the smell was still there as the room gradually cooled off. Norwegian law, he thought. In accordance with Norwegian law. It sounded ridiculous. He could say anything to her, but not that. It occurred to him that this woman had her own laws. And yet she had higher moral standards than anyone he knew. He felt like a schoolboy. Realised there was so much he didn't know, so much he had never tried. He was curious about people, he wanted to know about them, who they were and why they were that way. But right now he felt something wavering inside him.

The doorbell rang. Sara went to open the door. Jacob was sharp, for all that he looked like a schoolboy. Was the smell still there? His eyes stopped at the picture of Elise on the wall in front of him. She smiled back. She had no worries. She disappeared for an instant, seemed more dead than usual. It was harder to summon her back, her voice, her laughter. He felt a new kind of grief that she was about to disappear in a different way. Would it never end? He went out to the balcony. He liked the crisp autumn air and the bright colours. Liked this time of year better than the summer. He took several deep breaths. He thought he ought to work out more; he wasn't getting any younger. There was plenty of life left. Matteus would grow up, black in a white world. He had to be there for him. Sejer shook his head, bewildered. Couldn't understand his sudden gloom. And then, there was Jacob Skarre standing next to him.

"Smells good!"

"What do you mean?" asked Sejer, on the defensive.

"From the kitchen," Jacob said.

They ate and drank and talked about their jobs. Sara told stories from the Beacon psychiatric hospital, where she worked as a doctor. She wasn't the least bit stoned, at least not that Sejer could see. But now and then he would glance at her surreptitiously, and he scrutinised Jacob more closely than usual. One of the things about Jacob was that he was so tactful. If he noticed anything he would never say so. Should he mention it himself when they were alone? He brooded over this as Jacob talked about a shooting incident. It was a bad case, but, even so, an old story that repeated itself with few variations. Jacob was determined to confer with his God, to find some meaning in something which had no meaning. Because there wasn't any meaning or purpose, it wasn't part of any higher plan that would lead to anything good. Sejer was convinced of that.

"It was a bunch of kids who were going to have a party. It happened the same way it always does. The guys bought the alcohol and then picked up the girls. One of the boys, called Robert, had a rented room. And a stereo system. The landlord was gone, it was perfect timing. The idea was to get drunk, get laid, and then brag about it the next day." Skarre looked up at Sejer with the bluest eyes in the world. "Somebody also brought along some dope. They weren't really drug users, it's pretty much considered decadent to smoke a little hash at a party, and it's not exactly a major crime any more, not these days. To keep it short, the whole thing ended in the deepest misery. Drunkenness, then fighting. Robert got out a shotgun and shot his girlfriend right in the face. Her name was Anita, 18 years old. She died instantly."

He paused and stared into his glass of red wine. Held it by the stem, not wanting to leave any fingerprints on the bowl of the glass. It was amazing, Skarre's attention to detail.

"They were ordinary boys," he said to Sara. "I know it sounds as if they were nothing but the dregs at the bottom of society, but they weren't. They all had jobs or were students. They came from decent homes. Had never done anything criminal."

He started swirling the wine in his glass. "In a way it's impossible to understand, don't you think? Except to suppose that something took over. Something from outside."

"You can't blame the Devil," said Sejer with a smile.

"I can't?"

"Hasn't he been officially excluded from the Norwegian church, as being non-existent?"

"That's a great loss to human kind," said Skarre meditatively.

"Why so?" Sara wanted to know.

"If we don't believe in the Devil, we won't be able to recognise him when he suddenly shows up."

"Blame the Devil? For heaven's sake. That would cut a lot of ice in court."

"No, no." Jacob shook his head. "Try to think of it like this. We encounter the Devil all the time. The question is, how do we handle him?" He fell silent for a moment. "I don't really believe in the Devil, but I have doubts now and then," he said, smiling.

"For example, when I saw the photo of Anita – what was left of her – or Robert's face through the bars sitting in his cell. He's a good person."

"All of us are both good and bad, Jacob," Sara said. "It's not an either/or."

"You're right. Some people are fundamentally good. Others are fundamentally cynical. I'm talking about a basic tone that exists in every person. And in Robert, it's good. Don't you agree, Konrad?"

Oh yes. He agreed. And he didn't understand it. He didn't go to bed. Gave himself an extra hour. Sara and Jacob were going in the same direction, so they shared a taxi. He patted his leg, the signal for his dog to come and lie down at his feet. His thoughts whirled. Matteus, Sara, Jacob, Robert, and everything that happens. But life is not basically bad. The red wine had taken its effect, he had to admit. He'd drunk his fill, and a little more besides. Matteus would be fine, everyone was healthy, he was doing well in his job. And he would work out this thing with Sara. Later. He stared up at the picture of Elise. Since all was finally quiet in the building and anyway no-one could see him, he drew her a little closer.

Ingrid Sejer was also still awake. She had put Matteus to bed at 8 p.m., sung him a song and tucked him in. Later on she went to get his school bag to check that everything was there. Books and gym kit. She took it out to the living room and opened it. Glanced through his books, made sure the pencil was sharp, that the rubber and glue stick and scissors were there. A folded slip of paper fell out. The blue-tinted paper was not one she recognised. Perhaps it was a message from his teacher, intended for her.

"I'M GONNA CUT THREE GASHES IN YOUR BACK AND I'M GONNA RUB SALT IN THEM SO THEY HURT LIKE HELL.

YOU FUCKING BLACK!"

CHAPTER 6

As I said, Andreas was handsome. He had a flawless complexion. Fair and smooth, with rosy cheeks. And clean. I've always been cautious of the importance of cleanliness; it's something I learned early on. Nothing is ever left lying around at my house, either inside or out. I go out in the evening to check. The neighbours are not so meticulous. I've seen everything from bikini tops to dirty coffee cups on the patio table next door. Now, I don't mean it's a catastrophe, but I don't understand it. How can they stand at the window and see those dirty cups, and still sleep soundly? For myself, I am always considerate. I think that's important. We're not alone in the world, after all.

I sit in the red chair in the dark and listen. Even though it's quiet, I think I can sometimes hear someone outside. A warning of everything that is to come. A silent stream of people coming to the house, curious. Ingemar won't miss me, but he will do his duty. Put a notice in the paper. Send word to my two sisters, who are far away. But they always write at Christmas. Everything is fine. We keep in contact with other people.

We're not really afraid to die. We're only afraid of being forgotten. We know that we'll be forgotten, and the idea is unbearable, don't you agree? As time passes we become infrequent visitors in the minds of those left behind. The ones who clear out the house and divide up the belongings. Throw away the rubbish. And forget. If we knew that every evening someone lit a candle and sat down to think – thought about us if only for a few seconds – then we could depart this earth in peace. No-one will light a candle for me. Who would do that? But I've arranged things so that when my name is mentioned it will be with horror and amazement. A picaresque story. Maybe my picture will be in the paper. I've got rid of all of them except one which shows me almost young, 40 or so. The worst thing about dying is not being dead and buried. Something as proper and final as that: dead and buried. It's the hours before, when you fall into the hands of the living. They're only human, after all. I can imagine some of the things they'll say. I won't repeat them here, but they'll be said. I know what they are.

*

Andreas sauntered along, taking giant strides, with Zipp plodding diligently at his side. They were making for the river. It wasn't because of its steady roar or the way lights flickered in the black water, those weren't things they thought about. Nevertheless the water drew them. There was a raw wind, and Zipp stuffed his hands into his jacket pockets to warm them. They found a bench. Sat there in silence. When water is flowing past, it's not necessary to talk. Instead each was lost in his own thoughts, fantasising about falling in, struggling against the current and the cold of the water. A sense of solemnity came over them. Zipp was gloomily thinking about the girl in the striped jumper. Annoyed, he scratched his crotch.

"A nightcap right about now. That would be good."

Andreas nodded and squinted down at the river. Something black and heavy that never really got going. They had spent all of Gina's money.

"If an old lady with a handbag came along, I'd fucking grab it," he said. "Just grab it and run."

"We've done enough for one day," Zipp said. "And by the way, all the old ladies are in bed by now."

They fell silent again. A low murmur could be heard from the square behind them. Laughter and curses. Lots of people were drunk. They'd been drinking all night, at last finding courage and self-confidence, and now they were bent on showing it.

Ready for a fight, in other words. There were signs of a brawl in the taxi queue, and they could hear a few words: "You ape." "Damn Turkish devil."

"Shit," Andreas snapped. "Let's mug someone."

"Mug who?"

"Anyone."

"Calm down!"

Zipp couldn't understand what was bugging Andreas. He wasn't himself. Something was building inside him. But they both turned around to look at the city. Searching for a wounded animal, an easy prey. Most people could defend themselves pretty well, and it was also possible that they might get beaten up themselves. In their search for a release they were also frightened. Nervous of their plan, that was chafing deep inside. An intuitive sense of what it might lead to. As if they were coming to the end of a lengthy process that had begun long ago. Their fear gave them a dose of adrenaline, and it felt good. They headed up towards the taxi rank, passed the tent where beer was being served; it was still in use though it was early autumn as they had installed a heater. Clenched their teeth in irritation when they heard the glasses clinking. They cut across the main street, went past the Town Hall. Zipp realised that they were approaching the church. Andreas led the way, Zipp jogged along behind. He didn't understand why they were going there. No-one would be out tending the graves. No old people with pension cheques in their handbags. The church spread over a hill above the square and was without a doubt the building with the best aspect of any in the whole city. That's where the castle would have stood if the city had had a king, Zipp thought. They walked among the gravestones, reading the inscriptions. "I am the way, the truth and the life." Andreas stood with his hands on his hips and stared at the words. Zipp kicked at the ground, puzzled.

"It ends here," Andreas said in a low voice.

"What do you mean?"

"All of it. Everything that we are."

Zipp looked around in bewilderment. They were enveloped in silence and darkness. "What's with you? Skip work tomorrow," he suggested. "We can catch a lift out of town. We'll think of something. We could go to fucking Sweden."

"I've missed enough days as it is."

His voice had a dejected tone to it, Zipp noticed. Something was definitely up. Zipp was suddenly nervous.

"I'm kind of in the doghouse right now," Andreas said. "I've got to watch my step."

"But your boss is a woman. I can't understand how you can let some bitch order you around."

"A boss is a boss. She's the one who pays my wages."

"What about buck naked?" Zipp said. "A shag for a day off!"

"You have to draw the line somewhere."

"And where would that be?"

"At varicose veins and a moustache."

"What about the Woman? You like them that way, don't you?"

Andreas didn't reply.

"Hey!" A devil had got into Zipp, but he was trying to cheer Andreas up. "Do you lie on a sheepskin rug, or what?"

Andreas gave him a long look. Zipp couldn't restrain his laughter. He could picture Andreas, naked on a sheepskin rug. And an old lady with a brush and artist's smock. He was hysterical at the idea. Maybe Andreas was holding a brightly coloured ball in his hands. Maybe an orange. And then he laughed even harder. He roared into the silence among the graves, doubled over with laughter, and then stood there in the grass, gasping. He snorted several times through his upturned nose, followed by a few hoarse squeaks, then more snorts. Andreas gave him a weary smile. Pulled his hands out of his pockets, jumped forward, grabbed hold of Zipp's jacket, and started boxing him. Not hard, they were friends after all, but Zipp almost lost his balance. He stumbled backwards a few paces as he raised his hands in a half-hearted attempt to defend himself. But the comic image wouldn't let go, and he laughed so hard that tears poured down his cheeks while he fumbled to hold his friend at bay. Andreas launched a new attack. He lunged forward. There was grass underfoot and Zipp fell, but didn't hurt himself. He was still fighting to control his laughter. But then he caught sight of Andreas' face. There was something demonic about his expression, as if he'd gone berserk. And now he was on top of Zipp. What the fuck! Andreas had made up his mind, his strength was based on sheer will, and Zipp was helpless, overcome by hysterical sputtering; he was gasping for air while he wondered what was coming. A fist in the head or a knee in the stomach? Andreas looked so strange. Zipp waited for him to let go his grip, but he didn't. While he stared at Andreas through tears of laughter, he tried to remember what he had said that could provoke such a serious expression on the face he knew so well. This face that was now so close to his own. The shining eyes, the red cheeks, the teeth gleaming white in the darkness. Zipp felt warm breath against his chin. Andreas had locked his hands so that he lay helpless on his back in his tight jeans. And then, slowly, Andreas began thrusting against him in a steady rhythm. Zipp stared at him in surprise, couldn't understand what he was doing. He wasn't very bright, and Andreas seemed somewhere far away as he kept thrusting and thrusting. Suddenly he stopped. His eyes could see again; they looked at Zipp with such vulnerability. He loosened his grip. Zipp stayed where he was as he struggled to understand. And then, before he managed to work it out, he felt a hand between his thighs. It began rubbing him, the slender hand, it rubbed and rubbed. He was caught off guard. To his horror he felt desire seize him, and something terrifying struck him like thunder inside, a terror so great that he felt as if he would split in half. From the depths of his soul he managed at last to summon a scream. It came all the way from his feet, it sliced through his body and into Andreas' face, blasting him away, and with a mighty leap he was on his feet. He was still screaming, an incoherent bellowing, in a voice that he didn't recognise. He clenched his fists, ready to strike anything, to crush and rip, smash to pieces!

Very slowly, Andreas got to his feet, without releasing his gaze. Zipp was a raging animal, ready to attack. Andreas stood at a reassuring distance, keeping an eye on him and preparing himself. At that moment Zipp was the stronger one, strong enough to kill. One wrong move and he'd kill with his bare hands.

"Shit, Zipp," Andreas whispered. "I didn't mean to."

"Shut up! Shut up, you arsehole, you fucking poof!"

"I didn't mean . . ."

"I don't want to hear it! I don't want to know anything. Don't touch me, God damn it!"

Andreas raised his voice. Zipp could hear anger behind his words.

"That's just the way it is! It's always been that way!"

There was a plea in his eyes. Zipp was thunderstruck. He had never imagined this, not in his wildest imaginings. Anything but this. So what if he was particular about girls, if he preferred older women, that was all fine, appealing almost, it suited the way he was. But gay?

"What about the Woman?" he whispered, out of breath. "Was it all a bluff?"

"No." Andreas stared at his feet. "She's . . . a cover."

"What the fuck! A cover?"

"You believed it, didn't you?"

"Do you sleep with girls or don't you?"

Zipp couldn't control himself, his emotions were tied in knots. He'd been oblivious, hadn't suspected a thing, but now it was so clear. Andreas had never been interested in women, and Zipp, idiot that he was, had been blind as a bat. He felt such a fool.

"I sleep with her, but it's just a cover."

Now there was total silence. A floodlight near the church wall sent a white light over the patch where they stood, facing each other with fists clenched. Zipp felt as if everything had been staged by some higher power. Someone had placed them here, someone had put the words in his mouth. And what he had felt. The desire when Andreas touched him, and the urge to destroy him which followed. Confused, he stood there, stamping his feet. There was nothing to do but leave. This was too much for him. If only he had suspected something, thought it through over time, been able to prepare himself. But if he left now, everything would be over. For ever. He knew that, and Andreas knew it too. He was still waiting, his fists ready, whether to attack or to defend. From now on he would have to live with the knowledge that Zipp knew. That he might talk about it. And Zipp had to live with what Andreas had done. For several seconds desire had swelled inside him. It was just a hand, like all other hands, like a girl's hand. His head couldn't control what was between his legs, God damn it! There was a difference, wasn't there? Was there a difference? He wanted to knock down all the headstones, rip up all the plants, smash the whole town!

"The fact that you . . ." Andreas stammered. "It doesn't mean anything that you reacted that way. It's normal. Everybody . . ."

"Shut up!" Zipp was getting worked up. "I know that I'm not a fucking poof. You don't have to tell me that. For God's sake, shut up, Andreas!"

He tugged at his hair. He started sobbing, then wiped away the snot and tears, and looked at Andreas' yellow shirt gleaming in the dark. His world was in ruins, but the damn church was still standing, holding its own. He wanted to smash that too! You couldn't be friends with someone who was gay. People might find out and then obviously they'd think that he was one too. That's how people thought: that they were together, or something, had been fucking each other for years. He turned and walked away. Reached the corner of the church.

There, in front of the church, stood a bench. He sat down, had to think. Go home to bed and fall asleep, after this? Impossible. After the whole future had been wrecked. For years he had been living a lie, he had been duped. Maybe Andreas had wanted him at that time? Maybe he had been a figure in Andreas' dreams? Zipp's shoulders began to shake. He was crying soundlessly. Andreas, gay. So it was impossible to tell. God and the entire world could be gay! Perhaps other people he knew too, ordinary people. Girls even. He thought about Anita. What if Robert had been an alibi? Robert, and all the others she'd slept with. But Anita was dead now, so it didn't matter. Possibly, nobody was what he pretended to be. What about himself? Hell, no! He was a good friend. Was he? Did Andreas really expect him not to turn his back? That was asking an awful lot. At the same time, it was a matter of their friendship, all those years! He needed time. A few days to think things over, but he wasn't used to solving problems by thinking, and besides, he was freezing. Behind him he heard stumbling footsteps. It was Andreas, he knew. You'd think he would have gone a different way. Zipp stared at the gravel, wanting to be out of this situation, back to what they had before, but that could never happen. They would have to find a new way. What would people say if they suddenly stopped hanging out together? They were always together. It would make the rumours start buzzing. The story would be launched, at first as a joke. Have you heard? Zipp has broken up with Andreas.

His shoes were wet with dew. His feet were frozen.

"If you ever do that again, I'll kill you!"

Andreas put up his hands. "I won't!"

They both shrugged. Zipp got to his feet, almost mechanically. At the same instant they started walking at a slow pace to the stone gate. As they passed through it, it was as if something closed up behind them and was gone for good. Hidden in the dark among the graves. Zipp wiped his nose. He took some pride in his own generosity when he said: "Shit! People don't understand a thing. I hate this town."

Andreas nodded. It was a shitty town. Were there

any decent people in this place? What did anyone know about how hard it was, all those people sitting in their warm living rooms, staring at American soap operas and criticising anyone under 20? Fucking shitheads! And what did they say in *Blade Runner* when the storm was at its worst? "*You're our best and only friend.*" And then, in the dark, two faint voices:

"You're not going to tell?"

"No."

It was over. For a moment they had stared into an unfamiliar deep. Now it was closed again. For a few minutes they walked along as they had before, side by side. Zipp understood that Andreas needed him. Hadn't Zipp always given his friend the utmost respect? But what could he demand in return for keeping Andreas' secret? Something that he had never been given? THE UTMOST RESPECT!

He felt a singing inside, a brand-new sensation. He would no longer cower. Their relationship would have to have a new quality. Andreas was more handsome, more intelligent, more popular; he had more money and nicer clothes, but he was bloody gay! The word had unpleasant connotations for Zipp: a torn rectum, Vaseline and shit under his nails. Wasn't that what he had always thought? Life was basically great. He himself was totally normal. He suddenly thought about the desire he had felt at the touch of Andreas' hand. But what the fuck, he had been overpowered, and wasn't he in the prime of his life, surging with vitality? And no-one had seen them. They shared a secret, a strange experience that was both powerful and frightening, but they'd find something else. Something better. He was sure of that. No, not sure, but he hoped so. The way only a young man of 18 can hope.

They turned their backs on the dead and headed into town. They walked along without saying a word, on their way towards something cruel, something truly terrifying, worse than what had just happened. Both of them had stumbled off on to a detour, but now they were back on track. They scowled at everyone they met, turned down side streets, walking with their hands stuffed in their pockets. Andreas' knife swung at his hip. They had to find some way to remember the night that would overshadow everything else. Later, when they recalled that time, they would have to be able to talk about it to others, even though they both knew what it was about, that it actually had to do with that night when they landed in the grass, on top of each other. Zipp could feel the sharp hip bones against his thighs. But he pushed all of that aside. He had to move on.

It was almost midnight. They had to leave the town centre for quieter neighbourhoods. They kept their eyes moving, but took care to avoid looking at each other; it was too soon for that. Tomorrow, perhaps. They had to get through this night. They passed the cinema on the left and crossed the street. Walked past the Gotten kiosk, an optician and a second-hand shop. The streets got more deserted as they went. And there, sent by the Devil himself, was a woman on her own.

They noticed her at the same moment. A stout woman in a brown coat. She was wearing high heels, and it was clear that she wasn't used to them. Without a word, they picked up their pace, moving in unison – like a single, alert predator – with their heads close together, as if discussing something important. Sooner or later she would turn and see them. They didn't really know what they wanted with her. She had appeared at such an opportune moment; it was an exciting game for two capricious young men. There was something about the anxious figure that told them she was altogether alone, that no-one was waiting for her. A woman close to 60; or at least that's what they thought, who was walking along the street in the middle of the night, who hadn't been collected by a husband or by a son. Obviously she lived alone. And since she was walking, she must not live far away. Or maybe she didn't dare stand in the queue for a taxi. People had been killed waiting for a taxi; no doubt she read the papers like everyone else.

Then she turned. They looked into her pale face.

She quickened her step, but had trouble because of her shoes. She hadn't gone more than eight or ten paces before she turned again, cut across the street and crept along the windows of an estate agent's office. Light was flooding from the windows, and maybe that made her feel safer. She passed a park, turned left, and headed further from the town centre. They were now on Thornegata, approaching a hill. She turned left again. The street passed through an established residential area with older homes. Andreas had the idea that they should split up.

"I'll follow her," he whispered. "She'll relax if there's only one of us. You run up the hill through the back gardens so she can't see you from the street. We'll escort the old bag home!"

Zipp obeyed. He stared at the woman and thought about how scared she was, maybe afraid that she was going to die. Her shoes were tapping hard against the pavement. Andreas walked behind her up the hill while Zipp slipped into a garden and started running through shrubbery and fruit trees, invisible in the dark. Andreas kept going. He could hear her rapid breathing. She kept turning round to see him striding along behind her. He tried to saunter to look less threatening. He felt as cold as ice as he touched his knife. Was she praying as she walked? Halfway up the hill she made another turn. Now she's almost safe, he thought. He passed her, casting a glance in her direction, listening to her footsteps on the gravel. A gate slammed. A key in a lock.

Andreas had reached the far side of the house, he was pushing his way through the hedge, creeping into the garden, cloaked by the dark between the trees. He stood still and listened. Felt someone's breath on his neck.

"The old lady's inside. What do we do now?"

Zipp's eyes shone like delicate flames behind a dew-covered pane. *My best and only friend.*

Andreas thought for a moment. Then he took off his scarf and let it slide through his fingers.

"Shit. Are you going to strangle her?"

Zipp was pale. At that moment a light went on in the house. A faint glow from the window fell across the lawn.

"Do you think I'm a complete idiot?"

Andreas wrapped the scarf around his face so that only his eyes were visible. Then he took the cap from his trouser pocket and pulled it down over his hair. He put a hand on Zipp's shoulder, and was relieved when it was not brushed away. For a moment his knees felt weak with gratitude. They were going to share everything. The awful secret in the grass by the church, and what they were now about to do. Nothing big. Just rob an old woman of her money. Not a single objection occurred to either of them.

"You wait here. I'll go inside."

"Surely the old lady must have locked her door," Zipp said.

"I can get in anywhere." Andreas's voice was deep and resolute. He was going to make up for everything that had happened. The terrible pain had to be overshadowed by something; sheer terror would do the trick. The risk and the excitement overwhelmed his body, shaking him out of the paralysis he had felt back at the church.

"Shit, Andreas," muttered Zipp. "This is a dirty business."

"'I *am* the business,'" Andreas said in English, chuckling as he disappeared around the corner. Not the biggest or most dangerous animal in the forest, but the slimmest, the boldest and possibly the most cunning. Not an enemy was in sight, only an easy prey. Zipp crept closer to the wall around the garden. He couldn't see over it, but could glimpse the ceiling through the window and a chandelier in what must be the living room. Faint sounds were audible from inside. Zipp stood motionless in the dark. He prayed she didn't have a husband with a shotgun, or a fucking dog. He'd heard stories about what could happen, but at the same time he was giddy with excitement. The black night with the strange light. The silent trees, the dew on the grass that turned silver in the moonlight. He leaned against the wall and pressed his ear to the cool panelling.

CHAPTER 7

How handsome Andreas was. No doubt he could have any girl he wanted. It's easy to love what is beautiful. Those who are believers talk about God's perfect creation with an idiotic gleam in their eyes. But a number of people are uncommonly ugly. People like me, who have to work so much harder. Emphasise other qualities, so to speak. But even I found someone, or maybe Henry found me. I was so surprised when he proposed, so very moved by the courage it must have cost him, that I said yes at once. I didn't think anyone else would ever ask me. Would I, Irma Funder, get other offers? The woman with the eyebrows that had grown together and the fat thighs? The woman built like a horse? I didn't think much about whether I loved him; I didn't demand that much from life. Isn't marriage a job that has to be done? What is it anyway, this business about love? To need someone more than you need yourself? The lovely feeling that you've finally come out of yourself, taken off and flown inside another being? I don't know what in the world could ever free me from myself, except death. And what is sorrow? That you no longer have companionship? I don't even grieve for Henry. Or for my son, who never comes to see me. Does there exist an unselfish thought in anyone at all? I'm helping Runi with this now, because she helped me yesterday. If I love this child enough, he'll carry me in his arms later. When I'm old. Well, not Ingemar. But I had hopes. Equilibrium. Buy and sell. We will survive here, teeter around on this building site called earth, which is never finished. We build and build, we don't dare stop. As long as we keep building, we have the hope that one day something will tower above us and surpass everything else. Then we meet someone and heave ourselves out. The rest is all hormones that overflow, heat, dampness, a pounding heart. Everything that courses inside us. Biochemistry. Do you understand me? Henry and I, we even had a child. Lived like everyone else, or at least I think so. When he disappeared it was odd at first, the house was so quiet, but I quickly got used to it. I like being alone. No longer have to keep asking what he thought or believed. I'm lonely, of course, but who isn't? There are plenty of worse things. Illness and pain. Degradation. The way Andreas degraded me. He was thoughtless, but above all he was young. In that sense, he probably had a right to sympathy. Does everyone? I don't know why he chose me. Maybe it was random, the way life is random in a disgusting way.

Runi had called and wanted me to go to the theatre. It's been newly restored after the fire. The King was there for the opening, the chandelier alone was worth the ticket price, she'd seen it on television. The play was called *Chance Encounters*. I said yes when she called; I should have said no. I've always thought there was danger associated with going into town at night. They sell heroin in the square. But I didn't want her to get suspicious, think I might not be like other people, so I said yes. She is my cover. I have to show a little enthusiasm at regular intervals if I want to be left in peace most of the time. I got dressed up. It was still light and it didn't occur to me to worry about walking the 20 minutes into town. I chose a navy blue dress with a white collar. Underneath I wore nice underwear, silk panties and a tight vest to hold everything in place. My shoes had high heels, but I didn't have far to go. I left in plenty of time. I took note of the door labelled "Ladies", which is what I always do. Runi chattered and laughed the whole time, but every once in a while she would start complaining, as usual: about young people or whatever might occur to her. Life in general. I agreed with her at appropriate moments. There's something rather suspect about a person who never complains. Or at least

Runi would be suspicious, so I spent a while griping about the bus, even though I had walked. About how it never came on time. And about television programmes. The steady increase of crime in the city. There's certainly enough to talk about. Inconsiderate youths. Rubbish on the streets. All the synthetic additives in food. You know what I mean. She nodded and drank. It's nice to have someone agree with you.

We had good seats, but now and then I had trouble hearing what was said. We had a glass of port during the interval. I didn't understand the play, but I didn't say so. Just shrugged my shoulders expressively and said that, well, it wasn't that bad, but good Lord, I'd certainly seen better. And Runi agreed. But the theatre itself was magnificent. All in red and gold. And the chandelier was a dream in crystal. Hundreds of tiny little prisms, with light shining through every facet. Runi said it was made in Czechoslovakia, a gift from the Savings Bank. The old one from 1870 was gas lit, but in 1910 it had been converted to electricity, which is what subsequently started the fire. "Georg Resch," said Runi importantly, "he was the one who took the initiative." She loves showing off what little she knows.

It took a long time to get out at the end. People came pouring out from every direction, blocking the way. I was poked and jostled by strangers and I noticed all the different smells: expensive woollen coats, heavy perfumes and smoke from the first cigarettes. The buzz of voices. A surging roar which rose and fell. If I closed my eyes I might be carried along, just surrender. On the other hand, I have no trouble dealing with temptations. I just think about the day that inevitably follows. I fixed my eyes on Runi's coat. It felt as if the crowd was almost crushing me, it was hard to breathe. It's much more pleasant to watch television or read a book. But at last we were outside, and the crowd spilled away in all directions. Runi wanted to walk, it wasn't far. I said that I'd take a taxi. Hoped the driver would be Norwegian. I'm not a racist, but I can't understand what they're saying when they speak broken Norwegian, and then they get annoyed. And things aren't easy for them as it is; no, frankly, I simply didn't want to subject them to Irma Funder. So I hoped for a Norwegian.

It was two blocks from the theatre to the taxi rank on the square. I walked along the river and stopped at the corner. Stared at the endless line of young people who were pushing and shoving, cursing and yelling. I couldn't stand in that queue, not for anything in the world. For a moment I stood there, hesitating and cold, unable to make up my mind, and that's not like me. I would simply have to walk.

It was five to midnight. As I glanced up at the floodlit church, the way a child does, I thought: This is the witching hour. I looked around in confusion, but I saw only the noisy people queuing for a taxi and a few solitary souls, rambling about. An empty taxi glided past, turned off its light and vanished. What if I waited at the corner until the queue got shorter? At that very moment a couple walked up and joined the end of the queue. They each lit up a cigarette. I cut across the square and chose the main street. There was no danger as long as I stayed on the main street, which went all the way to the park. Only there did it get truly dark. The last hill was barely lit at all. I walked on the right side of the street as fast as I could, but my shoes hurt my feet. I tried to make myself uninteresting – because that's what I was, after all – but my shoes gave me away. I could just as well have had a bell around my neck. Come and get me, come and get me! shrieked my shoes. I had money in my handbag, but not a lot. I'm not stupid. Only enough for a taxi home.

I passed the optician's and the bicycle specialist. Thought I heard footsteps behind me, but didn't turn to look. If someone was there, panic would seize hold of me. It wasn't a long walk home. In a few minutes it would all be over. In my mind I pictured the house, my own house with its green paintwork, and the outdoor light that I had remembered to leave on, welcoming me home. I still thought I could hear something. Footsteps. Light, not tapping like my own. I couldn't resist a look. And then I saw them! Two young men. I admonished myself. There were people on the streets, they were going in the same direction, it was as simple as that. Yet it seemed as if they were staring at me, studying me as a possible target, but we women are always hysterical. We always imagine the worst, we know what it's like to grow up in a world of men. I started to walk faster. Turned around again to double-check. They were still there. I went all the way over to the shop windows, feeling safe for a moment in their light. Then I was in the dark again. When I turned around for the third time, one of them was gone. I sighed with relief; that was a good sign. He was already home! But I didn't slow my pace. I thought about everything that could happen. No, I wasn't afraid of dying. And I didn't pray to God. There were worse things that could happen to me than death. I thought it all through and knew that I couldn't allow that to happen to me. But that's how we think sometimes, and then it happens all the same. Like that time when I was ill and had to stay in hospital, with other people taking care of me.

I walked up the steep hill and thought about the

hospital and everything that had happened then. A nightmare that almost overshadowed the present. And that helped.

All the time I could hear footsteps. What frightened me was the fact that he didn't overtake me. A young man with long legs, he should have gone past long ago. Now I could see the roof of my house. I heard my own heart pounding, my legs hurt, and I was sweating inside the tight vest. I deliberately slammed the gate, as if someone in the empty house might be listening for it and get up from his chair. There were only a few more paces. The five steps up to the front door. I realised that I didn't have my key ready, I had to rummage in my handbag, in the little compartment. I stood under the light like a human bulls-eye. Then I found the key and stuck it in the lock. The door swung open. I could feel sobs rise in my throat out of sheer relief. That young man was going home to bed. Pull yourself together, Irma! I peered into the dark kitchen. Then I gasped out loud. A red eye shone in the dark. The coffee maker was on. It was half full of coffee. I had left the house with the coffee machine on, I could have burned down this lovely house, which is all I own. I switched it off. The kitchen smelled like a coffee shop. I turned on the light and lifted the pot from the hotplate. Had to lean on the counter for support. It had all been too much for me. The theatre, the crowd, the walk through the dark town at night, the strange man and the coffee maker on, in the old house. I straightened up. It would, I vowed, be a long time before I did that again. Then I went into the bathroom. Stood with my back to the mirror and dropped my dress to the floor. Pulled the tight vest over my head and then stuck my arms into a dressing gown. It's white; yes, out of sheer defiance it is white. I never stay over at anyone's house, so it doesn't matter. I stood in the doorway and peered into the kitchen, at the striped rug. Maybe a little pick-me-up would be in order. I had wine in the cellar, so I rolled back the rug from the trap door. I took the ring and pulled it open.

That's when something happened. I heard a sound; it came from the hallway. I hadn't locked the door! In my horror over the glowing coffee machine, I had forgotten to secure the latch properly. I had run to the kitchen with only one thought, to prevent a catastrophe. I stood there, frozen to the spot, staring, unable to believe my eyes. A man came walking into the kitchen with a knife in his hand. His eyes, which were all I could see under the peak of his cap, shone with determination. He had a scarf wrapped around his face, and he was looking at my handbag, which lay on the counter. There were 200 kroner inside. But I had jewellery and silverware and more cash in the safe in Henry's study. For a few seconds there was utter silence. He seemed to be sniffing at the room, as if the smell of burned coffee surprised him. Then he looked at me. He wavered a bit, the knife shook. I took a step back, but he came after me, pressed me against the counter, stuck the tip of the blade under my chin and snarled.

"Your cash. And fucking be quick about it!"

My knees started to shake. And that's when the accident happened, I couldn't help it. I felt a warmth sliding down my thighs, but he didn't notice, he was much too preoccupied with the knife, which was trembling, betraying his own fear. Just as scared as I was. I cast a glance towards Henry's study. I wanted to open the safe, but my legs wouldn't hold me. He got annoyed, waved the knife at me, shoved me aside with his fist. Not hard, but I flinched. His shouts were muffled by the scarf. "Hurry it up, you old bag! Hurry it up!"

I was just an old bag. And he was just a young kid. I could hear it in his voice. I hadn't moved. He pushed me again, and finally I managed to drag my feet across the room and into the study. I stood in front of the safe, staring at the dial, trying to remember the combination. My fingers shook uncontrollably, but my mind was a blank. I wanted to throw up, I wanted to run away. I was willing to give him everything I had, there wasn't really much inside, anyway, maybe 5,000 kroner. But I couldn't remember the combination. Now he really started to get nervous. Instinctively I thought that I had to keep him calm, tried to explain about the combination, that I had written it down. "In the teapot," I gasped, "it's in the teapot in the kitchen!" He screamed that he didn't have time for this. He seized hold of my dressing gown, up near the collar. I immediately pulled it tight because I was afraid, and he could see that this was for me the worst. I didn't want him to see me the way I was. With one hand he tugged at the belt and held it taut, then he raised the knife and cut my belt in two. The heavy white towelling fell away. I covered myself with my hands, but it was too late. He stared in disbelief, lurched back with a strange expression, not exactly disgust, but he couldn't comprehend what he saw. Just shook his head. He had forgotten what he came for. But the seconds kept ticking away, and eventually he understood. It was my intestine he was looking at. It sticks out through the skin of my abdomen and ends in a colostomy bag. It was almost full, and also split open. The knife blade had sliced it in two. The contents were running down my legs. I couldn't look at his face, I turned around and rushed out of the study, but he came after me. Stopped in front of me with his knife raised.

"I don't give a damn about . . . that! I want money!"

I felt it running down, it was thin, not fully digested, and the smell was starting to spread, and I'm so fastidious about things like that. Behind him, the cellar trap-door was open. He didn't notice it, he was jumping around, but I could see that he had reached breaking point. I thought he might end up stabbing me if he didn't get what he wanted. And so I pushed him. I heard a gasp as he fell backwards down the steep staircase. There was a crashing and thumping and thundering on the stairs. I heard a disgusting, dull thud as he hit the cement. A faint rattling sound that lasted a few seconds. Then silence.

*

Zipp was waiting in the dark. He heard sounds from inside: a woman screaming, footsteps crossing a floor. He stared and stared through the window, but he could see only the ceiling and the top of a painting. An eternity passed. Why didn't Andreas come out again? He looked for something to stand on. In the garden there was a small gazebo with several chairs inside. He crept over to it, picked up a chair and carried it to the window, shoving it down hard into a rosebed. He could feel the prick of the thorns through his trousers. He climbed on to the chair and peered over the windowsill. He saw a kitchen table and chairs and a striped rug. Nothing else, and nobody in sight. All was quiet. Confused, he stayed on the chair and waited. He couldn't imagine what had happened to them. Had this whole caper gone to hell? Had the worst possible thing happened? Were the police on the way? Damn it! He jumped down, but at that moment he heard a faint sound. Relieved, he spun round and stared at the corner of the house, but no-one appeared. Was Andreas playing games with him? Had he robbed the old lady and then run off with the cash? Was he standing down on the road counting the money, grinning and laughing at the thought of Zipp, still waiting in the dark? He climbed up on the chair again. Stood there for an eternity until his neck started to ache. Suddenly he caught sight of the woman in the house. She came through a door, wearing only a nightdress, and sank onto a chair at the table. She looked unharmed, which was a relief. He decided to stay where he was until she did something. Was she going to call the police? Had she called them already? Zipp jumped down, ran round the side of the house and stood at the corner, partially hidden. No-one came. He ran back to take one more look. She was still sitting there. He listened for sirens in the distance, but heard nothing. Just a faint hum from the town below. He was tired and bewildered after everything that had happened on this unreal day. He fumbled for a cigarette, inhaled deeply and watched the tip glow bright red in the dark. He badly needed to cough but managed to suppress the urge. He smoked the whole cigarette and then got back on the chair. She was still sitting there, for God's sake, in exactly the same position. The woman was clearly in shock, that much he could see. But he couldn't very well stay there all night. He was going to have to leave. Leave the dark garden all alone. He couldn't do that! But the clock was ticking. He had waited long enough. Without a sound, he slipped out through the gate, but the question kept churning through his mind: Where the hell was Andreas?

*

The pounding as he crashed down the stairs, the horrible sound of his head hitting the concrete floor, I can't describe it! The impact settled in my own body as a needle-like pain. I thought to myself: surely he must have died in a fall like that! That fragile body against the hard-as-rock floor. I closed the trap door. At least he wouldn't be able to come up and threaten me again. Of course, I would have to call somebody, surely someone would help me. Maybe Runi, or Ingemar. No, Lord knows, not

Ingemar! And the way I looked! I tottered out to the bathroom. Changed the bag. It was difficult to get the new one closed because my hands were shaking so much. I thought about what he had seen, what no-one was ever supposed to see. Or hear about, know about; well, only if necessary, if it was unavoidable. But see it? NO! The expression on his face, utter disbelief. Maybe he didn't realise what it was, maybe he thought I was some kind of deformed monster, a freak. A gleaming pink intestine on my stomach, that looks rather like . . . well, you have to forgive me, but it's so hard for me to talk about this. But it looks rather like a penis. And I'm a woman, after all.

I put on a clean nightdress. Sat at the kitchen table. I don't know how long I sat there. I felt encapsulated, with no room for any thoughts, not even despair. Then I raised my head, and my eyes automatically looked at the window. For a wild moment I thought I saw a face against the pane. I stared and stared, but it didn't reappear. I don't know how much time must have passed before I finally asked myself the question: What should I do now? When I reached that stage, the feeling of paralysis left me. And with the return of reality came the emotions. They nearly knocked me unconscious. I recalled his eyes. They were shining with fright and determination. To come here and force his way in had been important for him. How can money be that important? I was sitting a pace from the cellar door. If I opened it, the light from the kitchen would make it possible for me to see him. I had to get up and take a look, through the trap door. And then I remembered that I should call someone soon. Explain everything. There was so much that had to be done. Reluctantly, I got to my feet. Opened the trap door. I didn't dare to look. But I couldn't pretend that nothing had happened. If I went into another room and sat there until morning, he would still be lying in the same position. I stood with my back turned and counted to ten, to 20. He wasn't going anywhere. He had fallen to his death. Thirty, forty. Cautiously I turned. Why didn't he scream? I squatted down. The first step came into focus, then the rest. The light was slanting down over the stairs. The first thing I saw was his feet. They were lying on the second step from the bottom. His body was twisted into an impossibly contorted position. One arm was stretched out to the side, I couldn't see the other one, maybe he was lying on it. His forehead was a white patch in the darkness of the cellar, his cap was gone. No-one could lie like that and still be alive. The angle of his head gave me a terrible clue. I stood there as long as I could, staring at him. Listening for any sounds, but it was as quiet as the grave. I straightened up.

Realised that the worst had happened. He was dead.

The thought came to me with absolute calm, as something important but not dramatic. What would I have done if he were still alive? I should call for an ambulance. But the mere idea of having to explain everything was unthinkable. Strangers stomping into Irma's house? I put the trap door back in place. Laid the rug on top. It was simple. No-one knew that he had come into my house. I tried to think. It was a matter of making some important decisions. I took a deep breath, in and out, then another, in and out. I decided to stay at home the next day. I hardly ever missed work, so no-one would think it odd. I could say I was coming down with the flu. And then I felt it, the strange sensation that I had been in this selfsame situation before. I couldn't understand it. Fear must be playing tricks on me. But I had always believed that one day something terrible would happen. Whenever I sat in the red chair near the window I let my thoughts wander. In my mind I'd been through almost all the possibilities. The nightmare that would befall me. And now, here it was. Something that I'd been waiting for. When I realised the connection, I grew calmer. The worst imaginable thing had occurred; in other words, something was finally over. The problem was out in the open and could now be resolved. It was time for action. I told myself that first I needed to get some sleep. I felt worn out. Later, I would get rid of all traces. Had he left any traces? I looked around, went into the study. What about his knife? Was it down in the cellar? I was talking to myself in a low voice. "There's a dead man in the cellar. He came here to attack me. It was an accident. Nobody knows that he's here, and hardly anyone ever comes here. There must be a way out of this. There must be a way out!" I turned off all the lights except in the bathroom. Then I went to bed. Pulled the duvet over me and stared into the dim light of the room. I wanted to close my eyes, but I couldn't. They just kept running and running.

*

Zipp was perched on the top of a woodpile behind the house where Andreas lived. There was a faint light visible behind the curtains. The window was closed. He seemed to remember that Andreas always slept with the window open. He thought to himself: Here I am again, standing like a Peeping Tom. The bed was neatly made. He could see the black-and-white bedspread lying nice and smooth. And the poster of The Doors. On the desk stood an empty Coke bottle. No Andreas. Zipp had been convinced that Andreas would be at home in his own bed. But he wasn't.

Zipp jumped down. He would have to go home. Where the hell else could he go? Should he wait until morning and call? His concern turned to anger. And then he trudged off, past the church and the graves, walking fast with his hands in his pockets. Up and along the streets, feeling so damned alone. He had only to make it through this night. With daylight the explanation would emerge, something stupid. Andreas always had an explanation. He unlocked the door and went in. Ran downstairs. Pulled off his tight jeans. His skin felt clammy and stripes from the double seams ran down his thighs. He lay on the sofa with a blanket over him and stared into the darkness. Andreas had done everything, and he only stood there and watched. No-one had anything on him. A tiny feeling of relief began trickling through him. Just before the darkness swallowed him, he remembered the chair. He had left it standing under her window. What would she think? What had the two of them been thinking of? They hadn't thought, they had just charged ahead. Suddenly he pictured the pram striking the rocks, and the baby's tiny mouth with the toothless gums; the foaming sea; the angry cries. What we were ends here, he thought.

*

I lay in bed for a long time, shaking as if I had a fever. I felt neither good or bad, I was just a body living its own muddled life, without coherence. I dreamed that my intestine was growing, that it wriggled out, slowly but surely, until it was dragging along the ground. I had to gather it up and carry it in my hands for everyone to see. An enormous tangle of intestines. Look here! Then I woke up. I hadn't forgotten about the horror in the cellar. I had only pushed it aside for a while, like a mean-spirited dog some distance off, which couldn't get at me because it was chained up. But now it was growling. I opened my eyes and stared dead ahead at the flowered wallpaper. It growled again, this time louder. At the same time I was quite sure that I wasn't crazy. I'm not crazy. I'm perfectly sane, I'm describing everything exactly as it was, down to the last detail. Are you still reading this?

Then it was quiet again. Maybe the sound was the relics of a dream. Then it started howling. At first a long, drawn-out, faint howl, then it got louder. I've never heard such a sad howl before, it was coming from a creature in dire need, in the utmost pain. An insane thought occurred to me, but I pushed it away. It wasn't possible. The world couldn't be that evil! Things were bad enough already. But the sound was indeed coming from the cellar. A muffled cry, as if he didn't have much strength, and it had cost him everything to scream. I sat up in bed, shaking with terror now, and stuffed a corner of the pillow in my mouth. The man was alive! He was lying there in the cold cellar and screaming for help! I threw myself on to my stomach and pressed the pillow over my head. I couldn't bear to hear those screams, as if they came from a wounded animal. He was calling to me. Maybe other people would hear him. The neighbours? People passing on the street? They would stop and listen, make a note of my address. Maybe they would think I was hurting someone. I was going to be sick. What business had he coming here in the first place? If only he would shut up! Finally I got up and tip-toed across the room. I didn't want him to hear my footsteps overhead. Obviously he was in terrible pain. And he was only a boy. Imagine that he could scream like that. I've never heard anyone scream so horribly, with so much fear. A young boy. All alone in the dark down there, lying on the ice-cold floor.

I stopped in the kitchen. Turned on the light over the counter. I couldn't do anything without him hearing me. Turn on the water or open the door to the refrigerator. I pulled out a kitchen chair and sank down. Sat there with one hand on my stomach, feeling the warm contents in the bag through the material of my nightdress. It was quiet again. Maybe he had fainted or something, or maybe he was gathering his strength to scream even louder. I don't know how long I was there. Then he started again, this time louder. I stood up abruptly, went to the radio on the counter, and switched it on. Night-time programming. They were playing music. I turned up the volume. Found a level that blocked out his howls, so that I couldn't hear him. I listened in amazement to all the passion flowing into the room. "I will always love you." "Hold me baby, hold me now." I sat hunched over the table. I didn't belong in this world, I was an unloved human being. And now here I was, an old woman with a bag of my own waste at my stomach, taking up space. I suddenly started to retch, but nothing came out, just the taste of sour port wine. He had stopped screaming. Did I dare to open the trap door? Just take a quick look and shut it again? I began rolling up the rug, uncovering the door. I listened, holding my breath, didn't hear a thing. He must have lost consciousness. I could go back to bed, postpone the problem for a few hours more. I stared at the wall, at the calendar that showed September. It's autumn, I thought. It's going to get even darker and colder. Then I grabbed the ring and raised the trap door. Peered down at the pale face. The eyes above the scarf stared back at me, and I heard a scream so heart-rending that I almost fell down the stairs. But I regained my balance and dropped the trap door, dropped it with a bang. He was far from dead. He was going to stay alive for a long time; he had strength. He knew that I was up here, that I could save him. I turned the radio up again. Went back to bed. I could hear the music through the open door. A man was screaming in the most terrible despair. "I lied for you, and that's the truth." I sat up in bed until it got light outside. The grey light came through my window like dirty water. Someone like me, who is so meticulous, yet I couldn't stop it. He wasn't screaming now.

CHAPTER 8

September 2.

A slim, well-dressed woman came into the reception area. She paused halfway to the glass-enclosed booth and looked around. Then with swift, purposeful steps she moved towards the little window. Seen from the main entrance, there was something ridiculous about that little booth. But Mrs Brenningen felt entirely comfortable sitting inside it. She was protected there, didn't feel so much as a puff of breath from those questions she had to deal with. Didn't have to touch them. She was a sort of traffic light. Red or green. Usually red. Most people were told to sit and wait until someone bothered to come and get them. The woman was out of breath, making Mrs Brenningen think she was here to report a break-in or robbery. Something had been taken from her, and now she was indignant. She had bright red blotches on her cheeks and her lipstick at the corners of her mouth looked like dry crumbs. Mrs Brenningen smiled brightly through the glass.

"I need to talk to a police officer."

"And what is it about?"

The woman was evasive. She apparently had no desire to tell a lowly receptionist what her business was. But everyone had specific areas of expertise at the police station, and it was important that she was sent to the right department. And above all, it was important to ensure that the woman did in fact have a good reason for being there at all. For example, the passport office had moved to further down the street.

The woman seemed to sink into herself. She thought about the oppressive silence in her house. Even though there was never any noise this early in the morning, she could sense at once that something was missing. Something quite essential. She approached the door to his room, moving sideways, like a crab. Opened it and peeked inside. He wasn't there. Confused, she shut the door. Stood there, biting her lip. On the door he had hung a poster. It had been there for years. But this was the first time that she had really taken it in. "Kneel in front of this brilliant genius," it said. She was pulled out of her reverie because the woman in the booth cleared her throat, but still she didn't answer the question.

Mrs Brenningen represented an organisation serving the public and she didn't want an argument. She called Skarre's office and nodded towards the glass double doors. The woman disappeared down the corridor. Skarre was standing in his doorway, waiting. She looked him up and down, clearly not encouraged by what she saw.

"Excuse me, but are you just a trainee officer, or whatever?"

"I beg your pardon?" he said, blinking.

"This has to do with a very serious matter."

I assumed as much, since you decided to come here, Skarre thought. He smiled, after reminding himself of a passage in the Bible about patience.

"It's called an 'officer candidate'," he said gently. "No, I'm done with my training. Now tell me what this is about."

"I want to report my son missing."

He invited her to sit down.

"Your son is missing. How long has he been gone?"

"He didn't come home last night."

"So we're talking about one night?" Skarre settled himself behind his desk.

"I know what you're thinking: that there's no reason to worry. But that's really not something you can pronounce upon. You don't know him."

Skarre gave a mild shake of his head. The situation was so familiar. The son had been missing before. Now she wanted to take her revenge once and for all and make things hell for him. But it didn't matter; he still had to do his job. He picked up a Missing Person Report form and started filling it in. Place, date, time, his own name and title.

"The full name of the missing person?"

"Andreas Nicolai Winther."

"Nickname or any other name he uses?"

"No, none."

"Born?"

"June 4, 1980."

"Place of residence?"

"He lives with me. Cappelens gate 4."

"All right. I need a description of him. Height and build. Whether he wears glasses, that sort of thing."

She began describing her son. No beard or glasses, no distinguishing marks, nice teeth, eastern Norway dialect, normal mental state. Height: 185 centimetres; eyes: light blue – well, bordering on green, to be precise – long, curly, reddish-brown hair. Nothing special about the way he walks.

Skarre wrote it all down. In his mind he was forming a picture of the youth that probably didn't quite match up.

"Does he use a debit card?" he asked.

"He didn't want one."

"Has he ever been gone overnight before?"

"Surely that doesn't have anything to do with it," the woman replied, sounding sullen.

"Well, yes," said Skarre. "Actually, it does."

"So that you can file the report at the bottom of the pile and treat it as less important?"

"Your son is an adult," said Skarre calmly, trying to balance on the knife edge this woman represented.

"There's adult and adult," she said.

"I mean from a legal standpoint, and that's how we have to regard him too. You'll have to forgive all the questions, but I'm sure you understand that since your son is of age, and no doubt capable of taking care of himself, at this point we can't regard the situation as particularly dramatic. If he were a child, things would be different. I'm sure you agree, don't you?" His voice was exceedingly kind.

"But he always comes home."

"And I'm certain he will this time too. Most people turn up pretty quickly. Some are shattered after a trip on the boat from Denmark, or a party that got a little too wild. Has that ever happened before?" he asked.

"The boat to Denmark?" She gave him a wounded look. "He can't afford things like that. But it has happened before," she admitted. "Once. Maybe twice. But it's not something he usually does."

"I'm sure we'll sort this out. Together," he added, as a way of offering hope and encouragement.

She opened her handbag and took out a photograph. Skarre studied it. Andreas was an unusually handsome young man. Of course his mother would be worried.

"Who took the picture?" he asked with curiosity.

"Why do you ask?" she snapped.

"No reason." He shrugged. "I was just trying to be friendly. In my own clumsy way."

"Forgive me," she whispered. "I'm not myself. I got up at 8.00 and went to his room to wake him. He works at the Cash & Carry. I noticed that his bed hadn't been slept in. I waited until 10.00 to call the shop. He works in the hardware department, but he hadn't come in. He has skipped work before, I admit that."

"Are you angry with him?" Skarre asked. "Because he subjects you to these disappearing acts of his?"

"Of course I'm angry!" she said.

"More angry than scared?" He fixed his blue eyes on her.

"He's missing," she said in a low voice. "Now at least I've done something about it."

"I'll write up a report. Let me borrow the photograph. We'll send it out for distribution. At first to the PT."

"And what's that?"

"The police news bulletin. We have contact with the central authorities in all the Nordic countries. We live in a computer age now, you know. How's that for a start?"

"What about the TV and newspapers?" she ventured.

"Maybe not right away. It's someone else's responsibility to make that decision." He smiled. "I'm just a simple police officer."

He rolled up his sleeves. He didn't want her to think they weren't on top of things. If she only knew.

"What was he wearing?"

"Cotton trousers, a very pale colour. A T-shirt, with a light-coloured shirt on top, probably the yellow one. I didn't see him when he left, just heard him call from the hall, but the yellow shirt isn't in his wardrobe. And black shoes. He's good-looking," she added.

"Yes," said Skarre, smiling. "And what about his father? What does he say?"

"He doesn't know about it."

"Is he out of town?"

"He moved out," she murmured.

"Maybe he ought to know about this?"

"I'm not the one who's going to tell him."

She closed down a bit. Skarre gave her a searching look.

"It would be good if we could work on this together. Isn't there a chance that he's with his father?"

"Not a chance in hell!" she said vehemently.

"Have you called his friends?"

"He only has one. They were together last night. I tried to call him, but no-one answered. I'll try again."

"Do you think your son might be there?"

"No. I know his mother, and she would have sent him home."

"So in point of fact both of them might be missing?"

"I have no idea. I have enough to worry about with my own son."

"I'll need his father's name," Skarre said. "And the name of this friend. And their phone numbers. If it's difficult for you to contact the father, I can do it for you."

She thought for a moment, weighing up her options. Maybe it was a confrontation that she had been fearing for a long time. Diving down into the mud that had finally settled.

"What will you do now?" she asked.

"I have made an official note of your report. We'll contact you if anything turns up. I suggest that you stay at home in case he calls."

"I can't just sit at home and wait. I can't bear it."

"Do you have a job?"

"Part-time. Today is my day off."

"Try not to be cross. That may not be what he needs when he does get home."

"What do you mean? You're not worried about him? You think he's gone off on the boat to Denmark?"

"No," Skarre said wearily. "That's not what I'm saying. Let's just wait and see. Perhaps he's at home waiting for you now."

He reminded himself that this was what he had wanted, what he had always dreamed of doing. Helping people.

"Do you have any family you could talk to? Who could offer you some support?"

Mrs Winther rubbed one eye. She heard a little clicking sound as her poor eyeball rolled around in its socket.

"I need a taxi. Could you call one for me?"

Skarre put the form inside a plastic folder, called the switchboard and asked for a taxi.

"Please call and let me know when your son does turn up. Don't forget."

He put special emphasis on the word "when". And then Mrs Winther left. She strode solemnly into the corridor with the air of someone who was carrying out an unpleasant obligation for no pay. Skarre sat and stared at the photograph. Andreas Winther, he thought. Go ahead and admit it. You're lying under a duvet somewhere with a damn great hangover. Next to a girl whose name you can't remember. I'll bet she's sweet, or at least she was yesterday. You summon what strength you have left to think up an excuse for why you've missed work. Terrible headache. Coming down with a fever. With looks like that you could undoubtedly charm your boss into forgiving you. Whether it's a man or a woman.

Konrad Sejer was standing in the doorway. Skarre never failed to be struck by how tall he was. So eminently present. Sejer sat down with an expression that could have been crafted with his own hands. Then he leaned down and pulled up his socks. The ribbing around the tops was loose. "Anything going on?"

He caught sight of the photograph. Picked it up and studied it closely.

"Probably not. But he's a handsome young man. Missing since yesterday. Andreas Winther. Lives with his mother."

"Looks quite a charmer. Find out if he's attracted any attention in town."

"It's a good thing that Mrs Winther can't hear you."

"I'm sure he'll turn up soon. There's something about young men and their mother's cooking." Sejer was only moderately interested. There were many other things – some of them serious cases – that preoccupied him. Robert, for one, who was insisting on pleading guilty to the murder of Anita.

To the despair of his defence lawyer. It will sort itself out, Sejer thought. Press on home, Andreas.

*

The new day dawned. I lay in bed, waiting for 9.00. Dragged myself out of bed and out to the kitchen. The shuffling of my feet disturbed me. Did I really sound like that? Was it really true? I stared at the little lump under the rug, the iron ring. There's a dead man screaming in your cellar, Irma. The nightmare is real, and it's not going away! I went over to the telephone. Stood there for a long time with my hand on the receiver. Finally dialled my work number. I was surprised that I even remembered it, that my brain wasn't overwhelmed by the horror in the cellar, that it was still functioning. I could summon what I needed when I needed it. I think human beings are peculiar that way. But I had to make the call. At all costs, I had to prevent anyone from coming to the house. The mere thought of it forced an involuntary snort from me. I could have lain here dead, I could have lain here for days, until the smell reached the neighbour's. Merete answered the phone.

"Oh, Irma, are you really sick? I'm sorry, it's just that you're never sick! Don't worry, I can hold the fort. Take as much time off as you need."

She was quite pleased. All the others are younger than I am; I put a damper on things. Now they'd be able to really let loose and gossip about the customers to their hearts' content. And about me, no doubt. She wasn't the least bit sorry. I was right, as usual; I'm always right. In my mind I pictured Merete, in that tiny office behind the counter. A glance towards the shop, at Linda, the one with the fake fingernails. Conspiratorial smiles. No, that kind of thing doesn't bother me; it's always been like that.

"Thank you," I whispered. I could hardly speak.

"Have you been to the doctor?" she added, pleased with her own presence of mind in the midst of her delight.

"I'm just going to call him now. But it could be a few days before I'm back."

"Don't even think about us. We'll keep the shop running."

Oh yes, I thought, I've never considered myself indispensable. I thought: Now I'm hearing Merete's voice for the last time. It sounded shrill, like a bird chirping. Now they can dance on the tables over there. I'm never going back.

"Get well soon," Merete hurried to add. And then she was gone. She was sailing on her own sea, with no idea how far it actually is to the bottom. For a moment I felt sorry for her. For everyone who is young and knows so little.

I stood there for a moment and listened. Not a sound from the cellar. I thought: Now he's dead. He didn't make it through the night. If he had, he would have screamed by now, he would have heard my voice and screamed for help.

And then he did start screaming. Out of sheer terror I dropped the phone. He must have heard it hit the floor. The nightmare wasn't over. He was still lying down there, wailing. I had to call for help!

I stuck my arms into a knitted cardigan and stared at the striped rug. Call for an ambulance. Why hadn't I called before? How long had he been lying there? Since about midnight? Since midnight? Is that right? Why? *Because I thought he was dead.* What kind of an answer was that? I sank on to a chair. I fixed my eyes on the tablecloth with the flowers, the one I always use, I had embroidered it myself, every single stitch. I spent a year working on that tablecloth, it's my pride and joy. Sorry. I'm digressing, but the tablecloth is beautiful, it really is. A little coffee, maybe? I stared at the coffee maker. Things wouldn't be any worse if I had some coffee. I stood up and turned on the tap. He cried out again, a little fainter this time. I switched on the radio. What did he think when he heard the music? Probably that I was crazy. But I wasn't crazy, that's what terrified me. In fact, I felt completely rational. A space in my brain was still open, and absolutely clear.

It was cold down there. What if I crept down the stairs and put a blanket over him? I didn't have to look at him, just put the blanket over him and run back up.

I needed time. He would be found, of course. I would make sure of that, but first I had to arrange a way out for myself. There was too much to explain. The idea was intolerable; what would they think? And Ingemar. Everyone at work. What if it were in the newspaper? I peeked through the window. Into the garden. The gazebo and the top of the hedge. I could see the neighbour's roof. They could see my kitchen window from their first floor. I closed the curtains. Then changed my mind and opened them. They were always open at this time of day, and I wanted above all to avoid anything that might look out of the ordinary. I went to collect the blanket from the red chair. A woollen blanket with a fringe; it was almost too warm. When I took a siesta after lunch, I always kicked it off. I stood holding it in my hands. What would he think? Would he scream louder still? Would people in the street hear him? I started to roll the rug aside. The iron ring was a big one, I could put my hand through it. I listened again. Everything was quiet, as if he too were listening. Slowly, I pulled the trap door up. I knew that now the light would strike his face. I stood there with my heart pounding. Then I heard low moans. Maybe he thought that help was coming. And he couldn't do anything to me; he must have injured himself badly. I couldn't get my head round how this whole thing had happened, in my own house. I put my foot on the top step. It was a simple thing that I had to do: down the steps – there were nine of them – put the blanket over him, turn round and go back up. A good deed. Out of the corner of my eye I saw the white face. Or rather, what little of it was visible above the scarf. Why hadn't he taken the scarf off? Couldn't he move his arms? I kept my eyes on my feet, that's what I always did, I was afraid of falling, of breaking something and ending up in the hospital. When there were two steps to go, I had to take a little leap. His legs were up against the last steps. I unfolded the blanket, fumbling a bit because I was nervous. And then I laid it over him. I refused, at all costs, to look into his eyes, because then I might feel something. But I felt his gaze on me, knew that he was looking at me. I heard a few gurgling sounds. I stared at the floor to the right of his head. A pool of blood, and it had already congealed. I turned round and went up the stairs again. He started yelling. He was shouting for water. He hadn't had anything to drink for a long time. I couldn't let him die of thirst. I had to get him water and then go back down. The worst thing of all, I thought, is to die of thirst. Would he be able to drink from a glass? Or suck the water from a wet towel? I suddenly felt dizzy. Something was forcing its way into my consciousness, with no warning, something terribly moving. I walked up the steps, thinking. I owned nothing in this world. No-one's face lit up at the sight of Irma Funder. But this young man's life lay in my hands.

CHAPTER 9

Zipp sat bolt upright in bed. He had fallen asleep in the basement. Then he remembered everything. It was 11 a.m., so the newspaper would have arrived by now. Andreas was presumably at work. No matter what had happened the night before, Andreas would be at work now, walking around in the hardware department with that crooked smile of his. And he was gay. That was unbelievable. What's wrong with me? Zipp thought. What kind of signal was I sending out that he decided to make a move on me? Is it my tight jeans that he's always laughing at? Had other poofs also wanted me, without my realising it? He clenched his fists. The palms of his hands were sweaty. What should he say when next they met? Could they talk about sex and brag about things as they did before? Forget about what had happened? Yes, maybe, but could they keep pretending that nothing was going on – could they? When they were in a bar together, would Andreas sit there staring at the guys? Had he always done that? Where on earth was he? Zipp stared at the *Blade Runner* tape on the table. At the same moment he heard footsteps on the stairs. His mother stuck her head through the door.

"It was a late night, I see."

She said this with a smile. She didn't keep track of what he did as long as he stayed healthy and came home at night. She liked having someone in the house. Most boys moved out at his age, but she did what she could to hold on to him. And as long as he didn't have a job, he wasn't going anywhere.

"Why aren't you in bed sleeping?" he sneered.

"A quiet night shift," she said, sounding cheerful. "I actually took a siesta for a few hours."

She put her hands on her hips. "The phone rang. I didn't get to it in time."

Andreas!

"I've got to go to the employment office," Zipp said, getting up.

She stared at him. Was he finally going to set about getting a job?

"I was about to make some sandwiches. You'll have something to eat first, won't you?"

"Did you bring the paper in?" he said, looking at the floor as he pulled on his jeans.

"Of course. And I've already read it. Do you know what time it is?"

Since he didn't normally pore over the paper looking for a job, he had to restrain himself a bit.

He put the paper next to his plate and checked the front page. Nothing. He bit into a slice of bread and peanut butter, chewed and turned the pages. Just the usual stuff.

"The jobs are in section three," his mother advised him, watching him from where she stood at the work surface. She had another night shift ahead of her, which meant her whole day was free. That didn't really suit him. He liked it when she wasn't home. She was shrewd, the way mothers are; they could see right through anything.

"I know," he mumbled, as he kept turning the pages.

"You're looking for something," she concluded. "What are you looking for?"

"A disaster," he replied, shrugging his shoulders.

"Why are you interested in something like that?"

"A little drama in the daily round, I suppose."

He gulped down the first slice of bread as he scanned page after page.

"You're only reading the headlines," she said.

"Yeah," he said. "If I read all the main headlines, I'll be reasonably well-informed."

She shook her head with annoyance and let water run into the sink. Zipp has never in his life done the dishes, she thought. Would things have been different if she'd had a daughter? Easier, maybe. A little help around the house? She wasn't sure. Some of her friends had daughters, and they complained all the time about everything being so difficult. They had to explain so much to them. Menstruation. Sex. She shivered. No, it was better to have a son, even if he were unemployed. He was handsome and gentle. Things would turn out well for him, she was sure of that. There were plenty of young people who took a while to figure out what they wanted to do. But it was expensive having him live with her. He always needed something.

"I'm going to call Andreas at work."

He said it out loud. It sounded ordinary enough, and he was convinced Andreas would answer. He went into the living room, punching in the numbers with a practised hand. His mother gazed after him.

He gripped the receiver tightly. No, Andreas hadn't come to work today. Hadn't called in sick either. Didn't Zipp know that? His mother was worried about him. Had even been to see the police.

"The police?"

"To report him missing. He didn't come home last night."

"Is he missing?" Zipp asked. He knew his mother was listening, like a quivering cable reaching him from the kitchen; he had no choice but to play along.

"Didn't you see him yesterday?"

The question caught him off guard. Who in fact knew that they had been together? Someone must have seen them. And just think of everything they'd done! It would be best to stick close to the truth.

"Jesus, yes, we were together yesterday. Went out to the Headline. Watched a video afterwards."

"Well, it's odd, isn't it? I suppose he'll turn up."

"Yes. I know Andreas. He does whatever he likes." He tried to laugh, but it came out as a squeak.

"What's going on?" His mother was standing next to him.

"Andreas," he said, putting down the phone. "Didn't show up for work today."

"He didn't? Why not?" She gave him a hard look. Suspected that something was up and took in every detail. The way his eyes were flickering, the way he put his hand up to push back his unruly hair. He shook his head.

"How would I know? Everything was perfectly normal."

"What do you mean by normal?" She squinted at him.

"Well, last night, I mean."

"And why wouldn't it be?"

Silence. He searched for words but found none. Wanted to go back to the kitchen but was stopped by the phone ringing. His mother didn't move to pick it up. He shrugged and picked up the receiver.

"Hello? Zipp? This is Andreas' mother."

"Uh, yes?" he croaked, his mind churning like

143

crazy, thinking about everything that had happened and what he could say, or rather, what he couldn't say.

"Andreas didn't come home last night. I went into his room at eight this morning to wake him up, and he wasn't there! You and Andreas went into town yesterday, didn't you?"

"Yes," he said, casting a glance over his shoulder. It dawned on him that whatever answer he gave now was crucial. Crucial to everything that would happen later, because of everything they had done. The baby in the blue pram, the old lady in the white house. Something was badly wrong, but he didn't know what. He didn't understand why the woman was sitting at the table dressed only in her night-gown, why she just kept sitting there. And Andreas, who never came out of that house.

"You were with him. Where did the two of you go?" Her voice was suddenly sharp.

"Here. We came over to my house." The video was on the table downstairs. Did she think he was standing here and not telling the truth? "First we went to a bar. Afterwards we watched a film here. *Blade Runner*," he told her.

"What do you mean?" Her voice was uncertain. "He didn't come home last night!" she repeated. "Do you know where he is?"

"No," he said, in a firm voice, because that was

the truth, and again it was a relief not to lie. "No, I have no idea where he is. I called him at work and found out that he never showed up."

"So you heard that? I went to see the police," she said resolutely. "He needs to learn to take responsibility. He's an adult now, after all. He ought to start acting like one. But last night . . . When did you last see him? Where were you?"

He thought fast. "We were hanging out around town. At the square and stuff."

"Okay, and then what?"

"Nothing. We were just goofing around. We said goodbye around midnight," he said.

Around midnight. That sounded plausible. Around midnight. That's when they caught sight of that woman. Near the optician's.

"Where did you last see him?"

"Where?" Shit, did she have to know every last detail? "Where? On Thornegata, I think."

It slipped out. Why had he said that? Because that's where Andreas had told him to leave the street and sneak through the back gardens in the dark, while he continued following the woman.

"Thornegata? What were you doing out there?"

"Nothing," he said, feeling more and more annoyed by mothers who wanted to know everything, who felt they had the right to poke around and ask questions.

"But . . . Thornegata . . . Didn't you come home together? Where was he going?"

"Don't know. We were just roaming around," he repeated.

"Did anything happen?" Her voice was anxious. "Were you drunk, Zipp?"

"No, no! No, we weren't."

"Did he meet someone?"

"Not that I know of."

He wanted to hang up. To be done with all this pressure. "Tell him to call me when he shows up," he said. "Tell him that I'm going to have his guts for garters."

Speaking of Andreas only reminded Zipp of the night before, of what Andreas had wanted to do to him in the churchyard. He wished he could take the words back, but it was too late. From now on, he thought, everything's going to be difficult.

At last she hung up. His mother was standing with the dishwashing brush in her hand, dripping soap and water on to the floor.

"Well?"

"Mrs Winther," he said. "She's reported Andreas missing."

"And?"

"She just wants to get even. He's an adult, after all."

"Andreas is an odd sort," she said. She gave him an inscrutable look.

"What is that supposed to mean?"

"Just that he's different. He's probably come up with some wild idea."

"You don't know anything about it!"

His outburst surprised him. It surprised his mother too. She turned and went back to the kitchen. He grabbed the newspaper, ran downstairs and began reading through it. One article after another, page by page. It was a thick paper, so he was busy for quite a while. There was nothing about a woman and a pram. And nothing about the old lady, either. But then, that story had happened after the paper went to press.

*

"This had better not become a habit," Sejer said. They were in the King's Arms, drinking beer. In the middle of the week.

"No, that would be dreadful, Konrad," said Skarre, grinning.

They had not talked about the hash. Sejer had been thinking of mentioning it, but he didn't. If Jacob had any questions, he should for God's sake just ask them. Anyway, time was passing. And it was never going to happen again.

"Have you given it any thought?" Sejer said,

halfway through his second pint. "If the new police station is built in the Grænland area, and no-one wants to come up with money to extend the road network, we might end up waiting for a train every time we're called out."

"What fun," Skarre said. He pulled at a curl from the back of his neck and twisted it round his finger.

"Your hair is getting awfully long," Sejer said.

"I know. I'm thinking that if I hold out a few more weeks, it'll be long enough for a ponytail."

"A ponytail?" Sejer frowned.

"I'm telling you," said Skarre earnestly. "If I pull my hair back into a ponytail, it'll attract much less attention than it does now."

"But a ponytail . . . What about the dress code?"

"I've checked Regulations: 'Hair and beard must be well-groomed and kept at moderate lengths. The hairstyle must not prevent the proper wearing of headgear or other equipment. Long hair must be either pinned up or gathered in a ponytail or braid. Hair-bands and ribbons are forbidden.'"

"Jesus, you've got it off by heart! We're talking about a neutral appearance, Jacob."

"Everyone and his uncle has a ponytail," he insisted.

"What's it going to be next? Dangling earrings?"

"Studs, Konrad. I take them out before I come to

work. But I don't strictly have to. 'Small ear studs that sit close to the ear may be worn.'"

"I see. Well, you're not exactly a plain-clothes detective. But if we don't get the new police station soon, any kind of cooperation with the legal people is going to go up in smoke. It's just not working out right now, with them sitting 200 metres down the street. We need to be in the same building!"

Skarre lifted the bottle of Irish Stout and filled his glass. "If I put on some gel, it will look shorter. I'll tell you one thing, though: Gøran has longer hair than I do, just that his is so *thin*."

"But would that look good on you, Jacob? Having your hair plastered to your skull?"

"Don't know. But nobody takes me seriously with these curls. Mrs Winther thought I must be some kind of trainee or something." He took a sip of the dark beer. "How's it going with Robert?"

Sejer sighed. "Fine, given the circumstances. A cliché, I know but I have good reason to use it."

"Those kids who were with him. Couldn't they have stopped him?"

Sejer traced a stripe through the moisture on his glass. "Maybe they thought he was just trying to frighten her. Make the others lose face. If only he had settled for that."

"But there must have been something they could

have done! A chap who's dead drunk with a loaded shotgun in his hands, and they all stand there paralysed, looking on?"

"There's not always an explanation for everything," Sejer said.

Skarre didn't care for the idea that any human being could be prey, to such an extent, to their own primitive urges.

"They must have been totally taken by surprise," Sejer said.

"Too much so to coax him out of the rage that must have overwhelmed him. And they didn't have time enough, or the psychological insight."

Sejer felt something tugging at the back of his mind. He felt like rolling a cigarette, but he smoked only one a day, and usually last thing before he went to bed. If he rolled one now, he would use up his quota. To smoke two would be unthinkable.

"He had made up his mind to shoot. He needed some kind of release."

I could smoke half of one, he thought. And then the other half tonight. But that would be fooling myself.

"It's all so damned awful – forgive me," said Skarre, casting a glance at the ceiling, "the fact that they would just stand there and watch."

"There's nothing so difficult as stepping forward to intervene. Hardly anyone ever does."

"Maybe he'll drink a little less from now on," Skarre mused.

"Maybe he'll drink even more," Sejer said.

Skarre clasped his hands and piously bowed his head. "What if, as he raised the shotgun and took aim, Anita had burst into song, that beautiful and magnificent hymn, 'Onward Christian Soldiers'?"

Sejer burst into uncontrollable laughter. The sound carried through the whole bar. "What a splendid idea," he chuckled. "At least it would have been a surprise. It would have surely thrown him off balance for a moment."

"We're talking about the power of God's word," said Skarre. "Don't you ever think about that?"

"No."

"Everybody's at sea these days, drifting. No-one has an anchor to hold them down," said Skarre theatrically.

"Can I ask you something?" Sejer said. "Are you 100 per cent positive that you're going to go to heaven?"

"I don't know about 100 per cent positive. There are divided opinions up there, about whether I'll have a tussle with the angel." He took a gulp of beer from the bottle. "Mrs Winther called twice this afternoon," he sighed. "I hope he turns up. She's going to wear us out."

"Mrs Winther?"

"The mother of Andreas, who has been missing since yesterday."

"That's yours," said Sejer dryly.

"Okay, okay. Roger that. It's my job, I know."

Skarre gave a brisk salute. "Search, secure, collect clues that will make plausible the likely connections in the case, as well as the guilt of the accused."

"Do they still teach that motto at Training College? Well, she has asked for our help, at any rate. People are strange," Sejer went on. "They witness the most unbelievable things. But there's no guarantee that they'll come rushing to file a report with us. Obviously someone knows where he is."

"Why are you so sure about that?" Skarre wanted to know.

"As my mother used to say, when she could still talk: 'I just know'. A person might witness a murder and never say a word about it. They have a reason for keeping quiet, though it may not be a particularly good reason."

"I wonder what he's up to."

"Why are you devoting so much time to this one? We have plenty of other cases."

Skarre bent over his glass. "He's just so good-looking."

"What do you mean by that?"

"I reckon there are plenty of people who'd like to get their claws into him."

"Is this the sort of thing that occurs to you when you try to picture what might have happened?"

"He looks quite like an angel. If he doesn't turn up soon, people are going to take notice. You look like a lizard, people don't give a damn. I mean, they couldn't care less. It's a law of nature. Beautiful people, on the other hand . . . take that woman over there for instance. Everyone is turning to look at her."

Sara waved from the end of the room, ran her fingers through her hair and made her way to their table. She paid no heed to Sejer's shyness, bent down and kissed him on the forehead. Skarre beamed.

"Kollberg is tied up to the bicycle rack outside, against the wall," she told him.

She drank a glass of white wine with them. Afterwards, they walked across the bridge together. At the fountain on the square they watched Skarre disappear alone into the twilight of the streets.

"Does Jacob have a girlfriend?" Sara wanted to know.

Sejer shrugged. "Not that I know of."

"Lots of women must be interested in him. Good-looking man. Funny too. Maybe he prefers men?"

Sejer stopped in his tracks. "What are you saying?"

153

"Why does that make you so upset?"

He started walking again. "I'm not. I just don't think that's true."

"You're acting as if I had said something offensive."

"I think that's the way Jacob would have taken it."

"I don't agree. He would simply have answered yes or no."

"Don't ask him, Sara. For heaven's sake!"

"You're not scolding me, are you? Is that what you're doing?"

"No, no. But he might think that we've been wondering about it and gossiping. Don't take it up with him."

"You're so sure that I'm wrong. Why does it upset you so much?"

"It doesn't upset me. I'm just telling you that I know him. And you might put him in an awkward situation."

"So you don't think it's out of the question."

"Sara!"

Then he thought about what Skarre had said. "He's so good-looking." Why did he say that? And the ponytail and the stud in his ear. No, everyone and his uncle has a ponytail. They walked for a while in silence.

"How difficult it all is," said Sara, sounding surprised. "How fearful we are."

"Yes," he said. "I feel so uneasy myself sometimes. I don't know where I stand with you."

"Right here," she replied, squeezing his arm. "Let's have some fun. See that doorway?" she said, pointing. "The one over there next to the kiosk?"

"Yes?" he said, wondering what she had in mind.

"Why don't we go over there and make out?"

"Make out?" The words seemed to stick in his throat. "In the doorway? You must be crazy!" Embarrassed he stared down at his shoes. "It's 30 years since I stood in a doorway to make out."

"Well then, it's about time," she said, laughing as she tugged at his arm.

But he pulled her past the doorway, thinking all of a sudden that he felt so old when he was with her. Young too but occasionally old, because she was so playful. Because he couldn't let go of his proper demeanour and loosen up. Take chances. Kollberg's head came up to Sara's hips. She looked like a little girl walking a lion on a lead. They continued on in silence. Passed the Town Hall. THE COUNTRY SHALL BE BUILT ON LAWS. Sara admired the floodlit church.

"Could we at least walk through the cemetery and knock down a few headstones?"

Her voice was shrill and pleading. He coughed in dismay. "Knock down headstones?"

"Just one?" she begged. "A small one, that no-one takes care of any more?"

He gasped, astonished at his own raw feelings. No-one had ever managed to touch his ideas about death. Did it affect Elise, the fact that they talked this way? Did it affect how he felt? Should he raise his voice and tell this woman off, make her aware that this part of his life was, in fact, sacred?

"You're out of your mind," he mumbled.

"Don't you ever do anything illegal?" she said.

"No," he chuckled. "Why should I?"

"It's necessary and important. What if you die and you've never broken a single rule?"

"That won't happen. Of course I've done stupid things."

"Tell me!" she pleaded.

"No, no." He laughed in embarrassment. "That's all part of my past."

"I won't believe you unless you tell me some of it."

He thought for a moment and then reluctantly began to speak. "A long time ago . . ." he stopped and looked at her. "A very long time ago, in fact, when I was just a kid, just so you know. Youthful shenanigans, the usual things, that's all part of growing up. I assume that everyone . . ."

"Why don't you get to the point?"

"All right." He licked his lips. "A long time ago I had a friend named Philip. I also had an old Ford, and we were always driving around together. And every time I drove over to pick him up, I passed a tollgate where I had to pay. Five kroner," he said. "That was a lot of money for a young kid. It made me angry every time I came to that tollgate. There was a woman in the booth who collected the money. She sat there year after year, sticking out her hand through the hatch. I would hand her the five kroner, she would raise the barrier and I would drive through. Every single time I went to get Philip. I would always stare with fascination at her hand. She had what I'll call 'kitty hands'."

"Kitty hands?" Sara giggled.

"Soft white hands. And one day it occurred to me to put something else in her hand. Just for a change. Because she took it so much for granted that she was getting the money. Just to see what she would do if she one day got something else."

"What did you give her?" she asked.

"I had picked up Philip. We arrived at the tollgate and drove up to the booth. She looked at us and stuck out her hand."

"And you handed her a . . ."

"Dead mouse."

"A dead mouse!" she squealed.

"It had been caught in the trap in Philip's room. And its tail was missing. But boy, did she scream! Piercing is the only word for it. The mouse landed in her lap and she stood up so fast that she hit her head on the ceiling. And then she screamed again, and she didn't stop. Philip screamed too, while I stared at her with growing concern. 'Raise the barrier! Raise the barrier!' I shouted. And the barrier jerked up, and we raced out of there with the tyres of my old Ford screeching."

Sara smiled with satisfaction.

"But do you know what?" he said. "After that she was gone. She wasn't in the booth any more. Maybe she gave up because of the mouse. Maybe she was afraid that next time it might be a spider. Or a worm. Or heaven knows what. So actually," he mumbled, "we ended up chasing someone away from her job."

"Don't you think you're exaggerating?" she said with a laugh.

"Why else would she vanish like that?" he said, sounding worried.

"There could be all kinds of other reasons."

"I'm not so sure."

They walked on, keeping in step. Sejer took shorter strides than was natural for him.

"But honestly," she looked up at him, "is that really the only thing you can think of to put on your list of transgressions?"

"That one not enough for you?"

"Quite a sweet story," she admitted. "But pathetic too."

"Yours are, of course, better?"

"I'll tell you all about them one day. Late at night. Though it might be too much for you."

"You are already," he said. "You're too much for me."

"It's so hard," said Sara all of a sudden, "to live in the present. Right this minute. We spend most of our time in the past. Or in the future, about half in each. But to live in the present! Hardly anybody can do it. Except for children. Or idiots. Or sick people who have some kind of chronic pain that's always with them. And most of the time we're worrying about something."

"But not you, surely not you?" he said.

He wrapped his arm tighter around her waist, surprised at how different they were. They didn't really suit each other, or at any rate it wouldn't last for ever. *It won't last.* She dreamed up things, and he didn't know if he was up to all her whims. There was something unpredictable about Sara. He'd never known anyone like her. Was it even possible for him to get to know her properly? To follow the strange leaps she was always taking, to get used to them? Enjoy them? He liked them, of course. She made him laugh. But she could turn very serious. Her mood changes were abrupt, but at the same time she always had total control. As if she felt that all impulses ought to be followed. Not evaluated and suppressed, which is what he did. Think first and then act. Wasn't that important?

Later, when they finally reached his flat, he went into the kitchen. Sara appeared in the doorway, looking at him. Her expression took him aback.

"I'm just going to make some coffee," he muttered, turning on the tap.

"It's not coffee that I want." She walked across the room, turned off the water and pressed herself against him. He was still hesitating, but was drawn into a fierce embrace. He could feel how determined she was; she was not going to back down.

"Carry me to the bed," she commanded. He shook his head, but didn't let her go.

"Well, all right. The kitchen is good. On the table. I saw it in an American film."

"What do you mean?"

"It looks so exciting," she whispered.

He was in a fog. Didn't know if he'd even be able to do it. But he was still holding her and could feel something rising inside him. He could hold everything else down, but not this! At the same time his brain was buzzing, telling him to take it easy and not throw himself into it without inhibitions, like a teenager. But he didn't want to be taken to task. Not on this account. Other things, like the fact that he couldn't cook or that he couldn't control his dog, fine.

"Could you just stop thinking for a second?"

"You're not making it easy for me," he said. "I'm just a man."

"Yes," she said with a smile. "Poor man. How vulnerable he was when he stood up on his legs and walked for the first time."

She gave a husky laugh against his chest. "You men think everything is so hard for you, that your urges are so fierce, so much stronger than ours, but that's not true."

"It's not?" He cleared his throat. He was out of breath. God help him!

"Right now," she said, pressing against him, "right now when I want you so badly, do you know what that feels like? Has any woman ever told you?"

He tried, but it was impossible to think of any other woman at a moment like this, because he could feel her desire through his own body, and it amazed him that he could prompt such emotion in another human being.

"It's like having a fish between your legs," she whispered. "A soft fish with a blunt snout that's gently butting and wants to get through, and I'll go crazy if it doesn't get through!"

"A fish!" he said.

The phone rang. He reacted on reflex. He also looked at his watch: it was almost midnight. It would be either Ingrid or someone from work. He had to take the call. He picked up the phone and stood there for a few seconds, listening. Sara came over to him and watched him with her arms folded. He put down the receiver.

"You have to leave, don't you? Somebody's dead."

He nodded.

"That's what happens when you're in love with a police officer," she said nervously.

He tried to stay on his feet. Leaned against the old chest of drawers and felt one of his keys poking him in the back.

"Somebody's dead?" she said again.

"My mother," he said in a low voice. "My mother died. Two hours ago."

Then he gave a deep sigh. "While I was sitting drinking beer."

He walked past her, out to the hall. Turned and came back. "I have to call Ingrid."

"I know."

"What are we going to say to Matteus?" he whispered.

He was in no hurry going down to the garage. All the time he was thinking: This is the last time I'll be doing this, going to see my mother. Being on my way to the nursing home. Through the door, over to her bed, for the last time. He drove slowly through the town. It was actually a beautiful night. The red tower building was charmingly lit up, the reflected lights glittering in the river. Didn't it seem quieter than usual? As he turned into the car park, he realised that something was different. This was night-time, not the normal visiting hours, so the car park was deserted. Everything seemed strange and out of character. Being here, in the middle of the night. And the door being locked. He had to ring the bell and speak into an intercom on the wall. Practically plead to be allowed in. He managed to croak a few hoarse words into the microphone and then put his shoulder to the door. Once inside, he hesitated as he looked at the stairs. There were some things he needed to think about first. The senior sister saw him from the nursing station.

"Would you like to be alone there?"

He nodded.

"You take as much time as you need."

He walked to the wide blue metal door. For years she had lain in bed without being able to move, never recognising him when he came to see her. Because of a thrombosis in the brain stem. A tiny little clot in the wrong place, and she was gone. Except that her heart continued to beat. Her eyes would wander around the room, flickering, searching for something that they never found.

What was she looking at? Did she see everything for the first time whenever she looked around? Did she realise that the room was always the same? Did she have a need for some particular thing, without ever being able to say what it was? He had heard about things like that. Could he just as well have been a lamp? Or a coat rack? Did she have thoughts to add to the picture? Was anything going on in her ruined brain? Was anything whirring there, anything familiar or beloved, some meagre comfort? Not any more now, he thought.

For a long time he stood and stared at the door, thinking: Now they can see me from the nursing station, see me standing here and brooding. This is all too much for me. Not just this, but everything else that is bubbling up, all that happened long ago. No, not long ago. It might feel as if it had just happened, that Elise was torn from him again. But this was his mother, it was about *her*. Couldn't he even pull himself together enough to think about her for one last time?

So he went in. For some reason at that moment he checked his watch. It was 12.45. The door gave a plaintive creak as it closed behind him. The lamp next to her bed was on, but the shade had been tilted towards the wall so that his mother's face was in shadow. This thoughtfulness touched him. For a moment he was surprised by how normal she looked. But when he drew closer, he saw how pale she was. Her lips were pressed together a little more tightly than usual. That's not how she was, he thought. She was as gentle as cream, as soft as butter. He pulled a chair over to the bed, but not too close. He needed to keep a certain distance, had to approach with caution. He tried to summon up memories from his childhood, from in the past. Strawberry pudding. The little brown hens in the pen in the back garden. The bread dough rising under a tea-towel on the kitchen counter. Berries cooking in a pan. The smell of fruit and sugar. And her voice; he could hear it clearly. The delicate enunciation after so many years in Denmark.

Konrad. It's late now.

The words rang crystal clear in his head. She used to sit next to a lamp with her sewing. It was impossible to protest by saying "I don't want to go to bed." She would have burst out laughing. She would rise slowly to her feet, take him by the arm, and lead him upstairs to his bedroom. To think that someone so tiny and frail and peaceable could have had such power over him! But always with love, thinking of his best interests. He never had any doubt on that score. He raised his head and looked at her. He thought she looked beautiful, that she always had. Even now. If she seemed stern, maybe it was because she was standing at the gates of heaven, staring at something so grand that she felt quite abashed. Otherwise she had always been so good-humoured. But I don't believe it, he thought. He found himself in a state of emergency, on board a sinking ship. Gently he leaned over the bed. Her hands weren't cold, but not warm either, and very dry.

"Mother," he murmured.

How strange to say that word out loud and never to hear an answer again. He sank back on the chair, thinking that he ought to go home. He stood up, but left the chair where it was, as if it might yet keep her company. He happened to look as his watch again. It was 12.52. He did the arithmetic in his mind. Seven minutes. That's how much time he had granted her, to thank her for everything. Seven minutes to say thank you for a whole lifetime. *Take all the time you need*. He started shaking. Stood there with his shoulders hunched in shame. Turned round and went back to the bed. Sat on the edge, picked up her gaunt hands and held them tight. For a long time.

CHAPTER 10

September 3.

Mrs Winther seemed to have aged since her last visit. Her anger was gone, replaced by a growing panic, which was visible in the flickering light in her eyes.

"The fact that Andreas still hasn't come home is something that we're taking very seriously," said Skarre sympathetically. "But people have gone missing for longer than this and have still turned up safe and sound. There's always some explanation."

She was listening, but the words made no impression.

"By now it's serious," she stammered. "By now something must have happened!"

"Have you been in touch with his father?"

She opened wide her eyes. "Let's leave him out of this."

"We can't force you, of course, but I would strongly urge you to inform his father," Skarre said. "Maybe he could help us."

"They practically never see each other. That much I know," she said vehemently.

Skarre looked her in the eye. "Forgive me for mentioning this, but if anything has happened to Andreas, how do you think his father will feel if you've kept him out of the whole thing?"

"Dear God! Didn't you just say that he's bound to turn up? What exactly do you mean?"

Skarre wiped his forehead, which already felt sweaty. "For some reason he has disappeared. For two days now. I don't know why. But you shouldn't have to deal with this alone."

She wrung her hands, seemed to try to shape some words with her mouth, but no words came out.

"Excuse me? What did you say?"

"All right," she whispered.

"Does he live here in town?"

"Yes. You'll have to call him. I don't dare. There's certain to be trouble."

"Why will there be trouble?" Skarre asked.

"We're not on speaking terms."

"But this is about Andreas," he said quietly.

"Yes. We're not exactly on speaking terms when it comes to Andreas."

"Can you tell me a little about that?"

She didn't answer.

"If you want us to help you, you're going to have

168

to cooperate. Why will there be trouble?" he said again.

"We . . . He . . . Nicolai . . . His father . . . has the idea that Andreas is getting off on the wrong path or something. He says I have no idea what's going on. That Andreas has got involved in some bad things. But he doesn't live with the boy as I do!"

Skarre had been expecting this. He restrained an impulse at the last second.

"Andreas is a good boy," she said. "If there's anything at all, it's just a matter of those things that all boys do. Things that go with growing up."

"Like what, for example?" Skarre said.

"Partying now and then. Throwing apples," she said angrily.

"Throwing apples?" Skarre frowned. "An 18-year-old boy?"

"You know what I mean," she muttered.

"Not really."

"He has a friend. Zipp. His real name is Sivert Skorpe, but they call him Zipp. They're inseparable. I can't very well follow them, so I don't know exactly what they do, but I have no reason to believe that it's anything dangerous. Or illegal."

"But his father takes a different view?"

"To be quite honest, I don't really know what his view is."

"Is it possible that Andreas has more contact with his father than you realise?"

"You mean does he visit him on the sly?"

"He's a grown boy," said Skarre with a smile. "He may not tell you everything."

"Isn't that the gods' truth! But live at home and eat for free – sure, they want to do that!"

She regretted her outburst and hid her face. Mrs Winther was attractive, but her hands betrayed the beginnings of ageing.

"Why should I believe there's anything wrong when he never says anything? He gets up and goes to work. Dresses neatly. Goes out in the evening. I know that he's with Zipp. I know Zipp's mother and she's never said anything to me either. They watch a lot of videos. Drive around and look at girls. Zipp has an old car that his father gave him. If they have any money, they go to a bar. You're supposed to be 20, but they both manage to get in. Andreas is tall, 185 centimetres."

"I see," Skarre said. "Tell me about Zipp."

"He doesn't have a job and he doesn't want one. Andreas pays for his beer. I don't understand why he puts up with it; he's much too nice."

Skarre smiled. He had a dazzling smile, but he restrained himself, in view of the seriousness of the situation.

"I'll need a list of the people who know him.

Girlfriends, buddies. Everyone you can think of."

"He spends all his time with Zipp," she said swiftly.

"But there must be others who know him. He has work colleagues. And a boss."

"You don't understand," she said. "He spends all his time with Zipp. If anyone knows anything, it would be Zipp!"

Skarre fought back his impatience. "I'll need more than that to get things started," he said, trying to sound more stern. "What about a girlfriend?"

"Right now he doesn't have one," she said, sullenly.

"I'll settle for a former girlfriend," he said, smiling again. "Judging by his picture, there must have been quite a few over the years."

She shrugged. "Well, yes. But I don't know any of their names."

"None of them?" Skarre said.

"He never wanted to bring any of them home."

"I see."

"But I'm sure I can think of someone who can vouch for him, if that's what you need."

"That would be fine," said Skarre, and began writing as she gave him two names.

"You called his friend? What did he say?"

"He couldn't help me," she said. "But they had spent the evening together."

"And what did they do exactly?"

"Aren't you going to talk to him yourself?"

"Of course. I was just asking."

"They had a pint at the Headline. After that they watched a video together, at Zipp's house. And I guess that was about it."

"And when did Andreas leave Zipp's house? Did you get a time?"

"They went into town after they watched the film. Wandered around."

"So they parted somewhere in town?"

"Yes," she said, giving him an enquiring look.

"And where exactly did they part company?" Skarre narrowed his eyes and waited.

"Honestly! You can ask Zipp that question," she said, sounding resigned.

"I want to know what he told you," Skarre said. "Please. Just let me do my job!"

"But I don't understand . . ."

"It doesn't matter!" He took her hand. "Please just answer the question."

She pulled her hand away and started sniffling. "They said goodbye to each other around midnight. I think he said midnight. I asked him where and he said on Thornegata. Somewhere on Thornegata. I don't understand what they were doing there, in that part of town. Both of them live in the opposite direction."

"Thank you," Skarre said. "Let's move on. Does he like his job?"

"I don't know really," she said. "A hardware store isn't very exciting, after all. But that was all he could get through the employment office. What he wanted was a job in a music shop, but they couldn't find him anything in that line of work. I don't think they tried very hard, either. They write down preferences in their files, but that doesn't mean anything. You have to take what you can get."

"For an 18-year-old out in the job market for the first time, I can think of worse things than working in a hardware store," said Skarre.

"Like what?" she retorted.

"Has he ever been involved with drugs?"

"No. And don't tell me that's what they all say."

"No, I won't say that. But as far as you know, he hasn't?"

"No, he hasn't."

Skarre wrote a few notes. He was thinking about how he would act if he ever had children. Whether he would lose all perspective.

"How long have Zipp and Andreas known each other?"

"Since they were five. Zipp wasn't too bright, and when he was a little boy, he was fat. He looked like a Polish sausage that had been stuffed too full." She smiled. "Andreas took Zipp under his wing. It still surprises me that they've stayed friends, they're so different."

"Do you like Zipp?" wondered Skarre.

She thought for a moment, picturing his blond hair with the lock falling into his eyes. "Yes," she said. "Andreas could have found worse."

"Good. Does Andreas seem content with his life?"

"He's not lacking for anything. If he were unhappy, I would have known about it."

"And you and your son . . . You have a good relationship?"

"It's not possible to have a good relationship with a teenage son. No matter what I do, boys at that age don't want to listen to old ladies. Someday you'll understand what I mean."

"So we'll say that he seems content."

"With his life, yes. Not with me," she said bitterly.

I'm so naive, thought Skarre. I've always believed that good things await me later in life. But that doesn't seem to be true.

"Was there anything different about his behaviour lately? Anything special that you noticed?"

"I can't think of anything."

"Did he take anything with him when he left?"

"His wallet and some cigarettes. Nothing is missing from his room."

Skarre looked up.

"Not as far as I can tell," she added.

"I'm going to talk to his friend. You should stay home near the telephone."

She stood up and walked out of the room. Skarre had a strange feeling. There was something about this woman and everything that she wasn't saying. Who was Andreas Winther? It occurred to him that she didn't know herself. After a few minutes he left the room and went to Sejer's office. The door was locked. Surprised, he stuck his head in the door of Holthemann's office.

"Konrad?"

Holthemann shoved his glasses down his nose. "He asked if he could come in late today."

Skarre looked at him in astonishment. That was unheard of.

"Anything up?"

"It's his mother. She died last night."

The news prompted a solemn nod from Skarre. "We should send flowers, don't you think?"

The department chief frowned. "I'm not sure. Do you think we should?"

Skarre stayed in the doorway. Well, it was to be expected that people would die at the age of . . . he wasn't quite sure how old, but well over 80. It was the kind of thing that grown-ups had to deal with. Nothing to make a fuss about.

"I'll take care of it," he mumbled and left.

*

The gravity of the situation came creeping in like an ominous fog from the sea. A policeman at the door! Zipp put on a brave smile. My expression suits the occasion, he thought. I'm worried, for God's sake. Worried about Andreas.

"Jacob Skarre."

"Come in. We'll go downstairs."

His mother came out of the kitchen. "No, why don't you sit here and I'll make some coffee."

"We're going downstairs," said Zipp grimly. "I'm the one he wants to talk to."

In spite of her considerable weight, she was wearing a revealing white tracksuit. Her hair was gathered on top of her head and fastened with a red comb. She turned on her heel, offended.

"She always wants to know what's going on," Zipp said.

Skarre smiled. "It'd be good if I could talk to you in private."

They went to the basement room. Skarre looked around. He sensed that Zipp was nervous, but people mostly were, regardless. But he took note of it. Noticed his unruly hair and tight jeans. The basement room with the windows high up on the wall. Like Robert's room, he thought. A television and video. Posters on the walls. Genesis, Jagger. A full ashtray. Blanket on the sofa, which might mean that sometimes he slept down here. Zipp fumbled with the cigarettes on the table. Lit one and exhaled, looking at Skarre, who sat on a chair and gave him a friendly look in return. Minutes passed. The tip of his cigarette smouldered. The silence ran on. Grey dust whirled in the streak of light from the window.

"Are you going to ask me anything?"

Skarre smiled politely. "I'm really here just to have a talk. To find out who Andreas is. What he might be up to."

"I'd like to know that myself," said Zipp, nodding.

"Let's start with the facts. When you met, when you said goodbye. Things like that. The things that are concrete."

Zipp had now had time to think. The situation was impossible for him, considering everything they had done that he couldn't talk about. He wanted to help, but he couldn't. *No blabbing!*

He had to distance both himself and Andreas from the house of that woman. Most of the other things he could talk about. That they went to the Headline. That they had watched *Blade Runner* together. That afterwards they had walked around town for a while. But not the part about the pram. Or the part about the house and the woman. Or the part about the cemetery, either. Shit, that was a lot.

"First we went to a bar," he said.

"Which bar?"

"The Headline."

"What time was that?"

Zipp thought for a moment.

"Eight."

"Did you meet outside?"

"Er, yes. No." He made a quick decision. "Andreas showed up here."

"When?"

"About 7.30," he said.

"Okay." Skarre made a few notes. He needed to keep the boy calm. He accepted the times as reported, smiled reassuringly, listened politely, nodded, took notes. Zipp started to relax and became more talkative, smoking and smiling.

"I don't know what the hell happened. I hope he's all right."

"Let's hope so. He's your best friend?"

Zipp swallowed. "My one and only."

"I see. So he turned up here at the house around 7.30. Then you walked from here to the Headline. I suppose that takes about 15 minutes?"

"Something like that."

"Do you know where he had come from?"

"From home, I guess." Zipp gave Skarre a nervous look.

"No. He left his house on Cappelens gate at 5.30. Directly after his supper."

"Oh? Well, he didn't say anything."

Shit, thought Zipp. I could just as well have told the truth. That he came over before 6.00. That we drove around town. But then there was the whole thing with the pram. Zipp tried to stay clear headed. Repeat the parts that are true, he thought, and just say "I don't know" to everything else.

"So he didn't say anything about where he was between 5.30 and 7.30?"

"I don't know."

"You don't remember?"

"He didn't mention anything," Zipp corrected himself. He licked his lips. The guy looked unusually nice, but Zipp had seen enough videos to be sceptical. A shrewd mind disguised behind a friendly face.

"Okay. The two of you went to a bar together. Had a couple of beers?"

"A couple. Maybe three or four. After that we went to the video shop and took out a film. Which we watched back here. *Blade Runner*."

"Great film," said Skarre with enthusiasm.

"Yeah. Fantastic flick," murmured Zipp.

"And after the film you went back into town?"

"We went down by the river. And up near the church."

He swallowed hard at the memory of the church.

"The church? Why's that?"

"No idea. I just followed Andreas," said Zipp pensively. "So then we went back into town. Just wandering around. There were a lot of people in the square. We sat on a bench and talked. Andreas had to get up early to go to work, so he wanted to go home. We said goodbye to each other around midnight."

"Where?"

"At the square," Zipp said.

"At the square?" Skarre nodded again, but controlled himself, not wanting to give any indication of what he might be thinking. Zipp had told Andreas' mother that they said goodbye on Thornegata. Why was he lying?

"And Andreas. Was he the same as always?"

Zipp shrugged. "The same as usual. And that's all I know. I came home and went to bed."

"How did you find out that he didn't come home?"

"I called him at work. Around 11.00."

"Why did you call him?"

"Just wanted to talk."

"So sometimes you call him just to talk?"

"It was actually about some CDs that I wanted to borrow," he explained.

Skarre glanced over at the posters. "Do you know if anything was bothering Andreas? Did he tell you anything?"

Zipp counted the cigarette butts in the ashtray. No, don't mention that yet! Just let some time pass, and he won't come back to it again.

"Nothing that has anything to do with this," he said at last.

"I see. Well, you know him, after all. I'll just have to trust you on that. I suppose it might have something to do with a girl?" said Skarre.

"A girl? Well, it's possible."

"But you know who his friends are, don't you? I need some names. More people I can talk to."

"He spends all his time with me."

"But doesn't he have colleagues?"

"He never sees them outside of work. The only person is that artist," he said reluctantly.

"Artist?"

Zipp wasn't sure if he should go on. But it was good to have something to talk about. And for all he knew, well, what if Andreas was with her, in the middle of some big orgy! Reinforcing his cover.

"Once a week he goes to see an artist. A woman. She paints him," he said, clearing his throat.

Skarre gave him an alert look. "Do you know her name?"

"No. But I think she lives at the top of the ridge. An old green house. According to Andreas."

"You've known him a long time?"

"Since primary school."

181

"And you feel you really know him?"

Dear God. I thought I knew him.

"If he doesn't reappear soon, we'll be back to talk to you again," Skarre said.

"Okay." Zipp jumped up from the sofa. "And if I think of anything, I'll call you."

Skarre gave him a searching look. He stared at him for such a long time that it made Zipp squirm. He tried to stick his hands in his pockets, but his jeans were too tight. Afterwards he lay down on the sofa and stared up at the ceiling. There was nothing on which to fix his gaze, so he closed his eyes and tried to think of some explanation. He didn't hear his mother as she crept down the stairs, merely sensed that she was there, like a shadow, through his closed eyelids. He opened his eyes and stared at her. With the white tracksuit and the red hair-comb, she looked rather like a fat chicken. Then she pursed her lips.

"I know you. What's really going on?"

I know you. He hated that! He got up from the sofa, pushed his way past her, grabbed his jacket and walked out of the house. He reached the main street and, at a brisk pace, he set off past the square. Glancing neither to right nor left, he walked along with his hands stuffed in his jacket pockets. If he took the same route again, he would understand. He passed the optician's shop and the bicycle shop and the park. He climbed up the hill. The woman didn't get a good look at him so she wouldn't recognise him. He approached the house, staring at it as he slowed his pace. He looked at the windows. Didn't see anything. He continued on, hidden by the thick hedge. A short distance up the street he stopped. He poked his head as far as he could through the hedge, pushing aside a few prickly branches. The house looked quite ordinary. Pristine in the plant-filled garden. It was a one-storey building with a basement. He could see the cellar windows. Two of them, visible behind the flowers, which were starting to wither. He could hear footsteps further up the street. He pulled himself out of the hedge and walked back down the hill.

Something strange was going on. He felt like having a beer, but he didn't have any money. Even so, he headed into town and went straight to the Headline. He stood outside the locked door and looked through the window. He could just make out the table where they had sat the night before. In his mind he could hear Andreas humming "The End" by The Doors. The relevance of the lyrics made him nervous. Could it really be that he may never again look into his friend's eyes? He dismissed it out of hand.

CHAPTER 11

I could see the bare light bulb in the ceiling reflected in his eyes, two tiny points. He didn't move, just stared at me. I thought of a hare caught in a trap. How defenceless he was! I actually felt quite moved, and that doesn't happen very often. I saw a faint movement under the scarf and realised that he had opened his mouth.

"Water," he murmured. He barely managed to get the word out. I wondered why he couldn't move. His body lay so still, as if it didn't belong to him. It never occurred to me to refuse his request, but even so I stood there for a moment and looked at him, at those blue eyes. The rest of his face was hidden beneath the scarf. But his eyes burned into mine. They didn't blink, just silently pleaded. After a while I went back up to the kitchen. Turned on the tap, let the water run. What are you doing, Irma? Have you completely lost your mind? said the water as it trickled and ran. No, no. But for once I was taking the law into my own hands. He didn't ask me what I wanted or needed or desired. The answer was time. That's why I was taking my time. And then I went back downstairs. He caught sight of the glass. He blinked. At the bottom of the stairs I had again to step over his feet. He hadn't moved them; maybe they were broken. I didn't want to ask, just stood there with the water. His eyes began to run.

"The scarf," I said clumsily. "Take off the scarf."

But he didn't move, just stared at the glass, at me, and then again at the glass, blinking all the time. I didn't want to touch him, but I didn't have the heart to go back upstairs with the water. If I bent down, he might leap up from the floor with a horrible shriek and plunge his teeth into me. But he did look awfully weak. I stood there for a long time. He studied me in the same way that I studied him. The bulb in the ceiling held us locked in that peculiar moment. Frozen solid in a circle of light. Irma, I thought, call for help. You have to do it right now! But I didn't move. I stood there and stared into his pale eyes. On the right side of his head there was a sizeable gash that had bled a lot. The blood had coagulated into a big clot on the floor. I couldn't understand why he didn't scream. I was standing right next to him, after all. He didn't make a move to take off the scarf or to lift his head, and finally I realised that he couldn't. I didn't have any straws, but I didn't dare touch him. I took a sip of the water myself and stared at him over the edge of the glass.

I'll never forget his eyes, when he heard the sound of the water running down my throat. Silently he closed them. I didn't like that. The fact that he could hide by simply closing his eyes.

"I'll find a solution," I said. "Of course you have to have water. I'm not a malicious person."

His head began shaking faintly. Then he started coughing helplessly, and a gurgling sound came from his throat. His eyes rolled back into his head. And I thought: Now he's going to die right before my eyes. And that would have been terrible, but at the same time, it would have been beautiful and magnificent and agonising. But he didn't die. I plucked at the scarf with two fingers and pulled it down.

*

The resemblance to Andreas was striking. Nicolai Winther was about 50, tall and slender, with a beak of a nose and eyes that were set deep and close together, beneath delicate thin eyebrows. His hair was long and curly.

"What's he got himself into? Don't you know anything?" He fumbled with the buttons on his jacket, twisting them around and around so that at any moment they might scatter all over the room.

"No. Unfortunately. But there's no reason to believe that anything has happened to him.

186

Sometimes we all need an escape. A little time for ourselves when we don't feel obligated to explain it to the whole world. It happens all the time, and Andreas is an adult. But his mother is worried and it's our job to serve the people."

That was quite a little speech, Skarre thought, taking a deep breath.

"Two days," said Winther. "What the hell have they got into!"

"They? You mean Zipp?"

"Who else?"

"I should remind you that Zipp is at home. He doesn't know anything."

Winther had a coughing fit, and intermittent snorts of laughter. "Don't come here and tell me stories like that. Those two are inseparable."

"Well, yes," Skarre agreed. "It's true they were together on September 1, too. But they parted company around midnight, and no-one has seen Andreas since then."

Winther tried to relax. "I'm sure he's crossed the line. I've been expecting it."

"What do you mean by that?" Skarre pricked up his ears.

"Something was bound to happen sooner or later. I have always known it."

"How could you know that?"

"Because . . ." He stared at the floor. "Because

there's something about Andreas. Just something. I don't know what it is. He has no ambition."

He walked a few paces away. "It's hard to explain. You don't have any children?"

He looked at Skarre's youthful face.

"No. As you can see, I'm just a kid," he said with a smile, which made Winther grin, in quite an amiable manner.

"You've talked to his mother. I suppose you've had an earful."

"She's very worried," said Skarre loyally.

"And unprepared. I've been telling her for a long time. He's a strange boy. I hope to God he hasn't got mixed up with drugs or anything like that. If he's just off on a drinking binge, that's fine. He's probably drunk. Have you checked the hospitals and places like that?"

"That's always the first thing we do. There's quite simply no trace of him. Of course, we're expecting him to turn up at any moment. But to be on the safe side, we want to talk to everyone who is connected. When you say that he's different what do you mean by that?"

Winther thought long and hard. "No, what I mean is . . ." he said at last. "It all started out so well. We had a handsome and healthy boy, and we gave him everything a boy should have. With all the opportunities. And he grew up the way most boys do. He was never sick, he never misbehaved or was difficult to deal with. He did well at school, although he wasn't brilliant. But he has no plans or goals in life. He never shows any enthusiasm for anything. Never shows any enthusiasm," he muttered, as if astonished at his own words.

"He's never been interested in cars or bikes or the sort of things most boys care about. He seems quite content to sit around with Zipp. Andreas has no interests at all. Nothing seems to make an impression on him."

He rubbed at his gaunt jaw with a rough hand. "And you know what?" He stared at Skarre. "That scares me. What's going to become of him?"

Skarre had never heard anyone deliver such a frank and non-idealistic description of his own child before. And Winther wasn't doing it out of malice. Just that he felt flummoxed by something beyond his understanding.

"He walks around half asleep, but I have the feeling that something is ticking away inside him, lying dormant. Or maybe that's just wishful thinking."

They were both silent for a while. Skarre tried to place Andreas in some sort of category, but he couldn't find one.

"Are you and Andreas close?"

Winther walked to the window.

"He doesn't let anyone get close."

"What about Zipp?"

"I'm surprised that he chose Zipp. Andreas is far and away his superior. Zipp is forever running to keep up. I wonder if he needs him for some reason."

Skarre made a few notes.

"I don't really know him," Winther went on. "He's my son, but I don't really know him. Sometimes I think there's no-one inside him to know."

He said this with his eyes lowered, as if he felt ashamed.

Then he sat down, resting his chin on his hands and fixing his gaze on Skarre's knees.

"Surely he must have some interests," Skarre said in a feeble attempt to offer some form of consolation.

"He watches a lot of videos. In fact, I think he watches the same one over and over again. It's some kind of futuristic film. Don't you find that sick?"

"Not at all," Skarre said. "Haven't you heard about the man in London who goes to see *Cats* every single Saturday and has done so for eight years now?"

Winther answered with a grave crooked smile. "I'll have to take your word for that. But otherwise, I suppose that Andreas does have some interest in music. Well, not singing or playing himself, just listening to music. And not live music. Recorded music, on his stereo. A little more bass here, a little less treble there. Special speaker cones. Gold cables. Things like that. Maybe it's not really the music."

"Sound," Skarre ventured. "He's intrigued by sound?"

"Is that something which can intrigue a person?"

"Of course. It's a science."

"But he's not passionate about it," Winther said. "Just interested. He has a job and earns his wages, but he never has any money. He shares what he makes with Zipp. Why in heaven's name would he do that?"

"Because he's a good friend?"

Winther looked at him in surprise.

"So what do you have in mind when you say that Andreas might have got mixed up in something?" Skarre said.

Winther closed his eyes. "What do I mean? Well, that whatever it is ticking inside him has finally exploded."

He smiled at his own melodramatic words.

"As far as you know, has he ever been involved in anything criminal?"

"I have a feeling that he's tried a thing or two, together with Zipp."

"What gives you that feeling?"

"I just have it; it's the kind of thing you can sense with your own child. I've told his mother about it, but she doesn't want to listen. She wants proof."

"So would we, but we're talking about a good-looking, well-functioning young man," Skarre said. "Someone who gets up each day and goes to work and spends his free time with a close friend. And someone who has a clean record, because I have to admit that we checked on that straightaway. So it's hard to see what the problem could be."

Skarre had been prepared for almost anything. But not for what Winther said next.

"I'm going to tell you something." Winther stood up. "Maybe you don't think it's so strange, but you don't have children. Having children flings you into a whole other world, and I'm not exaggerating. Not having children, you live in a different reality from the one I live in."

"All right, I'll grant you that," murmured Skarre.

"I didn't think much about it when it happened, but I've been thinking about it now. Every time Andreas had to go to the doctor or dentist – to get an injection, or a tooth filled – the kinds of things that children need all the time. We were ready for a fuss, that he would be scared. Scream and shout. Or at least be a little nervous. But he never was. He didn't care. He would say 'All right', and off we'd go. And he would sit there as prim as a preacher while the dentist drilled or the doctor gave him an injection. Never made a sound. And I was proud of him, thought he was so brave. But now, when I think back, it seems rather . . . abnormal."

You didn't get the son you wanted, thought Skarre. No-one ever does. My father didn't either. Skarre remembered the fateful day when he went to see his father. After knocking three times on the heavy door of his office, he clasped his hands behind his back and said in the calmest voice he could muster that he didn't want to study theology; he wanted instead to enrol at the Police Training College. And he was certain to get in, because he had excellent grades and was in first-rate physical condition. He stood there wearing a mental bullet-proof vest. He steeled himself for what would follow, the devastating response. First he was speared by his father's furious gaze. Then his voice stabbed at Skarre's chest like a knife, and in two minutes he was completely flayed. Picked clean. His father's despair felt like boiling water against his raw flesh. His father didn't accuse him of anything or try to persuade him to change his mind. But he was perfectly entitled, as he pointed out, to express his boundless disappointment. And then he got up and left. Later, he asked Skarre to forgive him. Since his son had made up his mind, he would of course support him, provided he became the best police officer he could possibly be. The memory prompted a sad smile.

"You need to put pressure on Zipp," said Winther urgently. "He obviously knows something. And since he's not admitting it, it must be something serious. Something they did. Do you understand?"

"Yes. I do understand, and I believe you. We'll keep working on the case. We'll use this as a starting point."

After he left, Skarre thought about the promise he had made to Winther. At the same time he was seized with a strong feeling that something very serious might have happened to Andreas after all.

*

I screamed a loud, piercing scream that echoed through the cellar. He stared at me, tried to say something, but I turned and scrambled up the steps, knocking into the wire of the light bulb, which began swinging back and forth. The circle of light swept over the cellar. I slammed the trap door shut. Ran to the front door and opened it, trying to calm down. I stood on the steps for a moment, gasping. Then, as calmly as I could, I walked down the gravel path to the back garden. I didn't understand. Why was this happening to me? The flowers were starting to wither. I was withering too; I could hardly keep my knees from buckling. I was looking for something to keep my hands busy, some simple task, when I caught sight of the chair. One of the patio chairs – under the kitchen window! I stood there dumbfounded, trying to grasp what it could be doing there. Who had been standing on it, looking in? A horrible possibility occurred to me. There were two of them. Originally there were two! The other one had waited in the garden and carried the chair over to the window. I thought I was going to faint. But then I thought, no, it must have been the one in the cellar who had stood on the chair. And looked inside before he made his attack. I picked it up, and carried it with some difficulty up the two steps into the gazebo. If there had been two of them, and the other one was waiting in the garden, if he knew that his friend was still in the house, he would have come to the door a long time ago. I tried to force my body to stay calm, but my feet began to tremble, and the trembling spread upwards. I was shaking with indignation. I went back inside and stomped hard on the kitchen floor. In a fury, I lifted up the trap door and shrieked at him down the stairs.

"I don't own a thing. Just some old silverware! Why did you come here!"

"I don't know," he sobbed.

Crying was too much of a strain for his injured body, and his tears dried up. I stood there for a moment, looking down at him. He seemed so pitiful, so small and alone. I was sniffling, unable to control my emotions, and that frightened me. I usually have control of things. I felt as if I were breaking up. Even so, I went down again and sat next to him. Picked up the glass of water and held it out.

"Can't do it," he muttered desperately.

"You must. Otherwise you'll die."

He howled in despair, but I hardened my nerves and pressed the glass to his lips. He opened his mouth and I poured in the water. He coughed violently again, spraying water into my face.

"Can't do it," he sobbed.

"I'll arrange things so someone finds you," I said dully.

"Do it now!" he coughed. "What are you waiting for?"

I swallowed hard. At that second I felt thoroughly ashamed.

"I thought you were dead."

He didn't reply. Not a muscle moved in his body. To think that anyone could lie so still! I'm not an evil person. But something had entered my house that I couldn't control. I live alone. There was no-one to help me. For an eternity I sat on the cellar steps with my forehead resting on my knees. Not a sound from below. The only thing I noticed was the smell of mould and potatoes and dust. But later I heard a rushing in my ears that was very faint at first but grew louder. As if someone had turned over an hourglass. The sand had started running through.

CHAPTER 12

Skarre's curls always attracted attention. This time it was a teenage girl at the news-stand who was staring at him. To no effect, because he was preoccupied with other matters. Winther was right, of course. Zipp was hiding something. The certainty of this was as strong in him as his faith in God. What was it that Sejer had said? People always have some reason to keep quiet, and it doesn't even have to be a very good reason. At the same time, he understood the seriousness of the situation. This was no jaunt on the ferry to Denmark. He was jolted out of his train of thought because the queue moved forward. He was the fourth in line. In front of him stood an older woman wearing a brown coat. When he looked over her shoulder, he could see into her shopping trolley. It always amused him to look at other people's shopping. He would come to some funny conclusions, based on what they were buying. This woman had a baby bottle made of clear plastic, antiseptic and cotton-wool balls, three bottles of bleach and a lantern for tea-light candles from the hardware section. Didn't she need any food? He craned his neck and looked at other trolleys. Usually there was a sense of order, things that naturally belonged together, such as four litres of milk, a loaf of bread, coffee and frozen cutlets. Or a case of beer, two packets of crisps, a copy of *We Men* magazine and a pack of cigarettes. Or nappies, jars of baby food, toilet paper and bananas. But the items in the trolley in front of him seemed somewhat chaotic. He was having fun. He stared at the nubbly fabric of her coat. Now she was moving forward again, with a good grip on her trolley. She was average height, stout and heavy. Since he could only see her from the back, it was difficult to say whether she was in her fifties or her sixties. Her hair was grey and permed into tight, neat curls. She wore short boots with thick heels. He wondered about the baby bottle, it must be for a grandchild. He looked into his own trolley, which contained onions, paprika, rice, a litre and a half of Coke, three newspapers and a bag of Seigmenn jelly babies. He patted his pocket to check that he had cigarettes. Maybe he should get a pack of Magic too, which was in lines on a shelf behind the checkout counter. Maybe while staring deep into the eyes of the woman cashier with a brief remark: "Imagine, I nearly forgot the most important thing of all!" It was a game he played. Skarre moved forward. The woman in the brown coat put her shopping on the conveyer belt, paid and packed everything into a bag. Not a word spoken, not even a "please" or a "thank you". She didn't look the cashier in the eye. She seemed wrapped in her own world. Then she disappeared out of the doors. Skarre caught sight of something at the end of the counter. She had forgotten the baby bottle.

"I'll take care of it," he told the cashier.

She shrugged, and as soon as he had paid for his groceries, he ran in pursuit of her. By then she was quite a distance up the street. Perhaps on her way to catch a bus. She was carrying the grocery bag in her right hand, walking close to the buildings. Skarre had put the baby bottle in the inside pocket of his leather jacket and he hurried after her. She didn't notice him. Then she cut across the street and started up the hill towards Prins Oscars gate. He was close enough to shout, but he picked up speed so that he would be able to state his business without shouting. Skarre was very considerate. She was halfway up the hill, and Skarre was only five metres behind. He pulled the bottle out of his pocket and jogged a few paces towards her.

"Hello! Could you wait a minute, please?"

She lurched around to stare at him. Her fear was so apparent that Skarre stopped at once. He threw out his arms and waved the bottle.

"You forgot this! That's all."

She stood there for a few seconds, staring at him, then she turned and continued up the hill.

"What about the baby bottle?"

Finally she stopped.

"I was behind you in the shop. You left it on the counter."

He was quite close to her now. He could see her thin lips and her deep-set eyes. She had a heavy jaw and eyebrows that had grown together. Her face was pale, like something that been locked up.

"I thought it might be important," he said as he smiled and held it out to her. She took it reluctantly.

"I'm sorry," she muttered. "You gave me such a start."

"I didn't mean to," said Skarre with a bow.

"There are so many strange people," she said. "You never know who might turn up."

She gave him what passed for a smile. "You could have gone on your way and not done anything. This bottle is important."

"I thought so."

He turned to leave. She seemed to have calmed down.

"Have a nice day."

"A nice day?" She seemed to wake up. "You have no idea what you're talking about." Skarre hesitated. An expression of pure confusion appeared on her face. She turned abruptly and walked up the hill. Skarre watched her turn to the left, just short of a thick hedge. Behind the trees he could see glimpses of a white house with green paintwork.

*

I turned on the tap and let the water run. I was composed enough to show a little concern, and besides, I was responsible for him. I was all he had. The thought sang inside me, even though I knew that it wouldn't last; it was only for a moment that I would have a human being at my disposal like this. Someone who had to listen to me. He started groaning when I opened the trap door. It was odd to stand there with a baby bottle in my hand; it had been so long since I'd done that. I had thought everything through. If I placed a pillow on his chest, the bottle could rest there. I couldn't stand the idea of holding it for him. No, I couldn't. I was surprised that he was still alive. There was something wrong with his legs and arms, and maybe with his lungs too. His voice was weak, and he was struggling to breathe. I stood there holding the bottle in my hand. To think that I'd forgotten it! I had trouble remembering what I had said to that young man, and that made me nervous. But I had a lot on my mind. I went down the steps. He saw the bottle at once and opened his eyes wide. I put the pillow on his chest, on top of the blanket. The bottle was nestled on the pillow. He sucked down the water, not stopping. Bubbles rose in the bottle. I sat there, watching him, a few steps up so that his head was visible between my knees, like something I had given birth to on the floor. It was good that he finally had some water. Tears ran down his face the whole time he was drinking. I was absorbed by that beautiful face and those bright eyes and the water that trickled and ran down his throat. I had used scissors to cut a bigger hole so it wouldn't be so hard for him to drink. When the bottle was almost empty, it was so light that it fell off the pillow and on to the cement floor, making a tiny hollow sound as it rolled away.

"Thank you," he whispered. Then he closed his eyes. I was touched. Wasn't he going to scream again? Curse me? Threaten me so I'd call for help? It looked as if he were sleeping. I waited, in awe. He was having trouble breathing. I would have sat there all night if my back hadn't started to hurt. If I could have done it, I would have carried him up to my own bed. I would have done that for him, done it gladly. Nothing can compare with sitting there like that, looking at a person who is completely dependent on you. I decided there and then to take as good care of him as I possibly could. And the cellar, which was so familiar to me, gradually began to change. It was no longer dark and sinister; I could look at it properly. Cobwebs on the ceiling, the light shining through them so they looked like silver threads. The dim light in the corners, the yellow light bulb and the dull-coloured floor. Dreary old furniture that seemed now to have some dignity, resting contentedly against the cellar wall, having fulfilled its role. The worn steps on which I was sitting. The quiet room. Andreas had filled it with something. He was young and stupid. He had acted without thinking, the way young people do; they just barge forward. But surely he didn't deserve to lie here like this, freezing. I came out of my reverie.

"Are you in pain?" I asked.

A moment passed. He opened his eyes.

"No," he said, his voice feeble.

"Are you cold?" I asked.

"No," he said again.

He licked his lips. They had begun to split. The hair on the right side of his head was matted with blood. It was stiff and sticky.

"You're lying in such an awkward position. I'm going to move you."

"No! No!" He screamed. His eyes were filled with terror.

"But your legs are up on the steps – it looks as though it must hurt."

"No. Don't!"

I stood up and moved behind his head. Hesitated for a moment before I leaned down. He whimpered, begged me not to do it. But I hardened my heart and stuck my hands under his armpits. Counted to three and pulled him the last few paces away from the stairs. His shoes banged faintly against the floor. He didn't scream, which apparently surprised him. He looked better now, with his legs stretched out.

"I can't feel my body. I can't feel anything!" he said.

I was overwhelmed by what he said, by what I had done. What he had done, I corrected myself, he was to blame for all this. I was struck with great force by how serious his injuries were. I had to squash the despair I felt, that I couldn't bear to feel! I got rapidly to my feet.

"You should have thought of that before!"

He opened his mouth to cry out in reply, but he couldn't speak. He didn't have the strength. I went back upstairs. Closed the trap door. Could he have broken his neck? Cut off all connections below, so that everything would stop functioning? Could he live like that? Was he getting enough oxygen? It was too late to turn back. I had burned my bridges the first time I closed the trap door. There was no going back. No going forward, either. I sat down at the table and put my head in my hands. His face would appear at regular intervals to disturb me. But then I felt good again, warm and pleased. I thought that next time I would fill the bottle with warm milk, maybe with a little sugar in it. Or a couple of sleeping pills, so he would sleep. These thoughts gave me a kind of peace. There was so much good you could do if you only tried. I leafed through the newspapers again. In fact I couldn't find a single page without mention of violence or war or some other misery. A young man had shot his own girlfriend in the face. There were more kids like Andreas, there were lots of them. Each story was worse than the last. At regular intervals I would turn around to look over my shoulder. I was expecting something. A face at the window, a phone ringing. When the doorbell finally rang, my heart stopped beating. But it calmed down when I reminded myself that I didn't have to open the door. I am in charge of my own life and my own house. I let the doorbell ring, but it didn't stop. So I went over and looked through the peephole in the door. A figure loomed on the top step, and was I staring into a streaked face. It was my friend Runi. Andreas' mother.

CHAPTER 13

Robert came out of the jail escorted by two officers. He was very pale. Several blood vessels in his eyes had burst and he hadn't eaten for days. Not by way of some form of protest, just that he couldn't keep any food down. He was living on Coke and coffee and cigarettes. He didn't want to escape or to make excuses. Simply to understand. He had nothing else to contribute. Now he had all the time in the world, and he soon realised that the best path to the rest of his life lay in his willingness to cooperate. Besides, they were perfectly nice, they treated him with kindness. And that was true of everybody, from top to bottom. Like this police lieutenant, for instance. Robert slowly sat down. What was the rush? Where was he going to hide? It would always be with him, the fact that he had killed Anita. Dragging behind him like a lizard's tail. He hadn't done many bad things in his life. It's true that he wasn't a very good student, but he had no shortage of friends. He was a pleasant boy, it said so in his school report. And he believed the same as most boys, that good things lay ahead for him. That he wouldn't fall into any of the traps. But now here he was, charged with first-degree murder. Awareness of this fact kept striking him like a sledgehammer, with relentless precision, again and again. He had grown used to the pain.

"Sit down," Sejer said. "You can smoke if you like. And let me know if you need anything else. Anything at all."

"Thanks," Robert said.

He looked at the grey man. Sejer's towering height was impressive, but he didn't seem threatening. First and foremost, he was here to do his job. That felt good. He had done this before. Robert wasn't unique, not in this place, he was one of many. Sejer wished things were different. That Robert was the first, and for that reason would be remembered.

"The psychologist? He'll come if I call him, Robert."

"It's fine like this."

Sejer nodded, pushing back his grey hair. Robert sensed that behind his quiet demeanour slumbered mighty forces that might be aroused to anger if he didn't cooperate. He was wearing a shirt and tie and discreet charcoal trousers with sharp creases. His grey eyes were calmly scrutinising him.

"There's one thing I want to emphasise regarding this conversation. It might not be easy, but I want you to try anyway." He pulled his chair closer to the desk. "Through the whole course of events, as we go over everything that happened, try to avoid referring to the fact that you were drinking heavily all evening, or to how intoxicated you were the whole time. We both know that you were very drunk." He paused and looked at Robert, who was still staring back at him with his eyes wide open, nodding. "And we both know that this wouldn't have happened if you hadn't been drinking."

Robert lowered his eyes. He heard his lashes brush his cheek.

"We're simply going to review what happened, as you remember it, without emphasising that you were drunk. Placing the events in the context of your drunken state will come later. Your defence lawyer will take care of that. Do you understand?"

"Yes."

He rubbed his sweaty hands under the desk. Looked down at his shoes. Prison legs, he thought. Prisoner Robert.

"Let's go over the day that it happened. From when you woke up in the morning until the moment when Anita was lying dead on the floor. As detailed as you can. Take all the time you need," he added.

Robert began. "The alarm clock went off at ten to eight." My voice, he thought. It's the voice of a child. So shrill and strange-sounding. "I'm usually

208

tired in the morning. But it was Friday. It's easier on Friday," he said, smiling, "knowing that it's almost the weekend. We were planning a party. The day before, at work. And Anita said yes. She had got out of a baby-sitting job. And the landlord was gone, so we had the whole house to ourselves. Well," he took a deep breath, "it was an ordinary day. I was feeling good. Better than usual."

"Why was that?"

"Because of . . . Anita."

It took great effort to say Anita's name out loud. Anita. Anita. If only the name could be erased from all the files in the world. There were lots of Anitas. Each time he heard the name, it all came back to him. And knocked him flat.

"All the same," he said, clearing his throat, "I had a suspicion that it wasn't going to last. For ever, I mean. And if I thought about that, I felt resigned. Sometimes I thought about that."

"Why?" Sejer wanted to know. "Why did you feel resigned?"

"Anita was . . . great. I didn't need anyone better than her. But deep inside I knew that soon she was going to run off and find somebody else. Someone better than me. Sooner or later."

"How could you be certain of that?"

Sejer looked at the boy's shoulders. They were hunched up, as if against a cold wind.

"She acted the way most girlfriends do, but she wasn't exactly excited about me. It was a matter of time before she chose Andreas. Or Roger, or someone else. I guess that's the way it is when you have lots to choose from. I've never had lots to choose from. That's why this was so important to me. Having a girlfriend. No, not just having a girlfriend, I've had them before. But to have Anita."

Sejer leaned his chin on his hand. "Was Anita the prettiest girlfriend you've ever had?"

"I suppose she was. She always attracted attention, when I walked down the street with her. People would look at her hair and everything. And then they'd look at who was with her. Who the guy was with a girl like that."

Sejer studied him intently. The narrow face and the thin hair that hadn't been combed in a long time and was now sticking out in every direction. Dark blue eyes, flitting all over the room. A streak of a mouth, almost colourless. Thin fingers with nails bitten to the quick. Practically a child.

"How did your day at work go?"

"As usual. There's a lot to do on Fridays. I called Anita during my lunch break. Not because I had anything special to say, but I liked being able to call her when I felt like it. She worked at the department store. We talked for two or three minutes, then we hung up. I wanted to ask her to wear a dress, but I

210

didn't dare. Didn't want to seem like the controlling type. Girls don't like that. But she came in a dress anyway."

"What time was it when everybody had arrived at your room?"

"About 7.00. Anders arrived later. He works until 7.00, so he was probably there by 7.30. I don't remember exactly."

"What did you do?"

"Drank beer, of course. I mean, we talked. Played music. Discussed things."

"What sort of things?"

"Football. The Joe Cocker concert, which we went to, at the Oslo Spektrum. He was rubbish. We talked about that for a long time. The girls got mad, they thought he was so . . . what did they say? They thought he was great. You know, the way he stood there, with his body twitching like that, as if he had no control over it. They fall for that sort of stuff."

Sejer smiled. Robert relaxed. There was still a long way to go before the fateful shot. He was at a moment when he was not yet a murderer, and it felt good to be there and forget about the rest, but it was coming. Like a raging bull, the terrible deed stood tossing its head behind a fragile fence.

"Then we talked about politics. The election. Two of them were going to vote and they were arguing about it. Roger and Greta started to dance.

Anita was sitting next to me on the sofa. She sat there the whole time until late in the evening, except when she had to go to the bathroom. You know how girls are when they're drinking." Then he stopped. "I was so happy," he went on, quietly now. "I had everything. I mean it. My room. A job. A girl. Friends. We had two cases of beer . . . er . . . I didn't just have a weekend ahead of me, I had my whole life. Right at that moment I managed to convince myself that it was all going to last. But then I started getting really . . ."

"What were you thinking about," Sejer interrupted him, "when you sat on the sofa with Anita and looked around at everything that was yours?"

"That I could have sat there for ever. And about how everything would be when she left."

"What kind of life did you envision for yourself then?"

"I don't really know." He made an effort. "Something about starting again. And how hard it would be. That we don't really ever get anywhere, we just have to keep starting over all the time. New job, new friends. New girls. Around and around."

"Then Anita got up and went across the room. What did you think then?"

"That didn't bother me. She could move around if she wanted to. She didn't do anything, but I kept my eye on her. I kept my eye on everybody. On

Anders and Roger. They were looking at her, but everybody did that. I don't usually care. And even though I was . . . even though I wanted her all to myself, I didn't say anything, just watched her, and I watched everyone who was looking at her, just to keep tabs on them."

He bent his head and looked down at his prisoner feet.

"Anders was the worst; I know him. And I should have been prepared, but I guess he was jealous. Wanted to tease me a little, maybe. He's always teasing people, but he's not mean. Not at heart."

"What did he do?"

"He went over to Anita and danced with her. I never thought that she shouldn't dance with anyone else, I really didn't. Anders kept an eye on me, wanted to see what I would do. I didn't do anything. But I watched them. I felt really weird," he added.

"In what way weird?"

Robert's body seemed to have sunk a little, and his eyes had taken on a distant look. But he was thinking hard, digging into himself to find out what it was. Sejer said softly, "Can you describe it?"

"It's hard to remember."

"Think back. Imagine yourself there."

"I can see some pictures. But the sound is gone."

"What do you mean?"

"I couldn't hear the music any more. But the picture of Anders and Anita was crystal clear."

"Crystal clear?"

"I could see Anita," he said. "But everything else disappeared. She was dancing with Anders. They were dancing very slowly, as if everything was coming to a stop. The light, the sound, I couldn't move, I just looked at Anders and Anita. She had forgotten all about me. Mind you, she was really drunk. I mean, we're not supposed to mention that, but she had forgotten all about me!" There was desperation in his voice.

"But Anders hadn't forgotten about you," Sejer said.

"He was staring at me with a horrible smile. I've seen Anders smile before, but never like that. He had yellow teeth. I didn't smile back. I was thinking about the fact that everything was coming to a stop."

"And then?"

"Then he took a small step back. Pushed Anita away. And I thought, now he's going to leave. But that's not what happened. He raised his hands and grabbed Anita's tits. Grabbed them hard so I could see it."

"What did Anita do?"

"Well, she was really . . . She laughed," he said

grimly. "She just laughed. It was already happening. I was going to have to start again. It all seemed so impossible. I would rather die."

"Did you feel that you would rather die?"

"Yes," he said simply.

"What made you think of the shotgun?"

He took his time. Tried hard to remember. His efforts to concentrate affected his breathing, which became rapid and shallow.

"When I thought that I'd rather die. I remembered that it was in the cupboard in the hall. It doesn't take long to die, only a second."

"So the idea of getting out the shotgun, that occurred to you when you were thinking about dying?"

"Yes. The landlord had a shotgun in the house. I remembered that it was in the hall."

"At that instant, when you thought about the shotgun, is that when you looked at Anita?"

"They looked so unnatural. There was an eerie light."

"What do you mean by eerie?"

"Like they have in clubs sometimes. A blue, metallic light."

"What did you do?"

"I couldn't see anything in the room, just a bright pathway to the door. Suddenly I was standing in the hall. I still couldn't hear anything.

The only sound was a faint prickling. Like . . . ants in my eyes," he said. "I know that I shouted something at Anders, but I can't remember what. I opened the door. The shotgun was there, as it always was. Nice and shiny. All assembled. Waiting for me."

"And the ammunition?"

"Several boxes. They were up on the shelf."

His voice was hoarse and breathy. Sejer had to strain to hear him.

"Do you remember any feelings or thoughts from that moment?"

"No feelings. I was dead."

"What do you mean?"

"My face started shrinking. I remember my skin getting tight around my mouth. It was awful. I thought I had to stop time so I wouldn't have to start all over again."

"How were you going to stop time?"

"With a huge bang," he whispered. "If I fired a shot, there would be a huge bang. And everybody would wake up." He ran his hand over his forehead. "A bang. That would wake us up."

"Were you all asleep?"

"Everybody was in slow motion. About to vanish."

"You loaded the shotgun and went back into the room. What did you see?"

"Everyone looking at me. I liked it, the fact that they had to pay attention to me. They stopped smiling. Everyone except Anders."

"Did you hear anything?"

"My name. Someone shouted. It was far away."

Sejer leaned across the desk. "Why did you raise the shotgun and take aim?"

"I don't know . . ."

"Think hard, Robert. Why did you raise the shotgun?"

"I needed that bang!"

"But you took aim," Sejer said. "You could have aimed at the ceiling. But you aimed at Anders."

"Yes!"

"You aimed at Anders and pulled the trigger. Why?"

"I don't know. I can't say why!"

In a shrill, heart-rending voice he begged Sejer to stop.

"We're just trying to understand," Sejer said. "I won't laugh. I won't get rough with you. I just want to understand."

Robert sobbed and sniffed, concentrating on the blotting pad, which showed a map of the world. His gaze fell on the snow-white, ice-cold Antarctic.

"I was in a rage when I went to get the shotgun. It would have looked so pathetic if I aimed at the ceiling."

His head fell towards his chest. Sejer leaned back. His expression didn't change, but Robert wasn't looking at him anyway. He was still in the icy wasteland.

"I pulled the trigger, but nothing happened. The safety catch was on. It goes on automatically when you put the shotgun together. I remembered about that and took it off. I thought it was so embarrassing," he whispered. "That I made such a mistake. Forgot about the safety catch."

"Didn't you notice that Anders was hiding behind Anita?"

"Yes, I did."

"But you still decided to fire. Did you realise that you would hit her? Anita – the girl you were so fond of?"

Robert met his gaze for a second.

"No. Yes. I couldn't exactly ask her to move. 'Move over, Anita, I want to shoot Anders.' I couldn't do that. I had to shoot."

"Were you angry, Robert?"

"Angry? . . . I don't think so. But Anders was a coward."

"You were focused on shooting?"

"I needed that bang," he repeated.

"Why didn't you stop?"

"It was too hard. I was already in the middle of it."

"You felt you had passed the point of no return. And then it went off. How did that feel?"

Robert swallowed hard. Held back his reply. Couldn't believe his own words. "Good," he said. At the same time he began shaking violently. "It felt good. I got really hot. I could feel myself falling."

"The sounds in the room," Sejer said, "did they come back?"

"After a while. Like when somebody turns up the radio to full blast. I was shaking uncontrollably. They were bending over me, everybody was bending over me, and someone was screaming. The girls were wailing, and someone dropped a glass on the floor."

"What did you think had happened?"

"That a terrible accident had taken place. That I was injured."

"You. Injured?"

"Something had hit me. It was all a blur. The sounds were too loud. There was blood on the floor. I thought, somebody is going to come and help me soon. I fell down while I waited for help. I liked the fact that someone was going to come and carry me away. I liked it," he said.

"What about now, Robert? Do you want to go on?"

"Yes."

He had been making such an effort that his shirt had big wet patches on it.

"Why?"

"This time, starting again is different. It won't be the same things as before." He leaned across the desk, exhausted. "But I don't understand why. The psychologist can probably find an explanation. But how can he be sure that it's the right one?"

"He's not always sure, Robert. He does his job as best he can. He tries to understand."

"But is there anything to understand? It just happened."

"There are a lot of strange things that just happen. But it's important to go over things. And maybe you'll understand more as time passes."

"But I'm not crazy!" That was the one thing he didn't want to be.

"No. I don't think of you as crazy. But sometimes too many things can happen all at once and knock us over. But you can get up again. You're still the one controlling your own life."

"I don't think so. Not in here."

"Oh yes. You decide almost everything. What you say, what you think, how you're going to spend your days." Sejer took his hand. "I wish you would eat something."

"If I don't eat I get so foggy, and then I don't have to think so much."

"It's better to think, if you can. Don't put it off. It'll come back to you sooner or later anyway."

Robert's mouth was dry. He wondered if he could be picked up and carried back to the cot in his cell by this strong man.

"You can get up and leave," Robert said. "Leave this place and forget about us. I've become somebody's job," he said pensively. "You're paid to talk to people like me."

"Does that bother you?"

"A little."

"I don't mind being around people like you."

Robert was lost in his own thoughts. Sejer let him sit there. Robert was cautiously forming ideas. He would manage to bear what awaited him. Survive prison. Everyone in here had made similar mistakes. He was one of many, some might have even done worse things. He would toe the line, follow the rules, be a model prisoner. Day after day, for weeks, months. He would make it through. But afterwards . . . when he got out one day, what then? What would he say? What would he do when people found out about his past? Would he be able to handle that? Or would he make sure that he found a way back to this building, with its order and rules? Here it was easy. A few simple tasks, meals three times a day, money for cigarettes. Even kindness. Once again, he started to shake.

"But I want to know how I'm supposed to handle this!" he burst out. Tears welled up in his eyes, but he fought to hold them back and wiped his nose on his sleeve. Sat there in silence while the suppressed sobs shook inside him. He no longer knew who this Robert was. He had lost his foothold on reality. Slowly, he rose from his chair. He rose up higher and higher, felt himself hovering high above the desk. He could look down at his own empty chair, he could gently turn and circle the room. The chief inspector didn't notice; he was busy writing notes.

CHAPTER 14

Runi was standing on the steps, shouting. She was clearly upset and kept on tugging at the door handle. I ran back to the kitchen and turned the radio up to full volume.

"Irma, it's Runi. You have to let me in, Irma!"

I thought fast. Did I have to open the door? What would happen if I didn't?

"I'm not feeling well!" I shouted. "I stayed home from work today!"

I leaned against the wall for support. I had to keep her out! Why was all of this coming to my house, trying to force its way in!

"I have to talk to you!"

She wouldn't give up. I tried to think of an excuse not to open the door. Andreas would hear us and start screaming. She didn't usually come over like this, without being invited, it was unbelievably bold of her, and of course impossible for me to let her inside. But if I didn't open the door . . .

"Let me in, Irma! I beg you!"

Her voice had reached a falsetto pitch. I thought

about the neighbours; they would hear her. I was going to have to open the door. I turned the key and opened the door a crack. She barged into the hall. Her eyes were swollen and her coat was unbuttoned. It was awful to see Runi looking that way. I prefer her usual sweet self.

"Something terrible has happened!"

She sank on to a chair at the table and rummaged in her handbag for a cigarette. Gypsy music was coming from the radio, which she glanced at and then started shouting in despair. "I've called you several times. Why didn't you answer?" and then, "Can't you turn that radio down?"

I went to the radio and turned it down, but just a little.

"What's wrong?"

"Andreas," she gasped. "Andreas is missing."

"What do you mean, missing?"

I gave her a look of incomprehension. But I needn't have worried, because she was so absorbed in her own despair. That was actually quite typical of Runi. She didn't really see me at all, just stared down at her own unhappiness.

"He hasn't been home for two days. I've been to see the police."

"The police?" I was appalled.

"I reported him missing."

I pulled my cardigan tighter as I listened intently

for sounds from the cellar, but I didn't hear anything. Maybe he had fainted, or fallen asleep. Dear God, even though I don't believe in you, please make him sleep!

"But isn't Andreas often away from home?" I said. "Have you called his father?"

"He's not there. The police have been out to talk to him."

"What about his friends?"

"He only has one friend, and he doesn't know anything. Something has happened to him, I'm sure of it. Good Lord! I feel so desperate. What if he ran away? We're always fighting. I was never happy with him, and maybe now he's had enough. I'm going crazy with this waiting. It's driving me crazy, Irma!" She leaned forward and began to sob. She sobbed for a long time while I searched for something to say. I'm not very good with words, and I started to feel a little embarrassed. Besides, I thought I could hear a sound from the cellar. Some sort of clicking noise. Faint, but definitely there. But he couldn't move, so it had to be something else. I searched frantically for an explanation. What if Runi heard it? But she would never dream that Andreas was lying in my cellar with his neck broken. She didn't have that much imagination.

"Had he got himself mixed up in something?" I asked. It was like sprinkling water on frying oil: Runi at once started sputtering.

"Don't talk like that! You sound just like his

father. Andreas would never do anything illegal, if that's what you're insinuating. But so many strange things go on in this town, especially at night, so I fear the worst. I feel as if I'm going crazy when I think about everything that might have happened."

She kept on crying, but more quietly now. I should offer her something, I thought, but then she would stay even longer, so I didn't.

"Do you have any coffee?" she suddenly asked. I was annoyed, but couldn't very well refuse. She might get suspicious. Runi isn't especially bright, but she can be shrewd, in a primitive sort of way. I got up and turned on the coffee maker. That's when I heard the sound again. Runi was lost in her own thoughts. Her cigarette was sending a thin, disgusting stream of smoke towards the ceiling.

"You should try calling everybody," I said with my back turned. It's important to keep the conversation going, I thought. As long as we keep talking she won't hear the noise from the cellar. "What about his work?" I said. "Have you talked to them?"

"Of course I have."

"He might have run off with a girl," I said. "He's so handsome, that Andreas. Having himself a little adventure. Did he have much money?"

"I can't think that he did. He doesn't make much, and he's always sharing what he does earn with Zipp. If he had gone off with Zipp, I could understand it. But Zipp is at home. He's fine."

"Zipp?"

"His friend. They're inseparable."

"Oh? Inseparable?"

I took two cups from the cupboard, listening. A faint sound, from something thin and light.

"I'm going to ask the police if they can report Andreas missing on the evening news on TV. With a photograph and everything. Apparently every time something runs on the evening news they get lots of calls. They say that there's always somebody who knows something."

"That's not really true, is it?"

"That's what they say."

"They? Who are 'they'?"

"People I've talked to."

"But if anyone did know anything they would call, TV news or no TV news, wouldn't they?"

I fumbled with the coffee filter and spilled coffee on the counter, but she didn't notice.

"No. Because they often have good reasons for keeping quiet."

"What? What do you mean?"

I took a sugar bowl out of the cupboard and set it on the table. The sound from the cellar had stopped. Was he lying there listening to us? Did he recognise his mother's voice through the floorboards? Runi had such a shrill voice.

"Can't you turn off that music!" she said. "I can't even think!"

"All right, all right."

I turned it down a little more. She gave me a look of surprise that I didn't do as she asked. All my life I've done what people told me to do, but not any more. I left the radio on. She shook her head.

"What should I do?" she said.

"I'm sure he'll come back soon," I said clumsily.

"You don't understand anything! You don't realise how serious this is. Two days. Just think what could happen in two days!"

"But he's not exactly a child," I objected.

"Oh yes, he is. He's my child!"

"I mean, he's probably off doing something. Something that he might not . . ." I stopped and shrugged my shoulders.

"What are you talking about?"

"I'm just thinking aloud. You don't usually worry about him."

"But this time he's disappeared!"

"Yes."

I put my hand on her arm. It was odd. Not once, in all the years that had passed, had I ever done that before. She looked at my hand in astonishment.

"If they come over here," she said, "the police, to talk to you. Will you promise me one thing?"

"Come over here?" There was a knot in my breast.

"Well, you know him, after all."

"No, no! I don't know him!" I felt the colour

leave my face. "He's never been at home when I've come to visit you. Once or twice, but no more than that."

"What are you saying?" She looked at me with dismay.

"I just mean that I've hardly ever set eyes on him, Runi."

"But you know perfectly well who he is! Don't talk like that!" She threw out her hands. "I'm just begging you to put in a good word for him. They're going to ask you what kind of a boy he is. I don't want them to think that he takes drugs or gets drunk, or anything like that. You just have to tell them the truth, that he's a good boy!"

I was starting to sweat under my arms. I'm usually so dry and unflustered. "But I don't know much about what he does in his free time."

"Good Lord, Irma, just do this for me, will you?"

"I can't lie to the police." She looked so upset that I bit back my words.

"Lie to them? I'm not asking you to do that. You just have to tell them the truth. Andreas is a decent young man with a steady job. I don't want them to get the impression that he's mixed up in anything bad. Then they won't put any real effort into looking for him. They'll leave him to his own devices. If only he were a girl. Then it's a different story; so many other things could happen. That's how they think. It's been hard enough, let me tell you, to get them to take this seriously!"

"I'm sorry, Runi. I didn't mean it. But I hope they don't come here. They won't come here if you don't give them my name. There must be others who know him better. You know I don't really know him."

"So you won't help me?"

She looked stunned. As if at any moment she might fall off her chair.

"Yes, of course I will."

"I gave them your name a long time ago. They want to talk to everybody who knows him."

I stood up and started tidying the counter, even though it didn't really need it. I moved the spice jars around and the potted plants. I didn't want her to see that I was on the verge of falling apart myself. The police at the door. And then I heard that sound again. I turned up the radio and stared out of the window in a panic.

"Oh, please."

"It's just that you make me so nervous," I stammered.

"What's the matter with you? And why aren't you at work?" she asked all of a sudden, as if she were seeing me for the first time. It was horrible.

"I'm not feeling very well. It will pass."

She fell silent. I said nothing either. Outside, the wind was blowing faintly. The birch trees leaned over the roof of the gazebo, as if they were stroking the green shingles, like a cautious warning of fiercer storms to come later in the autumn.

"Do you know what I was reading about in the newspaper?" said Runi quietly.

"No."

"I was reading about a bunch of teenagers who had a party in the room one of them lived in. You know, the kind of thing they're always doing. Perfectly innocent. Maybe a beer or two."

"And?" I tried to think about my own youth. I never went to a party in anyone's room. Henry and I would walk down the street by ourselves. He was very shy.

"One of them had a new girlfriend. But then one of the others began to . . . you know. Chat her up. And then the first boy got so angry that he took a shotgun and shot her in the face. She died instantly."

"I read about that. Why are you talking about it now?"

"I was thinking about Andreas. And about everything that could happen!"

"But surely you don't think anyone has shot him, do you? You don't believe that, do you?"

She started crying again. "No. But no matter how terrible it might be, I'd rather know about it than go around with this uncertainty. What did I do wrong, Irma?"

At this point I could have rattled off a whole long list of things, but it was too late for that.

"I think you should go home and go to bed," I said firmly.

"Go to bed?" She looked at me in disbelief. "Why should I go to bed?"

"You look worn out. It would do you good to get some rest. And you should stay near the phone. In case he calls."

"In case he calls," she repeated, like a faint echo.

"Or the police. When they find him."

"I can't bear to be alone in the house. I'm going out of my mind."

Good Lord! She came here to ask if she could stay with me, I thought. To stay in my house! I got up and moved nervously around the room.

"What is it, Irma? You look really upset."

"No, well, I just feel so uneasy. When you tell me all these things. And I'm not feeling good, either. I really should be in bed."

Runi got to her feet. She looked different. I waited to hear what would come next.

"Okay, I'm going," she sounded bitter and she looked dumbfounded, hurt beyond words. I stayed where I was, giving her a guilty look.

"I don't understand you," she went on. "I've never understood you."

"There's not much to understand," I snapped.

232

Something started tightening inside me. I could feel it quite distinctly. I was moving away, towards somewhere safe where she wouldn't be able to reach me.

"Aren't we friends any more?" She gave me a searching look.

"There's so much you don't know," I said.

"But you never tell me anything."

"It's not worth hearing. I am best off alone."

She pulled on her coat. Picked up her handbag from the chair. Stood there for a moment, wavering. Her eyes filled with tears.

"When Henry left you, I tried to give you support. You weren't so high and mighty in those days. Have you forgotten that, Irma? And that time when you were sick. I've tried, at any rate. Just go to bed. I won't bother you any more."

She made for the front door. I could have cried, I was so relieved to get her out of the house. At the door she stopped and gave me a quizzical look.

"What's that noise?"

"What noise?"

"Something in the cellar. Can't you hear it?"

"No, I hear . . ."

"Hush. Be quiet."

"Oh. That."

I glanced over my shoulder, towards the trap door to the cellar. And told her, as I realised what it must be.

"It's the boiler. It clicks like that when it's on."

"Goodbye, Irma."

I said nothing, just stared at her, thinking: Go now, Runi. Leave me in peace. As soon as the door closed, I turned the key in the lock. I stood there for a long time, leaning against a chest of drawers. When I raised my head, I saw my face in the mirror. Perfectly composed.

"My name is Irma," I said aloud. "And this is my house."

I went down to the cellar and sat on the steps. I had the lantern in my hand. It's beautiful, I thought, the tiny flame and the light flickering across his face. Andreas opened his eyes. He didn't look scared. He just lay there, waiting. Then he caught sight of the lantern. I held it in front of his eyes. He frowned.

"Now you're making me very happy. I'm going to read to you from the newspaper. There's something I want you to hear."

I smiled as I spoke. I liked the fact that he had to lie there and couldn't escape. That he had to listen to me. A man had to lie still and listen to Irma Funder and everything she had to say. A handsome man. One of those who thought everything in life was for him, the immortal type. You have to understand that this means a lot to a woman like me. I was making the rules now. Imposing them on him. It feels good to make the decisions.

"Listen to this. I can't understand things like this, I can't understand these kinds of people." And then I read aloud: "'The Central Hospital today reported a story about a woman who contacted the casualty department on September 1 with her infant son.'"

Andreas looked as if he were bored, or maybe asleep. But I knew that he was listening, I could see it in his face, and the hours dragged down there in the cellar. He had to take what little he could get.

"'The child was examined, and the doctor determined that he was unharmed. The mother went home, reassured.'"

Now Andreas was breathing rapidly and calmly, almost like a little child.

"'Later the same night the woman telephoned the hospital. She had found her baby dead in his cot.'"

Andreas opened his eyes.

"'When asked whether the child had suffered any blows or a fall, the woman reported that earlier that day she had been attacked by two young men while taking a walk along the shore at Furulund. The men had stolen her handbag. The child, a four-month-old boy, fell out of the pram during the affray and had hit his head. She could . . .'"

A gasp came from Andreas' lips. The eyes staring at me were like two black wells of terror. I looked at him in surprise, couldn't understand why he was so affected. He actually seemed frightened by the story.

As if something so monstrous had actually made an impression on him. I thought: There's hope!

"'She reported that the child cried normally at first, but in the following hours, he seemed to sleep more than usual. The police have now instigated an intense search for the two men who may indirectly have caused the child's death. The Medical Examiner will perform an autopsy, which is standard procedure after a cot death – but the examination is expected to reveal whether the child may have died from head injuries as a result of the fall.'"

I paused and looked at Andreas.

"Do you want more water?"

His eyes as he looked at me . . . I've never seen anything like it.

"Dead?" he whispered. "Is the baby dead?"

I looked at him. "That's what it says. She found him in his cot. But they're not sure yet. It might have been a cot death. When they open us up," I said, "that's when they find everything out. How we lived, what we ate. Isn't that strange?"

A spasm flitted across his face.

"A little boy," I went on. "Only four months old. Couldn't they have left her alone, a young mother with a pram? Cowards. Do you want more water?"

"I'd like a hammer in my head," he groaned.

I sat in silence, looking at him. "Were you with Zipp? Did you come here together?"

Alarmed, he opened his eyes wide. "How did you know that? How the hell do you know his name? How . . ." The outburst made him whimper. "Tell me!" he cried hoarsely. "How do you know!"

"I know everything," I said. I liked the expression on his face at that moment, the utter bewilderment. Then it changed to something else.

"He was here with me. He was waiting in the garden. He'll be here soon to find me. If he shows up, just tell him to leave."

The chair, I thought. "He's not coming," I said aloud. "He would have been here long ago, if he was coming. He has abandoned you, Andreas. Your best friend. How unpleasant for you."

A gurgle came from his throat; it sounded like laughter.

"You're crazy. Do you know that?"

"Who's the crazy person here!" I shouted. "Do I go around with a knife demanding money from people?"

His face was shiny with sweat.

"I don't really know what I want," he muttered.

"It doesn't matter what you want," I told him. "You don't have any options."

"A person always has options," he said, with his eyes closed. That little shit, always closing his eyes.

"You're lying to me. You're in pain," I said softly. "I don't want to cause anyone suffering. I have some painkillers upstairs."

"Give me an overdose," he said.

"I'll see to it that someone finds you."

"When are you going to do that? When? I'm lying down here rotting!"

"When everything is ready," I said. "I'm not ready yet."

"You've never been ready."

"Do you want some water?"

He didn't reply. I went and fetched the water. I had an extra pillow on my bed, so I got that too. And a heater that I wasn't using. I crushed two sleeping pills and sprinkled the powder in the bottle. Carried it all down to the cellar. He couldn't lift his head, I had to do it for him. Put the pillow underneath. He screamed. I tucked the blanket tighter around him. Plugged in the heater and turned it on high. It started glowing. Then I put the bottle on his chest. I caught sight of something on the floor, behind his head. It was the blue cap. I picked it up.

"There's something fizzy in the water," he said.

"Sleeping pills. They'll help you sleep for a while."

"Thanks," he whispered.

CHAPTER 15

Zipp bummed 200 kroner from his mother. She sensed a certain desperation in his voice. Something was definitely going on, she was sure of that. Her curiosity gave way to fear. They were no longer young boys, and she didn't really want to know what they were up to. Just the small things, whatever lay within the normal boundaries of youthful rebellion. Her own cowardice had overpowered her, and she thought about his father, who was no longer alive, and wished he could be here. This thought also struck her with horror. She didn't miss him, but he would have taken care of this.

Zipp went straight over to the Headline. He wanted to sit at the same table and retrace his steps of that evening. Find an explanation. But the table was occupied, and for a moment he felt bewildered as he stood there with a beer in his hand. He found another table, drank his beer slowly. It was 9.00 and starting to get dark. He was planning to go back to the house, ring the doorbell, and ask the woman straight out. Provided she opened the door, that is.

He was drinking to muster his courage. It occurred to him that if Andreas never came back, he would be all alone. He had never made any other friends; he hadn't needed anyone else. Or had Andreas arranged things that way? A bigger circle of friends would have meant greater danger. He had actually been used, functioning as a kind of life insurance for Andreas, who was a tactician. But he had liked the way things were, had never had any reason to complain. So why should he complain now? Except for the fact that he was totally alone and might have to beg to be admitted to a new group of distant acquaintances, who might not want to have anything to do with him. But why doubt him? Damn it, all he had to do was ask. When he finally turned up, and of course he'd turn up soon, and pat him on the shoulder. With that slender hand of his. Touching him. Andreas, gay. Zipp wiped his nose. Life had become so difficult. Where should he turn for help? Should he go to the police, tell them the truth? He almost choked on his beer. My buddy and I, we robbed a woman out at Furulund. And by the way, her kid fell out of the pram and started screaming his head off. And then we had a lot to drink, and everything fell apart in the cemetery. He jumped on me, and it was all so fucking awful. For him, and for me. We had to get rid of that shit! And so we chose an old woman who lived alone.

Andreas went in, holding a knife. And you know what? He never came out again.

Zipp emptied his glass and went to get another. He was determined to find out what had happened. He would ask the woman what it was all about, tell her everything, that they were both in on it. If only she would tell him what happened. Andreas' mother had called again, and he had been through the whole story a second time. He knew he sounded as though he was having trouble remembering what he had said the first time. He had told her a different story from the one he told the police officer with the curly hair. Not that it mattered; he could always blame it on the fact that it was late, and dark, and he really wasn't sure about anything. He was feeling desperate, and it was fucking nasty. He wasn't used to such outbursts of emotion. He watched people coming and going. Most of them caught sight of others they knew and started shouting and yelling. Shit, is that you? Things like that. One or two people gave him a distant nod, but nothing more. Andreas had always been his anchor. Organising a definite perimeter around them, in order to keep his disgusting secret. That's what he thought: a disgusting secret. But at the same time, he was ashamed of himself. Andreas was his friend, after all, and for the most part he was still the same person. The way he walked and laughed.

The way he held his cigarette. He still lived in the same house, still did the same job. He was better-looking than most men, pretty bright too. The only thing was that when he got horny, he had to have a man. But sex, that was important. It said a lot about who you were. Zipp read men's magazines and there were always articles about how sexual urges governed people's lives, even influencing what profession they chose, which car they bought and of course their likes and dislikes in general. So Andreas and his attraction to men must be part of everything too, even Zipp himself. Andreas had chosen him as his friend, and it had often surprised him. Had Andreas wanted him ever since junior school? Never given up the hope of turning him over on his stomach? On his fucking stomach, the mere thought of it! He squirmed on his chair. At that moment it all came back to him. The shining eyes close to his own, the white teeth, the hand in his crotch. He was sweating fiercely, had to chug down more beer. Damn it, he wasn't feeling good. Not to mention that he'd been assaulted. Well, theoretically. Andreas had forced himself on him. And now he couldn't stop thinking about it. But then he thought about his expression. The narrow shoulders, the stubborn gaze. A new Andreas he had never seen before. It couldn't be true. He had been chosen as a friend. He jumped up and left.

It was almost pitch dark as he started walking along the street. He wasn't scared, just anxious. A great anger was growing inside him. He wasn't going to come back without an answer, not tonight. He walked so fast that he was sweating. He stopped in front of a mirror shop and looked at the dozens of tiny Zipps. It suited how he was feeling. Shattered into thousands of pieces. He continued walking, reached the hill, and had to slow his pace. There was the gate and, across from it, the thick hedge. He decided to sneak into the garden first, to look through the window and see if she was at home. He squeezed through, scratching his cheeks on the jagged branches. The chair had been put back into the gazebo. He picked it up and crept to the wall of the house. He set it carefully in the flower bed, fearful that it might bang against the wall and she would hear it. The curtains were partially drawn, but there was a gap big enough for him to see into the kitchen. And there she sat! He saw papers lying on the kitchen table, and a coffee cup. Satisfied, he got back down and walked round to the front door. For several seconds he stood there, gathering his courage. He read the name on the door plate: Irma Funder. Then he pressed the doorbell. Nothing happened. He didn't think she would open the door straightaway, but he refused to give up. He rang the bell again, decided to keep ringing it until she came to the door. Sooner or later the ringing would drive her crazy. And probably she didn't have enough technical cunning to disconnect it. He didn't hear any sound from inside. He ran back to the garden behind the house. Climbed onto the chair. The opening in the curtain had been closed. He could no longer see inside. She had drawn tight the damn curtains! He went back to the front door and rang the bell again. Finally he put his finger on the bell and held it there. The shrill ring reverberated inside. He heard footsteps, but then they stopped. No-one opened the door. He put his finger back on the doorbell and held it there. Suddenly he felt afraid. What if she called the police? This could be considered a form of harassment, couldn't it?

But just then, she opened the door. Only a crack. He looked at her white face, and her eyes, as sharp as glass.

"What do you want?"

A hoarse voice, dry as tinder.

"Andreas," he panted. "Where's Andreas?"

For a long time she said nothing as she studied him, almost with curiosity. That was when he was sure that she knew! He felt braver, angrier.

"Tell me what happened!"

He tried to slip his foot in the door, but she was too fast for him. The door slammed shut.

"Shit!" he shouted. "I have to know where he is!"

"You have no right to know anything."

"Okay!" he shouted. "But can't you at least give me a hint?"

"Why should I be nice to you?" she said flatly, her voice barely audible behind the heavy door.

"Because I'm begging you," he whimpered.

She opened the door again. "I'm not easily moved," she said. "Go home. I'm sure they'll find him."

The door closed for the second time. Zipp pressed his finger on the doorbell, but this time nothing happened. He ran to the back of the house, climbed up on the chair. Under the bottom of the curtain was a tiny gap. He peered in, trying to decipher what little he could make out inside. Something blue appeared in his frame of vision, and what looked like a white cross. It was Andreas' cap.

*

Andreas opened his eyes. I was standing halfway down the steps, watching him. I have the upper hand. I loomed on the steep steps while he lay on the floor beneath me. I had the feeling that if I stretched out my arms, I could take off and fly. Hover above him in perfect circles, staring down at his helpless form.

"Did you hear the door bell? A friend of yours. Zipp."

"You're lying," he whispered.

"He was asking about you. He begged on his knees." Andreas' chest rose and fell almost imperceptibly under the blanket.

"That stuff you have on your stomach," he said in a low voice. "That's nothing to be ashamed of."

"I'm not ashamed!"

I shrieked the words. Bellowed at him. "I'm not ashamed! It's not my fault!"

"You're sick, aren't you?"

I backed up two steps and put my hand on my stomach.

"It's not your concern. I've never bothered anybody!" Then I sank down on to the steps, exhausted after my outburst and also surprised at my emotions, at screaming like that. Right in his face. Aiming at someone and pulling the trigger. I felt relaxed and at ease. I wanted to laugh out loud. But then Andreas would have more fodder for that idea he kept pulling out, that I was a crazy or something like that, but I wasn't. I'm not.

"Irma is very odd," he said.

"Why do you say that?" I stared at him.

"That's what my mother says. Every time you come to visit her."

"You recognised me?"

"Of course."

"You shouldn't talk like that. It's going to be difficult for me to let you go."

"You're never going to let me go," he breathed. "I'm going to die down here. My body is disintegrating. Don't you think I know what I smell like?"

"It's the wound to your head," I said. "It's started to get infected."

"That colostomy bag," he went on. "That's nothing. If only you knew. I walk around carrying my own burden, my own secret. Well, I won't be doing any more walking. But it's damned heavy nonetheless." His voice sank to a whisper. I moved a step closer. "It's fucking awful," he said, sniffling. He couldn't get enough air into his lungs to cry properly, and that made him seem so pitiful. It was better to be angry, it's an easier emotion, more detached. But now other, more troublesome feelings were slowly coming to life. I felt overwhelmed. That handsome face was most handsome when all malice was gone and only the child was there to see. His lips quivered, and he blinked to stop the tears from spilling out. I remembered when Ingemar was little, the smell of him, the soap and lotion. His round skull, so terrifyingly fragile. The way Andreas was fragile now.

"The baby," he said. "At Furulund. The baby that died. That was Zipp and me."

His jaw went slack. For a moment it looked as if he had slipped into a coma. A big bubble of spit grew between his lips.

"The baby?" I said in surprise.

He swallowed with difficulty. "We were going to steal her handbag. She was taking a walk along the shore. I don't care what happens to me now. You can do what you want."

For a long time I sat there, stunned, listening. His voice was growing more faint. "Go away," he said.

"I'll go when I feel like it. This is my house. We need to talk about this. How could the two of you be so thoughtless!"

"I know. I understand everything now. But that handbag was just a minor thing."

"Stealing handbags from people? A minor thing?"

"I understand everything now. Now that it's too late. You're fucking crazy, but there's nothing you can do to me any more."

"Watch your mouth!" I shouted. "This conversation is over when I say so. And don't try to use what little time you have left to humiliate me. Do you understand? Get a hold of yourself. Or I won't give you any more water."

"Dear Irma." His lips contorted. "You don't control me. I do. And I don't want any more water."

"So you're planning to die of thirst?"

"You die faster without water."

"Go ahead and try it. You haven't understood anything at all. If you had, you would have kept a lower profile. You should have shown me a little respect."

"I'm lying on the floor of your cellar, dying," he said dryly. "I can't get any lower than this. Death is a liberator, Irma. I've abused my place here on earth. It's time for me to withdraw."

I didn't understand what he was babbling about. He was beginning to get confused. I stood up angrily and left. Sat at the kitchen table for quarter of an hour, thinking. After that I went back down with some warm sugar milk in the bottle. I was sure he would drink it, in spite of his little speech. He reminded me of a baby as he lay there. I had put on a knitted cardigan so I wouldn't be cold, but it was warm down there because of the heater. I liked sitting there, looking at him. When he was done, he was about to doze off again, but I shouted his name, over and over. "Andreas, Andreas." And then he opened his eyes. I took the newspaper out of my apron pocket and showed him the article about him, with the nice picture. "HAS ANYONE SEEN ANDREAS?"

Then he started to cry.

Listen to me! Again and again I went down to the cellar. Day after day. I asked him if he needed anything. Changed the light bulb, tucked in the

249

blanket. He started to smell. His face looked sunken and his lips were almost grey. I felt instantly happy every time I caught sight of his head with the dark curls. Knowing that he was still there, making no noise. I didn't think about the future. Or about the past, either, and that was something new for me. I was used to worrying about the next day and everything that might happen. But not any more. I was living in the moment. Finally, a sort of peace.

CHAPTER 16

September 4.

Three nights had passed. Zipp opened the phone book to the letter F. How easy this is, he thought. Open the phone book, look for the name, and make the call. Just like that, I'm there, right in her ear. Threatening and pestering.

The phone rang and rang. He clutched the receiver in his hand.

"This is Zipp!" he cried when she answered. "I want to speak to Andreas."

There was a moment's silence. He could hear a faint rustling sound and someone breathing.

"Andreas is not available."

Her voice was rough. What did she mean by that? Not available? She was sitting on the truth with that fucking big arse of hers, like the bitch that she was. He was so distraught that his knees started to give way. That shitty feeling when you knew that someone was lying through their teeth or, right in your ear, to be precise. So easily, so utterly without shame. His own fury was roaring inside his head.

"I know he's there. Damn you!"

"You don't know any such thing."

Her voice was calm. The polar opposite of his own pounding heart.

"His cap is lying on your kitchen counter."

Silence again. That gave her something to think about! He stood there fidgeting, trying to compose himself.

"You should clean up better after yourself," he snapped.

"I'm doing just fine. But have you cleaned up after yourself?"

He listened to that composed voice, trying to decipher what she was thinking. How could she be so calm?

"Yes," he replied. "I just need Andreas."

"What about the baby?"

"I don't have a baby!" he shouted. "And I don't feel like playing your games. I just want Andreas!"

"Andreas is crying," she whispered. "He's crying for the baby."

He felt a sudden stab of terror.

"The baby at Furulund. It's dead now."

Zipp stood and stared at the phone book. Funder, Furnes, Fyken. What was she talking about? He stared at the newspaper on the table, felt sure she must be bluffing.

"A head injury," she said softly. "Infants are so

fragile. If you don't stop bothering me, I'll call the police and tell them that you killed him. A little boy, only four months old. They're looking for you."

"I tried to stop the pram!" he yelled.

A tiny click, and the line went dead. Outside the window he could see the spire of the church. A crack in the blue sky. He was still shaking. A tiny baby. He had to look through the newspapers, make sure that she was lying. She was just testing him. He would read the papers himself later. First he had to try to relax. He stumbled downstairs, lay on the sofa, closed his eyes and fell asleep. Two hours later he woke up. His mother was calling from the top of the stairs.

"Telephone! The police. They want you to go down to the station."

He was shaking so hard that he had to use both hands to put a five-kroner coin into the parking meter. The news about the baby was in *Aftenposten*, for God's sake. The woman was right! Could the attack come under the heading of manslaughter? It was the mother who had failed to set the brake properly. Damn it! He felt the ground shifting under his feet, as if he were walking through a bog. A trickle of sweat ran from his temple, and he couldn't move his eyes the way he wanted to. They were staring, like two balls of glass, saying: Guilty, guilty, guilty! He was sniffling as he fought with the fucking parking meter, that damned money hog, this damned world he'd been thrown into. Had he asked for this? Was anyone happy that he was here? He pressed his shoulders back and thought: Pull yourself together, man. They just want to talk about Andreas.

As he walked to the front entrance, he repeated to himself: I don't remember, I don't remember. If they realised that he was lying, or hiding something, they would have to prove it. He entered the reception area and gave his name at the desk. Had to stand there, alone, and wait. A man came towards him, wearing a uniform. Not the young guy with the curls this time. This was going to be worse. He straightened up, wanting to meet the situation with confidence, only to discover that the man was a head taller than he was. He was struck by the feeling that his case was hopeless, it would be impossible to fool this monolith of a man. The aura of friendliness surrounding him was just a veneer. It didn't for one second hide what he was truly made of. Zipp was reminded first of iron and steel, then oiled wood and finally lead crystal as he met the man's grey eyes. He felt a prod on his shoulder. It directed him to the lift, into a corner.

"Konrad Sejer."

The voice was deep, threatening. This was undoubtedly one of the bosses. Why? The office surprised him. It looked like any other office, with a child's drawings, photographs, thank-you cards, things like that. A good chair. View of the river. He could see the sight-seeing boat gliding past, must be one of the last tours of the season.

"Zipp," Sejer said. "I'm going to order some coffee. Do you drink coffee?"

"Jesus, yes."

It hadn't got off to a good start. His voice wavered. I don't remember, I don't remember. Sejer left the room. Zipp wondered what the consequences would be if he lied. This was just a conversation, wasn't it? He thought of what his mother had said: "I know you". There was something about this man that gave him the same feeling. He must try to maintain a friendly tone. As long as the tone remained friendly, he was safe. Sejer came back with a coffee pot and two Styrofoam cups.

"Good of you to come," he said. As if Zipp had had a choice. The grey man knew this, he was just playing a game. Suddenly he seemed terribly dangerous. Dejection swamped him. A dull fear that he wasn't going to get out of this in one piece.

"Sure. But I don't understand what I'm doing here," he stammered. "I told you everything about that night."

The man shot him a glance that felt like a blast in his eyes.

"It's more serious now," Sejer said curtly. "Before, it was one day, now it's three; that's a whole different story."

Zipp nodded mutely.

"For your sake, I hope we find Andreas," Sejer went on. He watched the stream of burning hot coffee trickling into the white cup.

For your sake? What the hell did he mean by that? Zipp was about to ask that very question. What the hell do you mean by that? Wasn't there some sort of insinuation in the question? That if they didn't find him . . .

"He's your best friend, right?"

"Yes he is." Zipp said. Now he felt as if it were being used against him, the fact that they were friends, that Andreas was his best pal. Stay calm, he told himself, just answer the questions.

"I'm going to be honest with you," Sejer said. "I'm an old-fashioned kind of man." He gave a winning smile, which made Zipp think that either he really was nice or he was one hell of an actor. He decided the latter was more likely. "One of my officers, Jacob Skarre, has already talked to you. I'll get directly to the point. In his report, he made it clear that during the course of your conversation he had the strong impression that you weren't telling the truth. That's why you're here. Do you understand?"

Zipp shrugged. Calm, stay calm. Breathe from your stomach.

"The thing is, I've had experience before with Officer Skarre's intuition. And I have no choice but to take it seriously."

Zipp stretched out his legs and laid one foot over the other.

"What I've been thinking, just as a possibility," Sejer said, "was that the two of you did something together that evening that may have had an unexpected outcome. Something you've decided not to tell us, because you're afraid of the consequences."

Zipp was rolling some spit around in his mouth. Finally the deep flow of words stopped. He was apparently waiting for an answer.

"No objections?" he said at last.

"We were in a bar," Zipp said.

"So tell me in your own words all that happened that night," said Sejer. He was now sitting in his chair.

"My own words?" Zipp stammered.

"What you did, what you talked about. Maybe that will give me some idea of what's going on."

Did he know more than he was saying? Had the woman with the pram described them down to the last detail?

"Sorry." Zipp hesitated as he searched for what the inspector called "his own words".

"You don't have to feel embarrassed. This conversation stays in this room. You're not being taped or recorded. You can speak freely."

Such phrases the man used! Now he was trying to give the impression that he was an ally, but he wasn't, was he?

Zipp straightened his shoulders. "Well, there's not much to tell. We were in a bar having a beer. After that we went to my house. Watched a video. Wandered round town for a while. Andreas went home to bed. That's all."

Sejer nodded encouragement. Zipp started to believe that this man wasn't here to ask him about the baby after all. He was indeed concerned about Andreas, and nothing else. Zipp tried not to take a defensive position.

"But he didn't go home to bed," Sejer said, smiling. A new kind of smile: broad and open.

Zipp had to smile at his own stupidity. But it was entirely innocent, it had just slipped out, apparently to his advantage, judging by the man's response.

"No, of course not. But that's what he said."

"Exactly. He had to get up early?"

"At 8.00."

Sejer drank some coffee. "What film did you watch?"

Did that make any difference? Did he think they watched a film that might have steered them into trouble?

"*Blade Runner*," he mumbled, a bit reluctantly because he didn't want to show any kind of enthusiasm. Sejer noticed his slight irritation.

"I saw that one a long time ago," he said. "I didn't much like it. But then, as I said, I'm old-fashioned."

Zipp relaxed. "Andreas insisted on watching it. Even though he's seen it hundreds of times. Or something like that."

"Is that right? Hundreds of times? Were you bored?"

"I'm often bored."

"Why's that?"

"I don't have a job."

"So you wait all day for Andreas, until you can have some company?"

"He usually calls after dinner."

"Did you make any arrangements to meet again when you said goodbye?"

"No, we didn't have . . ."

He checked himself. The words had come pouring out of him. I don't remember, I don't remember. He was floating away like a scrap of paper on the rushing stream that was this man.

"You didn't have what?"

"He met someone." The words just popped out.

"Ah! He met someone?"

Zipp didn't look up, but if he had, he would have seen Sejer's wry smile.

"Who, Zipp?"

"I didn't know them."

He stifled a silent curse. Who the hell had put that reply into his mouth? Now he would be asked why he hadn't told this to the other officer when he came to his house. Okay, so he'd forgotten about it. That wasn't so bad. This man would have to prove he was lying. It wasn't enough that the air was thick with lies. Though it was.

"Excellent that you remembered that," said Sejer with satisfaction. "That's what I always say. Things come back to you more clearly over time. And you're in a difficult situation, after all. Your best friend is missing, and you're worried about him."

In his mind Zipp pictured Andreas trapped somewhere. Alone in the dark. That white house. He didn't understand it. A lump was forming in his throat and tears came to his eyes. But maybe that was to his advantage. Showing how worried he was.

"Two guys," he said, with his eyes lowered. "They came over to us in the square."

"Two men?"

"Yes."

"Young men?"

"Older than us. Thirty, maybe."

"Have you ever seen them before?"

"No."

"But Andreas knew them?"

"It looked like it."

A long pause. Way too long. Either he was thinking over this information, this utter lie, or he was amused by these wild fantasies. What if Andreas showed up and told his own version? Am I assuming that he's never going to show up? Have I written him off? No, I'm a good friend!

"All right. Tell me more."

"Tell you what?"

He was on thin ice now, suspended precariously over the cold deep. Images flew past his eyes: Andreas' burning cheeks, the baby with the toothless gums.

"We sat on a bench. They were standing near the fountain. Andreas said he had to take off. And then they left. I don't know where they went. I was actually a bit pissed off."

Then Zipp shut up. His coffee cup was still untouched. He would have taken a sip, but he didn't trust his hands. Sejer had no such problem. He took sip after sip, without making a sound. Zipp's last words hung in the room: "I was actually a bit pissed off." He had made it up, but there was truth in the lie. If that had really happened, if they had been sitting on the bench and Andreas had suddenly taken off, he really would have been irritated. He reached this conclusion with a certain pride.

"But Andreas – didn't he spend all his time with you?"

Zipp squirmed. "I thought so."

"Thornegata," said Sejer suddenly.

Zipp glanced up.

"You mentioned to Andreas' mother when she called that you said goodbye to each other on Thornegata."

"I don't remember," he said swiftly.

"I mention it because there must be some reason why you would have thought of that particular street. You remembered wrong, of course, we've already ascertained that, but for some reason your brain still made that choice. Maybe you were in the vicinity of Thornegata sometime that evening?"

Zipp felt bewildered.

"It just slipped out. A short circuit," he said.

"It happens," Sejer conceded.

He got up and opened the window. The September air swept in.

"What do you think has happened?" Sejer said. He was sitting down now.

"Shit. I have no idea."

"But you must have some thoughts about it."

"Yes."

"Could you tell me?"

He thought hard. It occurred to him that what had started as "just a conversation" now felt very much like an interrogation.

"I've thought of everything!" he said with a sudden, fierce sincerity. "That he went off and hanged himself. Anything at all."

"Is that something he might do?"

"No. Or rather, I don't know." He thought about the cemetery. "I don't know," he repeated.

"Was there something bothering him?"

"He never said so."

"Did he talk much about himself?"

"Never."

Sejer went over to a green filing cabinet, took out some papers and leafed through them. Zipp craned his neck, but he was sitting too far away to see. Sejer took out something from a folder and pushed it across the desk towards Zipp.

"What do you say, Zipp?" he said solemnly. His eyes were piercing. "Is he still alive?"

Zipp stared at the photograph of Andreas. "I just don't know!" he stammered.

"Is there any reason to assume that he might be dead?"

"I don't know!" he stammered again. He had a horrible feeling that he had fallen into a trap. "Do you think he's dead?" he said flatly.

Sejer propped the picture up against the coffee pot.

"Zipp. Why are you lying?" he said.

There it was at last! He knew it would come sooner or later. He was fully prepared for it! The question hit him like a rubber ball and bounced back. There wasn't a mark on him.

"I don't know anything," he intoned.

"Those guys at the square. Can we drop them?"

"I don't know where they were going," Zipp said.

"Were they really there at all?"

"I only saw them from a distance."

"How many were there?"

What had he said before? Two? Or three?

"Two or three. I don't remember."

"Are you worried about your best friend?"

"Of course!" Zipp gave him a hurt look. At the same time he tried to work out what the man wanted.

"Then why won't you help me?"

"I am helping. But I don't remember!" He lost control. He was totally out of it. "I've told you everything I know. Can I go now?"

"No."

"I'm not under arrest, am I?"

"You can't go yet."

"Why not?"

"I haven't finished with you."

Zipp felt as if he were slowly falling. The truth began to look like an easier solution. He understood everything. Why people confessed to things they hadn't done, anything to escape interrogation. He swayed on his chair. Danger was threatening from every direction. It was blowing in through the window, crawling up his legs. A ghastly future that he didn't want. Prosecution and sentencing. The baby's mother in the front row, staring at him as he stood in the witness box. A judge, clad in black robes and with a huge gavel crashing against Zipp's chest. Knocking his heart off of its rhythm, making it falter, he couldn't breathe. Years alone in a space two metres by three metres, Zipp thought. He felt faint. A rushing and a sinking feeling in his head at the same time. He wanted to hide. He reached for the coffee cup, he saw his own hand come into view to pick up the cup, but he missed and it fell. Coffee splashed over the desk.

Dripped down his thighs and burned through his clothes.

*

I told Andreas that Zipp had called. I thought he would shout at me, but he didn't have the strength. He didn't look as if he cared. I didn't understand it. Perhaps he was using the time to reconcile himself with the worst possibility, that he might die down there in the cellar. Alone, among the potatoes and spiders and mice. We human beings are amazing. We can handle most situations, given time. He didn't want to talk. He shut me out. I didn't let it upset me, just stood there for a while and tormented him with my presence. Fiddled with the buttons on my jacket. Then I went back upstairs. Started rummaging in the drawers and cupboards. I was particular about what would be left behind. I'd collected a lot of papers and the majority of my clothes in sacks. I didn't have much time. Andreas was worn out. I liked him better when he whimpered and pleaded, but now he didn't want anything. He closed his eyes when I stood on the stairs. I slammed doors and stomped on the floor. I was the only one he had! He said he wasn't in any pain, but I didn't believe him. He didn't want to give me the satisfaction of knowing that he suffered. Maybe he didn't want to go on, in any case. Get out of this cellar and go to a hospital. Roll along in a wheelchair. With all those memories. Some lives are too difficult to endure. Maybe that's what he was thinking. I couldn't comfort him. He didn't deserve any comfort. He shouldn't have come here.

Despair would seize hold of me now and then. Unpredictable attacks of panic. I didn't recognise myself. None of us deserved this, none of us wanted this. Andreas was a bolt from the blue. I was the one he had struck. Then I started laughing. These past few days, and everything that had happened, it was all incomprehensible. Unreal. A young boy on the cellar floor in the house of an old woman? What a story! I pulled myself away and went to the window. Sometime I would have to eat something. I hadn't eaten in ages. I saw an end to my despair, a sudden clarity. I let go of everything I was holding. It couldn't get any worse than this. It was important to put an end to this ridiculous performance once and for all. He had suffered enough. He had learned his lesson. I stood up and opened the trap door. Yelled down the stairs to him: "I'm going to the police station. They're going to come and get you soon!"

He probably didn't believe me. I was very tired. The police could do what they liked with me, I didn't care. Andreas could explain. He was the one who had started it all.

*

"Do you feel sick, Zipp? You look pale."

Sejer wiped up the coffee on the desk, using some paper towels from the holder by the sink. Zipp was busy holding on to the edge of the desk, so he didn't answer. His body had betrayed him. But it didn't matter. The policeman was now a genuine enemy, no longer pretending to be friendly. Now he would use other methods, strike harder, maybe even threaten him. It was a relief, in a way. He knew where he stood, could no longer be seduced or duped. He ground his teeth. Sejer recognised all the signs from hundreds of other conversations. It was a relief for him too. They had reached a new phase. He knew the pattern, the gestures, the body language. The tension in the room was still rising, with a hint of anger, but underneath there was fear. What could those two have done on that fateful night? He looked at Zipp, genuinely curious.

"I hope, both for God's and Andreas' sake, that you have good reasons for keeping quiet," he said sharply.

Zipp didn't let himself be provoked. He was a solid wall with no openings, not so much as a crack. The truth felt heavy, but secure inside him. He was impregnable.

"Is Andreas alive?"

Zipp took his time. He was not in a hurry.

"I don't know."

That was true. It was too easy. He almost had to hold back a smile.

"What did you fight about?"

"We didn't fight."

Sejer folded his arms. "This isn't just about you. He has a mother who's scared and a father who's worried. You know something that might help us. If he ends up as something that we have to carry home in a bag, you're going to blame yourself for the rest of your life."

That was harsh, but Zipp had to admit that it was true.

"None of this is my fault," he said.

"What do you mean by 'this'?"

"I don't know."

He put on the brakes again. It surprised him how difficult it actually was not to say anything at all. The grey eyes were so intense, demanding something from him, drawing him out.

"Have you ever seen a dead man?"

He hadn't. He hadn't wanted to see his father, back then, a long time ago. He didn't answer.

"The first time is always overwhelming. It takes your breath away. The reminder that we're all going to die."

Zipp was listening. The seriousness scared him. It was because of all he didn't know. He felt a fool. He pushed the feeling aside. He wasn't a fool, just very unlucky.

"If the dead person is someone you knew well, the feeling is doubly strong. He's lying there, but he's not lying there. A wall falls away."

Sejer paused. His mother's dead face appeared in his mind's eye. "The two of you shared so much, the way best friends do. How are you getting along without him?"

Zipp pursed his lips. His throat felt tight, his eyes stung, but he didn't blink. He just hoped that the water filling his eyes wouldn't spill over the edge and become tears. Although that might look good. He was in despair, God damn it. But the inspector had more up his sleeve, he could hear it in his voice. This was only the beginning.

"How would you feel if you were indirectly the cause of someone's death?"

The question almost made him choke with laughter, but he controlled himself. They might never find out who had been responsible for the business with that baby. Maybe it would be best if Andreas were dead. The thought crossed his mind, sudden and unasked, yet pragmatical. That scared him. Did he wish Andreas dead? No, that's not what he wished, but if he did turn up, wouldn't everything come out? Who they were, what they had done? He'd rather be alone for the rest of his life than have to take the blame for that baby. He had to fix his eyes on something. Study every little detail, describe it accurately and exactly in his mind. The way prisoners did when they sat in their cells. The man's tie. Grey-blue with a tiny embroidered cherry motif.

"Zipp. There's something I have to tell you."

Now it was coming! He knew it! His hairline, straight and even, and his thick hair the colour of steel.

"You've wrapped yourself up in a great feeling of calm. That's no art. Anyone can do that. I can't reach you. But what you're doing demands deep concentration."

Some speech! He must have learned it on a course. His hands were big, the fingers long, the nails clean and white. Fucking meticulous, this man. In his lapel there was a pin that looked like an umbrella.

"The problem is that deep concentration takes so much energy. You can hold on to it for a while, but then it slips away from you. Tell me what you know. What you are doing is just a delay. And a delay wastes time. Time we could be using to find Andreas. We could call his mother and say: 'We've found him, Mrs Winther. And he's all right'." He leaned across the desk. "'Thanks to Zipp, who came to his senses.'"

I'm not coming to my senses, it's as simple as that. I don't care, I just don't give a damn.

"It's impossible for anyone to hold on to anger for a prolonged period of time. It's driven by hormones, and that's not something you can control. It can shoot up like a geyser. You're at that age. In time you'll stop feeling what you feel now and slip into something else . . ."

"Shut up!" Zipp was shaking violently. "You can't touch me!"

Sejer smiled sadly. "Are you so sure of that? Don't you read the newspapers?" He lowered his voice. "If you only knew how angry I can get." He stood up and pushed back his chair. Straightened his jacket. Looked at Zipp. His smile was almost jovial. Zipp tried to steel himself.

"You can go home now."

He stayed where he was, gaping. There must be some mistake. If he got up and walked across the room, maybe he would stick out his foot to trip him.

"G-go home?"

"Lie down in your warm bed. Send Andreas a kind thought."

Zipp tried to be happy that he'd managed to keep his mouth shut, but he didn't feel happy, just empty. What about the baby? he thought. They didn't know anything about that. That was something, at least. The minutes passed. He was still whole. He slipped past the man. He reached only as high as his lapels. But he saw the pin. It was actually a little gold sky diver.

CHAPTER 17

Anna Fehn opened the door and looked at Sejer. She liked what she saw, but at the same time she felt anxious. The painting of Andreas stood on the easel, half finished. And now a policeman had come here to ask questions. How much should she tell him? What would he think? He didn't sit down when she pointed to the sofa.

"Why are you here? How did you find me?"

He smiled briefly. "This is a small town. I'm just curious. Would it be possible to see the painting of Andreas that you've been working on?"

She led the way into another, bigger and brighter, space. The easel stood to the right of the window so that the light fell on it from the left. Sejer didn't recognise Andreas because the boy stood with his face tilted down, his eyes fixed on a spot on the floor. But the hair, maybe, the wild curls. Otherwise it was his body that she had wanted to portray. Sejer was struck by just how naked he was, more naked than he would have looked in a photograph. The body was in violent

273

motion, more defined than his age would indicate. He was painted in blues and greens, only his hair was red.

"Does he like it? Posing?"

She nodded. "He seems to. He's good-looking, and he knows it." She laughed softly. "The first time he saw it, he said: 'Shit, that's fucking awesome!'"

Sejer stuck his face close to the canvas. "It must take a certain kind of person. To pose like that."

"Why so?"

He shrugged. "I'm trying to imagine myself in the same situation. How uncomfortable I would feel."

"Maybe you take yourself too seriously."

She noticed his eyes, which weren't brown, as she at first thought, but deep grey. His hair must have been raven black at one time. She guessed that he was a practical type; his hair was cut very short and he carried himself with controlled grace, without being ostentatious. Mature, she thought.

"Do the two of you do anything else besides pose and paint?"

She had been afraid of the question, but was unprepared for the speed with which it came. Was he being impudent or just unusually acute?

"Sometimes," she said evasively.

"Have a bite to eat together, or sometimes a beer?"

She coughed. "Er, yes. Sometimes."

"Sometimes what?"

He stared her down. A tiny smile took the sting out of his dark gaze. She started fidgeting with a brush sticking out of a jar. Stroked her chin with the soft bristles.

"We sleep together."

"Who took the initiative?"

"I did. What did you expect?" The reply was followed by dry laughter.

Sejer looked at the painting again, saw the enthusiasm in every stroke. The young body in which everything was tautly in place. And the force in it, the youth. Anna Fehn was in her early forties and Andreas was 18. Well, it was a familiar story.

She looked at the floor. "To be honest, he never really seems to like it. But he does it anyway. As if he thinks it's expected of him, or that it's required, I'm not really sure which. I often wonder. Why he puts himself at my disposal like that."

Sejer could understand perfectly why a young man like Andreas would grab such a chance if it was offered to him. Anna Fehn was not a dazzling beauty, but she was very attractive. Blonde and voluptuous.

"Do you know his friend? Zipp?"

"Andreas has mentioned him. In a patronising kind of way. As if he's impossibly hopeless."

"They've been friends for years."

"Yes. And I wonder whether his dissatisfaction is just a cover. That it's actually hiding great emotion. So great that it bothers him."

"What are you getting at?"

She went over to the window where the pale light fell across the naked body on the canvas.

"Call it woman's intuition, but I think that Andreas . . . There's no passion in him. You can feel . . . a certain lack of interest. I think he prefers boys. I think he's in love with Zipp."

Sejer stared at her in shock.

"Forgive me if I'm starting a hare. But I think I'm no more than a cover for him. Something he can brag about to others."

To Zipp, Sejer wondered. "He doesn't spend time with anyone else except Zipp."

"I know."

"But you're not positive about this?"

"At times it's quite blatant. I've had lots of models over the years, and many of them have been homosexual."

"What are the signs that make you think so?"

"I think we girls can see it faster than men. Think about it. I look at you. You look at me. We each think our own thoughts. We do this in a split second, before anything else. We appraise one another. Will I make love with this man, with this woman? Yes or no? When we've decided that, then we move on and attend to whatever is our real objective. And we can put the tension aside. But its always there to begin with. A tension that we get so used to throughout our lives that we don't even think about it. Until one day we're confronted with a man, and the tension isn't there. That's a strange experience. It makes us relax. Girls enjoy the company of homosexual men," she said. "Men evidently don't feel as comfortable in the company of lesbians. Isn't that strange?" She suddenly looked a bit hostile. He listened, astonished, as he retreated into himself. Was that the first thing he thought about when he met a woman? Surely that couldn't be true? Except for Sara, when he met her. But first of all Elise. And, very rarely, Mrs Brenningen on reception. But other times? Yes, if the woman was beautiful. But what if she wasn't attractive in any way? Then he rejected her. After first ... He stopped what he was thinking. "Will the painting be finished soon?" He nodded at the canvas and the face that was still missing a nose and mouth. The eyes were only indicated, two green shadows beneath the red shock of hair.

"It will be a while. But I'm not going to do anything more with the head. I promised that no-one would be able to recognise him, and I'm going to keep that promise. Where is he?" she asked.

"We don't know. All we have is Zipp, and he's not very informative. What will you do now?" he said. "He's missing, and you won't be able to finish the painting."

She shrugged. "I'm sure he'll turn up. And if not, then he'll never be more than a sketch. Would you consider posing for me?"

Sejer was so taken aback that he almost choked.

"I thought I made clear what my feelings on that score were."

"It's important to break down barriers," she said. "To take off your clothes and let someone study you, to allow yourself to be properly seen through someone else's eyes – it's hugely liberating."

Stand in front of this woman, he thought, without a stitch on. With her eyes everywhere, analytical eyes examining him until all that was left was an impression. And not what he really was. Just the impression he made on her. Which was unique to her. What would she see? A 50-year-old, sinewy body in good physical shape. A trace of eczema in a few places. The line at his waist where his skin was paler than elsewhere. A scar running down his right thigh, shiny and white. Hour after hour, until he was fixed on the canvas for all time. And someone would own it, hang it on their wall. Look at it. But why is that so much more frightening than being photographed? he thought. Because the lens is dead and can't judge. Was he afraid of being judged? Would he overcome something if he agreed to pose? And if so, what would that lead to? Sejer decided he could live with his own curiosity.

His expression was polite and proper when he thanked her for her help.

*

Andreas opened his eyes. His mien, when he finally understood, how shall I describe it? A tiny light that suddenly goes out.

"You didn't go there," he said, exhausted.

"Yes, I did!"

I wrung my hands and felt ashamed. Because I had failed him. But I was also furious at all the prejudiced people who don't really see us. Who just give us a quick look and jump to conclusions.

"I was there. But he didn't understand a thing. A young man, I don't think he's worked there long. I tried to explain, but he just asked me whether I needed a lift home. As if I were a foolish old woman. And you know what the funny thing is? I've seen him before, but I can't think where. It's so odd!"

Andreas uttered a whimper. He must still have had some hope until now, but it was gone, the very last bit of it.

"Shit. You mean you went to the police station, and then you just left?"

He started wheezing, as if his throat were full of mucus. He couldn't cough it up. His lungs wheezed.

"Get out of here!"

"I'll leave when I feel like it. I tried to tell them."

"No, you didn't! My God, you're so pathetic!"

"You're the one who's pathetic. Just look at you! Don't provoke me; I can't take much more."

"Poor Irma. The world has been so unfair to you. No-one understands what it's like for you, is that it?"

He was crying, but his tears were mixed with laughter. It wasn't attractive.

"Be quiet, Andreas."

"I'll talk as much as I like. It's the only thing I can do."

"I won't give you any more water."

"Do you enjoy this, Irma? Tormenting me? Where do you feel it? Does it turn you on?"

"Leave me alone," I snapped. "If you only knew what I might do."

"But I do know. It's the same for me."

"You have no idea what you're talking about."

"Go to bed. I want to be left in peace."

"You want to be left in peace? You should have thought of that earlier. You know what? I do too. But did you take that into consideration?"

"No," he said mildly.

"You weren't counting on Irma!"

"I didn't know that you were the one who lived here."

"Liar!"

"I didn't recognise you until it was too late."

"Don't give me that! Because if you'd noticed it was me, you would have gone to the next house! And stuck your knife into someone else's face. Some stranger. Because that would have been easier!"

I was trembling with anger, and it felt wonderful, those fierce emotions burning my cheeks. I was a live human being, justifiably shaking with indignation, in fact I was standing at the front, fighting one of my most important battles. And best of all, he had to listen to me! He couldn't even lift his hands to block his ears. His face went blank. He had closed me out again, but I knew he was listening.

"You're a spoiled child."

He didn't answer, but I could see his eyelashes flickering.

"What did you ever do for your mother? Tell me that. What obligations have you ever had?"

His smile was weak. "I took out the rubbish. Every day."

"Oh, how marvellous. You took out the rubbish! I'm so impressed, Andreas."

"How long have I been lying here?" he whispered.

I counted to myself. "Three days. Do you want to get out of here? Try to find my weak points. My maternal instincts. The key to your freedom. I've had a child, so I must have them. Try to see if you're a good judge of character."

"I am a good judge of character," he sighed. "But it's not necessary in this case. Even a child could see it a mile off. You're totally insane."

I stood up and shook my fists. I wanted to howl out loud, show him how furious I was.

"You damn little brat!"

Surprised, he stared up at me with his light blue eyes. "Your cheeks are burning, Irma!"

I spun round and left. This time I turned off the light, wrapping him in thick darkness.

"Call them, for God's sake!" he shouted. "You fucking bitch. Call for help!"

I knelt down and shoved the trap door shut. I opened it and closed it, over and over. It banged and slammed like an earthquake through the house. Worn out, I sank to the floor.

CHAPTER 18

September 5.

Mrs Winther called. Skarre tried to explain.

"No, Mrs Winther, that's not possible. We're not unwilling, but I'm speaking from experience. The TV news doesn't report this kind of case. Only if we think it probable that a crime has been committed. And in this case . . . Yes, Mrs Winther, I realise that. But I know the man in charge, and he's not easily persuaded. You can call them, if you like, but I'm trying to spare you the disappointment. Only very special cases. Of course Andreas is special to you, but people disappear every single day. Between two and three thousand a year, to tell you the truth. A girl of ten would get more attention? Yes, that's true, that's how things work. We managed to get a photograph in the local paper, and that was difficult enough. The head of the news section? Of course you can call, but I don't really think . . . Yes, of course we'll call you at once, but there's a limit to how much we can do here. Actually, we've already done much more than we would usually be able to.

I realise that you don't see it that way. But we can't rule out that Andreas may have left because he wanted to. And in that situation . . . Yes, I know you don't think that's possible, but no-one ever does. The thing is, if we do find him, we have no right to say where he is. To you. If he doesn't want us to. Unfortunately, those are the rules. He's an adult . . . Goodbye, Mrs Winther."

*

Ingrid Sejer was sitting in front of the television, watching the evening news. Matteus stood behind her chair, staring at the screen, barefoot and wearing thin pyjamas. His mother turned round and saw him.

"Matteus. It's late," she said.

He nodded, but he stayed where he was. His mother looked a little depressed. She put her hands on his thin shoulders.

"What are you eating?"

"A liquorice Porsche."

She smiled sadly. "Pappa says that I shouldn't pressure you, but I wish you would tell us who wrote that note. That awful note in your school bag."

"It doesn't bother me," he said.

"It doesn't frighten you?"

"No," he said. She gave him a searching look,

surprised at his reaction, and realised that she believed him, though she wasn't sure why.

"I'm not going to run to the headmaster and tell him, or anything like that," she said. "If you tell me who wrote it. And I won't call his mother. Or hers, if it's a girl. I just need to know."

Matteus was fighting a silent battle. It was hard when his mother begged him like that.

"All right," he said at last. "It was Tommy."

His mother was struck dumb. She sat for a moment with her eyes wide, shaking her head. "Tommy?" she stammered in confusion. "But he's . . . he's from Ethiopia. His skin is darker than yours!"

"I know," Matteus said, shrugging.

"But why would Tommy, of all . . ." She started to giggle. Matteus giggled too, and they were both laughing hysterically. His mother hugged him, and Matteus didn't understand why she was so happy. But she was. She stood up and got him a glass of Coke. Then she sat down again to watch the news, from time to time shaking her head. Matteus was on the sofa. Imitating the grown-ups, he opened the paper and found himself looking at a photograph of a young man with dark curls. He was smiling at Matteus with white teeth. In the picture he looked nice, much nicer than he had that day in the green car. It was him, he was sure of it.

"Why is this boy in the newspaper?" he asked.

His mother glanced at the photograph and read the story underneath.

"Because he's missing," she told him.

"What do you mean, missing?" he wanted to know.

"Missing, gone, disappeared," she explained.

"Gone like Great-Grandmother?"

"No. Or rather, they don't know. He left his home and never came back."

"He's driving around in a green car," Matteus told her.

"What are you talking about?" She gave him a doubtful look.

"Him and another boy. In a green car. They asked me how to get to the bowling alley."

"Is that one of the boys who were bothering you down the street the other day? When you came home from the party?"

"Yes."

"Are you sure?"

"I'm sure."

She grabbed the newspaper and read the text again. Missing since September 1.

"I have to call your grandfather," she said.

"But I don't know where he is *now*," Matteus said, sounding worried.

"That doesn't matter. I still have to call him. Go to bed now."

"I want to talk to Grandpa."

"You can have two minutes." She dialled her father's number and waited.

Skarre was chewing on his pen. It was leaving a metallic taste in his mouth. How could someone just disappear off the face of the earth like that? At the same time, he was thinking of what Sejer had said. There's always someone who knows something. And Zipp knew. His thoughts were interrupted by the phone ringing.

"Criminal Division. Jacob Skarre."

There was a strange rushing sound on the line. He listened for a moment, waiting.

"Hello? . . . Hello?"

The silence continued. Just the faint rushing sound. He could have hung up – they had plenty of calls when people never said a word – but he decided to wait.

"You'd better come soon. He probably won't live much longer!"

There was a click. The conversation was over. Skarre sat there bewildered, holding the phone.

A woman. She sounded hysterical, almost tearful. And at that instant something occurred to him. He stood up so fast that his chair fell and went clattering into the filing cabinet behind him. Those words. That despair! Where had he heard them before? He leaned against the cabinet, thinking. That hoarse voice, it reminded him of something, if only he could remember. Something recent. He sat at his desk again. Thought hard. But he couldn't pin it down. How could he make himself remember?

He tried thinking of something else. Finally it came back to him what she had actually said. He probably won't live much longer. Did it have to do with Andreas Winther? Why did he think of Andreas? He fished in his shirt pocket for a cigarette. A folded piece of paper came out with it. He unfolded it. "A woman of about 60 arrives at the office at 4 p.m. She seems confused." And then he remembered. The confused woman in the brown coat who had come to see him the previous day. *It has to do with a missing person. He probably won't live much longer.* She was that strange woman with the baby bottle too. That's why she had seemed familiar. What on earth was she up to? He lit his cigarette and went to the window. Opened it and blew the smoke out.

The phone rang again.

"This is Runi Winther. I just want to apologise for being such a pest."

Skarre cleared his throat. "That's quite all right, Mrs Winther. We know this is difficult for you."

"Have you talked to my friend?"

"Not yet."

"But you promised!"

"I will see her. Tomorrow, Mrs Winther."

"She'll vouch for him. She has to!"

"As far as Andreas' conduct is concerned, we have no reason to believe that it's anything but what it should be."

"But I want you to hear it from someone who knows him."

"All right, Mrs Winther. No, call us by all means, that's why we're here. Fine."

Sejer put his head round the door. "I wonder what those two have been up to. Zipp is lying about the time. They were seen together at 6.15."

"And I wonder," Skarre said grimly, "whether we could be running out of time."

CHAPTER 19

September 6.

Skarre drove along the river, turned left off a roundabout and changed down into second gear at the bottom of a steep hill. He didn't often come to this part of town, but he liked the neighbourhood, the overgrown hedges and the craggy apple trees. Prins Oscars gate.

Prins Oscars gate? He listened in amazement to his own thoughts. A thick hedge on the left-hand side. Number 17. Damn, he had passed it. Had to drive to the top and turn. He parked next to a wrought-iron gate. Took in a white house. He frowned. This white house with the green paint-work? Was this where he was to go? He got out and locked the car. Read the name on the postbox and saw that it was the right one. Irma Funder. He walked down the gravel path. Rang the doorbell and waited. Something was bothering him, some vague unease. He could hear nothing from inside, but he had no means of knowing whether someone might be looking at him through the spyhole in the door. He did his best to assume a trustworthy expression. A chain rattled. The lock clicked. A pale face came into view as the door opened a crack.

"Irma Funder?"

She didn't nod, only stared at him. He could see no more than her nose and eyes.

"What is it?" she said. Her voice was hoarse. He must have come at an inconvenient time.

"I was given your name by Runi Winther. Andreas' mother. You know that he's missing?"

More rattling. Feet shuffling on the mat inside.

"She told me about it."

The door opened a little wider. Skarre looked at the woman in disbelief. He studied the curly grey hair, the thin lips and the strong jaw. A bell started jangling in his head. It was her! The woman who turned up in his office. The woman who – he tried to compose himself – she was the one who left behind the baby bottle in the shop. It was a bizarre coincidence. For a moment he was thrown off balance. An eerie feeling started creeping down his spine and his brain whirled, trying to remember exactly what it was that she had said, when she stood in front of his desk. The very same thing the woman had said on the phone: "He probably won't live much longer." The hairs stood up on the back of his neck, as they had when she had been in his office.

"Could I come in?"

He was so agitated that his voice shook, and two bright red patches appeared on his face. She noticed, of course. She grew frightened and wanted to withdraw. The door closed again until only a narrow opening remained.

"I don't know anything!"

"Mrs Winther would like me to talk to you. She's very worried."

"I know that. I'm sure he'll turn up."

"Do you think so?"

Skarre stuck a shiny regulation shoe in the door and he smiled as warmly as he could.

"It's a routine matter. Your name is on my list," he told her. "And it's my job to come up with a few sentences to add to my report. That way we can cross you off the list and be done with it. And move on, to more important things."

I'm talking too fast, he thought. Dear Jesus, help me so I don't scare this person off before I find out more!

"I know I'm not important," she snapped.

He looked at her. Beneath his curls, his mind was racing.

"This isn't a very good time."

She was about to shut the door on him altogether.

"It will only take a minute."

"But I don't know anything!"

"Now listen . . ." Skarre got a grip on himself. He had to get into this house and find out who the woman was, even though he couldn't see any connection between her and Andreas' disappearance. Except that she knew his mother. She was a woman who lived alone, cut off from the rest of society. Why would she know anything? But one sentence kept echoing through his memory: "I know where he is".

"If you won't speak to me, my boss will come here himself," Skarre said. "You know the type, a chief inspector of the old school."

It was a threat. He could see that she was weighing it. Finally, she opened the door and he stepped into the hall. It was a tidy house. The kitchen was blue, with a striped rug lying at an angle on the floor.

"May I sit down?" He indicated a chair.

"I suppose so, if you can't stand for as long as a minute," she said curtly. Skarre shook his head. What kind of person was this? Was she a bit crazed? Mrs Winther hadn't suggested anything like that. Mrs Winther was perfectly normal herself. Why would this woman be her friend? May the Lord forgive my arrogance, he thought. And he sat down. Didn't take out a notebook or pen, just sat there, looking at her. She was busy with something on her kitchen counter. He looked about him, saw the baby bottle. It was standing next to the coffee maker. What was she using it for?

"Your name: Irma Funder. That's what it says on the postbox," he began.

"That's my name," she said, dismissively.

"It's not usual. Generally the man's name is on the postbox. Or the names of both husband and wife. Or simply a surname."

"My husband is gone," she said.

Skarre thought for a moment. "He's gone? You said he was sick."

She spun around. "When?" she snapped.

"The last time we talked."

"I don't know you!" Her face was contorted with anxiety.

"No," he said. "But we've met before. Quite recently. Have you forgotten already?"

He gave her a searching look. "Tell me what you know about Andreas."

She turned her back and shrugged. "That's quickly done. I don't know anything. He was never at home whenever I used to visit Runi."

"Used to? Don't you visit Mrs Winther still?"

"I'm not feeling very well," she said.

"I understand," he said, but he didn't understand a thing. Only that something was amiss.

"Tell me about your husband," he went on. And then she did turn to face him. Her thin lips were colourless.

"He left me," she said.

"How long ago was that?"

"Eleven years ago."

"And now you think he's dead?"

"I never hear from him any more."

"But you manage on your own?"

"As long as I'm left in peace," she said. "But all this coming and going makes me nervous."

"All what coming and going? What do you mean by that?"

"Nothing. But there are so many strange people out at night. I don't usually open the door. I keep it locked. But since you're in uniform, I took a chance. It's not easy to see what people are made of."

"What is Andreas made of?" he asked.

"Oh, Andreas," she said. "He's a funny one. Almost synthetic."

"What?" Skarre was startled by her reply. "Do you have any children of your own?"

"I had a son. Ingemar."

"Had? Is he dead?"

"I don't know. I haven't heard from him in a long time. For all I know, he could be dead." She turned away again. "Time's up. You said one minute."

"So you haven't seen Andreas?" asked Skarre.

"Many times," she said. "He doesn't interest me."

She's not all there, Skarre decided.

"Do you think he's got mixed up in something?" he asked.

"I think that's highly likely. I know that Runi wouldn't agree; she begged me to put in a good word for him. But I'm sure you want to hear the truth."

"Of course." He looked around the blue kitchen, at the two doors, leading to a bathroom and bedroom perhaps. The voice on the phone. The same voice. He was positive. Why did she come to the station? What was she trying to tell him?

"I would like to know the truth," Skarre said.

"I'm sure he's capable of a little of everything. Him and that friend of his, the one he's always with."

"Do you know him?"

"He calls himself Zipp."

"We've talked to him, but he says he knows nothing."

Irma Funder smiled at him. "That's what they always say. Time's up."

Reluctantly, Skarre stood up. There was something about this house. Something not right. During those few minutes he had taken note of most of the details. A notepad and pen lying on the kitchen table. Three bottles of bleach on the counter. Two black bin bags against the wall. As if she had been cleaning up. As if she were getting ready to leave.

"What did you want when you came to my office?" he said sharply. "What did you want when you called?"

At that instant he felt his stomach lurch. Something about this woman made him nervous.

She rolled her eyes. "Called? It would never occur to me." Suddenly she lost her composure. She looked at him, her heavy body trembled. "I don't have long to live," she said.

There he saw the flame again, in her eyes. The words struck him like a blow. Her face didn't expect an answer; it was a statement. Bewildered, he stood there looking into her eyes. How should he handle this? What could he do? Nothing. Just leave and report to Sejer. The blue walls of the kitchen closed around him, together with this person, and now they seemed to be getting closer, and the room getting smaller, and everything outside became distant and indistinct. The view through the kitchen window, the pretty gazebo and the big birch tree, it was all just a picture. Outside these blue walls there was nothing.

"So the evening started at a bar," Sejer said. "Did you go there to calm your nerves?"

"Don't know what you're talking about," Zipp said.

They had called him in for the second time. Did

that mean they had found something out? Was it about the theft of the handbag? This is wearing me out, he thought, standing so long on the edge of a precipice. I'd rather fall off.

"Be good enough to tell me again when you met."

"As I said, at 7.30."

Sejer tapped his pen on the desk. The tapping sound made Zipp stare at him alertly.

"There's something I don't understand," Sejer said. "I don't understand why you're lying about this."

"I'm not lying."

"You met much earlier than that. Something happened."

"We met at 7.30!"

"No. Andreas left his house at 5.30. You drove around town."

Zipp thought so hard it hurt. Who had seen them, other than that woman at Furulund? Was the moment coming when he would be confronted with the dead baby? For short periods he'd managed to forget about it. Those periods held promise for the future: one day the memory would be erased, as something unreal.

"In that case, somebody's pulling your wick," he said sullenly.

Sejer put down his pen. "You stopped someone and asked for directions."

"Huh?"

"A little boy. Perhaps you thought you'd have some fun with him." Sejer was looking down at his own hands. "Perhaps you just wanted to frighten him."

Zipp was so relieved that he almost felt like laughing.

"Oh, that's right. Of course. A little black kid. We weren't trying to give him a hard time. And we met him on the way to the bar. A bit before 8.00, I should think."

"That little black kid," Sejer said, "is my grandson, so don't give me any crap about not giving him a hard time. He was wearing a watch, and you were driving a green car. Andreas commented on his jacket. It was 6.15."

Sejer's voice had taken on a threatening undertone.

"Your grandson?" Zipp damn near hiccupped with astonishment. At that moment it actually seemed possible, he thought, that the chief inspector might reach out and punch him. And what did he know about police methods? Shit, this was getting serious!

"Is Andreas in love with you?" Sejer said. Zipp felt dizzy. Who had they been talking to? No-one knew that, certainly not that black kid. Was the word out around town?

"Sorry," he croaked, still trying to follow this man's whims. "But I think you misunderstand."

"Sometimes that happens. In which case, I apologise. Is Andreas homosexual?"

Zipp thought he might be able to use this. It might send him off on the wrong track. Keep his thoughts away from other things.

"Yes," he said meekly. "At least, I think so." *You won't tell. Yes, I will, God damn it!*

"Why do you think so? Has he ever made a pass at you?"

"No! He's not stupid."

"We all have our weak moments. Do you think it was difficult?"

"I don't know what you're talking about."

"Maybe you couldn't stand the thought that he was keen on you? Were you furious?"

"Just surprised," he muttered eventually.

"Did you hit him? A little too hard?"

At last Zipp began to see where he was heading.

"No," he murmured. "I wanted to, but I didn't."

"So you're taking your revenge in a different way. You're withholding information. Are you trying to save your own skin?"

No answer.

"My dear Zipp." Sejer lowered his voice to a whisper. "How are you going to get yourself out of this?"

"Out of what?"

"Whatever it is you've got yourself mixed up in. Would it be to your benefit if Andreas never turned up again?"

"No, God damn it!"

"I'm looking for a reason," Sejer said. "A reason why you won't tell the truth. As I said the last time, it had better be awfully good. Is it?"

Zipp wrung his hands. "Yes," he gasped. "It is. And I'm not going to say anything else! I want to go home! You've no right to keep me here."

"Like most departments, we have a little loophole."

Zipp stared at him doubtfully.

"The time between 6 p.m. and when you went to the bar. How did you spend that time?"

"In the car. Cruising around. Looking at girls."

"*You* looked at girls," Sejer corrected him. "What happened?"

"Nothing."

"Then why did you hide the fact?"

"I don't remember."

And that's how things went on. Zipp was amazed at his own stubbornness. That he had so much willpower. That he could almost drive a man crazy, he would never have believed it. But the inspector had willpower too. They tugged and tugged, each at their own end of an invisible rope. Zipp alternated

301

between sighing with exhaustion and inexplicably having the upper hand again. For the first time in his life he was fighting with someone. A sheer battle of wills. And it was strange, all the emotions that came and went. At times he even enjoyed it. Liked the man on the other side of the desk.

*

Now it was simply a matter of time. Soon the police would be at the door. I saw it in the young officer's face, he could smell something was going on in the house. His eyes, which raced around, taking everything in, were full of purpose. It was nice and warm in the cellar. I stood still and looked at Andreas. He really didn't lack for anything. I had taken good care of him. A thought occurred to me like a box on the ear: He would never have done the same for me.

"I'm leaving now," I whispered.

He tried to focus his eyes on something. It required a certain amount of effort. His gaze settled on the light bulb hanging from the ceiling.

"They'll soon be coming to get you, they were just here. The police. I'll leave the door unlocked. Are you listening to me?"

He closed his eyes. Didn't say anything. Wasn't even happy.

"After all that you've done!" I said, resigned. I squatted down on the steps. "Can't you explain who you are? Why you came here? So that I'll understand?"

"You wouldn't understand," he said. "No-one will."

"You're not giving me a chance. There's always an explanation. It makes it easier to bear."

He sniffled a bit. "I'm no worse than anyone else."

I frowned. "I know plenty of people who would never force their way into the house of a woman who lives alone. With a knife and things like that. So don't trivialise matters, Andreas."

"I had to," he said. "I had revealed everything about myself. Had left it all behind at the cemetery. I had to find something . . . something to disguise myself with. Because he saw me as I really am. Zipp. He saw me. And suddenly there you were. I needed you."

"No. You chose me. I want to know why."

"I had to go on, don't you understand! Had to go into your house and come back out again – as something else."

"As a simple criminal?"

"No! I left that behind at the cemetery. I needed something new."

"I don't understand you. You talk such nonsense."

"You didn't call for help," he said in a low voice. "You chose not to. Why?"

"It wasn't my choice! I've tried to understand it."

"No, someone like you can't choose. You just have to sit and wait. And then no-one comes. It makes you crazy, doesn't it, Irma?"

How could he be so shameless when I was finally going to get help for him? God knows, he would get plenty of help. Nursing and tending to him. Fair treatment. He was so young, after all. An insignificant sentence. His personal psychologist. I had to give him one last stab.

"The fact that you do have a choice has destroyed you, Andreas."

"I've never been able to choose."

"I have my own thoughts about that."

"There's a lot that you don't know."

"I'm going to leave you now. Maybe you've learned something. Leave people in peace."

"I've never bothered anybody," he murmured.

I cleared my throat, trying to sound threatening.

"Not until now," he went on. "I don't give a shit if you believe me or not. I know who I am."

"Is that right? Is there anything worth knowing?"

"Yes," he muttered. "It took me a little time. But now I know."

I kept quiet, sighing. No-one is as wise as the young when they've just begun to understand.

"Where are you going?" he said.

"Out. But I have to get dressed first."

"But where are you going?"

"Away," I said vaguely.

"You don't have to do that," he sighed. "I'll take all the blame."

It took a moment for his words to sink in and I understood his meaning. That was too much for me. I stood up, shaking. "TAKE ALL THE BLAME? ANDREAS – THERE'S SOMETHING IMPORTANT HERE THAT YOU'VE MISSED! YOU *ARE* TO BLAME! DO YOU UNDERSTAND?"

He blinked in horror at my outburst. There's more strength in old women than young boys know. They ought to watch out. I was still shaking, spreading my legs apart so as not to topple over from sheer outrage. Andreas started to cry. Tears and snot ran down his face. The room smelled of him, a cloying smell from the infected wound on his head. From his unwashed body. It smelled of mould and potatoes and burning dust from the heater, which glowed red. Oh, how he cried. It was necessary for me, right now before I left, to hear this. To take it with me. Then his sobs stopped.

"You're never going to call. You won't keep your word. You're a coward and crazy and a liar."

I bit my lip so hard that tears came to my eyes.

"You asked why I chose you? It was because you're so ugly, Irma."

I started to shake.

"Ugly and fat. With your intestines hanging out. No-one could love somebody like you."

"You be quiet!" I shouted.

"I can see the veins through your stockings. They're the size of fucking grapes."

I was still standing there, wanting to crush him with my bare fists. He looked evil when he said that. I lost control, stood there flailing my arms around and looking ridiculous, I could feel it, but I couldn't stop the rage from coming. I had to destroy something, let loose, all of a sudden I had too much strength. A violent surplus that threatened to rip me to shreds. It turned into pain, it burned like fire, and I looked for something in the dark cellar, something I could use to crush and destroy, but I didn't see anything. Just old plastic furniture. The bin of potatoes. An old windowpane leaning against the wall. And a box of tools. It stood under the workbench. Open. I pulled out a hammer with a rubber handle. Went back and stood in front of him. And then it happened, as I stood there, wielding my power, demonstrating that I had the upper hand, that he'd better watch out. He laughed! And I snapped. I can bear most things: not being seen, not being heard, people bickering and banging things around. But not that. Not someone laughing. I lashed out. Hit hard. Struck somewhere on his white forehead, and his laughter was cut off, it stopped with a faint groan, and I struck again. The hammer hit the floor several times, white sparks flew up every time the steel hit the concrete, but I kept on hitting, sensed that what was under the hammer slowly lost its shape and grew soft. I caught a reflection of my own face in the old windowpane. He was right. I was ugly. So I kept on hitting until I had no strength left. It felt good. I was empty. My body gradually grew calm. I looked around with stinging eyes. Heard a tiny sigh. Whether it came from Andreas, a last sound from his lungs, or whether someone saw us, I don't know. Just let them try! For a long time I stood there with the hammer raised, staring into the shadows.

CHAPTER 20

Zipp could see the outline of his face in the black of the television screen. Something cowardly and wavering. He stomped up the stairs and slammed the door behind him. The goal had finally become clear to him. The white house with the green paintwork. Hadn't he withstood terrible pressure? Look what inner strength he had! This time he wasn't going to settle for just talk; he wanted inside, God damn it!

He made his way up the hill, taking long, determined strides. From behind, his round arse could be seen energetically swinging and twisting as he walked. Even if he had to force his way in and manhandle the old woman, he was going to find out the truth! He was rarely so resolute in his life, but he liked the feeling of such certainty. He could do anything! Fifteen minutes later he came to the gate.

He heard a door slam. Rapid footsteps crunched across the gravel. There she was. The Funder woman! He watched her shuffle off and then he slipped into the garden. He crept up the steps and tried the door, but of course it was locked. Slunk round to the back, making sure that no-one could see into the garden. With a crowbar he should be able to pry open one of the cellar windows and get in. But he didn't have a crowbar. In the rose bed lay a rock the size of a cabbage. He rolled it over and brushed off some sort of crawling insect. Then he knelt down and tried to see in through the windows. One of them was covered with a sack or something. He could look through the other one if he cupped his hands on either side of his face. He picked up the rock and flung it at the glass. It made only a small opening and it took him a while to break off the rest of the shards from the window frame. Then he stuck both feet inside, turned himself around and let go. It was a long drop. His knees almost buckled. He brushed off his jeans and his hands then slowly turned round and saw a door in front of him. He paused for a moment, waiting for his eyes to get used to the dark. Shelves with bottles and jars. An old sledge, a rotting parasol. And a door. He opened it, his heart pounding. It was heavy, maybe spring loaded. Inside there was another room. A strange glowing red light broke through the darkness. It was hot inside, and it smelled bad. He stumbled a few paces across the room, his heart trembling like a chicken under his jacket. He put his hands on the wall and felt his way forward, one hesitant step at a time. He needed to find the light switch. Then he stepped on something soft. It gave way under his foot and made an odd crackling noise. He stopped at once. There was something lying on the floor. What the hell was it? He stepped back and stopped to listen. Cautiously he moved a few paces in a different direction. Something crashed with the sound of metal striking the floor. He had knocked over a heater. And then he found a step. A stairway leading up from the cellar into the house. That must mean that a light switch would be at the top. He crept up the stairs, his ears pricked. What was the soft thing he had stepped on? What if the woman came back? Why would she? Maybe she had forgotten something. That was always happening, at least in films. He kept on up the stairs, counting the steps. His head hit the ceiling. An old-fashioned trap door. He searched for the switch, running his fingers along the walls, getting a few splinters in his skin. There it was at last: a switch. He twisted it on, heard a reluctant click, and the light went on, a bare bulb hanging from a cord. It lit up slowly, as if the cord were worn out and needed to take its time. He turned round and stared down into the circle of light. Caught sight of a plastic tarpaulin. It was covering something at the foot of the stairs. Good

God! For a dizzying second he thought it looked like a body underneath. It did look as if it was a body. But that wasn't possible. No. It was probably just an old blanket that hadn't made it to the rubbish heap yet. She must have just thrown it down here. He would go back down and find out what it was. Because it couldn't possibly be . . . He crept down the stairs. What the hell am I doing here, what the hell is going on? I'm really asleep on the sofa at home. He sniffed, wiped his nose on the back of his hand. He was at the bottom of the steps. Looked around, running his eyes over the filthy plastic. Something white and moist. He bent down, but he was blocking the light and had to move to one side. Picked up a corner of the plastic, which rustled.

"No! Dear God, no!"

His shout slammed against the walls, reverberating around the room. He lurched back, throwing out his arms to find some kind of support. It searched the dark corners, saw a workbench, an old bicycle, a bin for potatoes. Potatoes, he thought. Everything was so strange. Get the fuck out of here! Then a door slammed. Someone walked across the floor overhead, swift footsteps. He glanced at the light, caught sight of the door he had come through. Then he didn't think any more, just dashed out, closed the door carefully behind him, and squeezed into a corner. Waiting. She had come back. She was insane! He imagined her coming down the stairs with an axe. A chair scraped overhead. Zipp stared at the door. If she opened the trap door, she would see the light. He had to escape without making any noise, get out the same way he had come, through the window. But he couldn't reach it. What about the sledge against the wall? He could stand on that. Claw his way out and run. Call the police. The woman was off her head, she had to be locked up. Suddenly he heard new sounds. Creaking wood, jangling chains. Footsteps on the stairs. She would see the light was on. Zipp thought: I'll strike first. He looked around for something to use as a weapon. A bottle would do. They were lined up on the shelves, containing juice and wine. He crept over to them, shifting his weight with care from his heel to the ball of his foot. Took a bottle from the shelf and got a good grip around the neck. He stationed himself at the door and stood there with the bottle in his shaking hand. He was trembling so hard that his teeth started to chatter. Come on, God damn it, I'm going to knock your fucking head off! He heard the footsteps. And then all was quiet again. What was she doing now? Wondering about the light? Horrible shuffling footsteps moved across the cement. He pressed his body against the cold wall and stared at the narrow opening in the doorway. Slowly, it opened wider. He took a deep breath and raised the bottle just as her head appeared in the doorway.

In a flash he saw her heavy jaw and the deep-set eyes. Then he slammed the bottle down onto the side of her head. Her knees gave way and her back struck the heavy door. She fell forward, right against his chest. Zipp screamed like a wild animal and leaped back. She fell to the floor, landing on her stomach. Her forehead rested on his sneaker, and he had to yank it away. Her head hit the floor with a little thud. He was amazed that the bottle hadn't broken. He stared at her for one wild moment, then dropped the bottle, which did then break, and he recognised the smell of sour wine spreading through the cellar room. Her heavy body filled the doorway. He tried to step over her, but his foot touched her back and he nearly toppled over. He staggered, then regained his balance. Ran out, past the tarpaulin. Reached the stairs, heard his own rasping breath and knew by the way he was breathing that a terrible thing had happened. The body under the plastic had been smashed to pulp. Inside him a voice shrieked: Your fault! Your fault! The trap door stood open and a light was on in the kitchen. He scrambled up the steps and stood looking around the blue room. He went back to the opening and looked down. The cadaver under the plastic seemed to gape up at him. He grabbed the trap door and let it fall. It's over, he thought. Like a gunshot, the trap door slammed shut. It's over. Destroyed, smashed to pulp, unrecognisable. But that yellow shirt! Then he stormed out.

Sejer could only think of a dead tree. The woman was still upright, but all her strength had gone. It didn't matter to her whether or not he caught a couple of miserable purse snatchers. Her baby was dead. For more than three decades she had lived without the child. How attached could she be to a child she had known for only four months. Until death do us part, he thought. He also thought about the phenomenon of time and how it had a capacity to make things pass, to make things fade, if nothing else. He let her stand there in silence. In the meantime he remembered what the doctor had said. That an autopsy would be performed on the boy. That, in all probability, his fall from the pram had nothing to do with his death. It was just a tragic, frightening coincidence. It wouldn't do any good to tell that to the mother now. She had made up her mind. Two young men had killed the most precious thing she possessed. Not that she was thinking about them. She wasn't thinking about anything; she was just letting time run listlessly along. Now and again she would blink; her eyelids would droop and then, with what looked like great difficulty, they would open wide.

"Won't you sit down?"

She dropped on to a chair. Her beige coat no longer looked like a piece of clothing, but rather a big stretch of canvas that someone had draped across her shoulders.

"Tell me everything you can remember about what they looked like," he said.

"I can't remember anything," she replied. Her voice was flat. She may have taken some kind of medication. A kind-hearted doctor hadn't been able to stand seeing her pain.

"Yes, you can," he told her. "It's possible to recall bits and pieces if you concentrate."

Concentrate? The word made her raise her head and look at him in disbelief. She barely had the strength to keep herself sitting upright on the chair.

"Why should I help you?" she said, her voice faint.

"Because we're talking about two men who need to understand the gravity of what they did. We won't be able to prove that they're responsible for your son's death, but it will give them an almighty shock. And perhaps prevent them from doing any such thing again."

"I don't care about that." Once more she raised her head to look at him. "And you don't even believe what you're saying. If they kill a baby every week from now on – I still don't care."

He searched for something to say that might rouse her. "Maybe you don't care right now," he said, "but what about a year from now? Then you'll start to worry because you didn't do anything. You'll worry at the thought that they're still going around as if nothing had happened."

She gave a tired laugh. Sejer got up and walked to the window, as he often did. Rain was streaming down the pane. So unaffected, so untouched. And that prompted the thought that something would still be untouched after everything else had vanished. And would keep running, floating on the wind, pounding against the rocks, salty and hard.

"But you're here," he said, turning round. "So I have to think that you might be able to help. Or else why did you come? I had given up hope, and we have lost a lot of time."

His words made her look at him, she was more alert now.

"Well, no," she stammered. "I was hoping for an explanation. There's always an explanation, isn't there?"

An explanation? As if he had one. Instead he shook his head. "You can help me," he said softly. "Even though I can't help you. And in that sense, it was a little awkward to ask you to come here. But if we cannot – with your help – resolve the matter, you may end up feeling regret, and by then it will also be harder to remember things."

"One of them wore a cap." The words slipped out, quietly, reluctantly.

"A cap?" he said. "Let me guess. It was probably red."

He saw a glimpse of a smile as she said, "No, it was blue. With white letters. And a little white cross. Do you hear me? A white cross!"

He could feel that something had broken the ice. For the first time she relaxed.

"They were driving a small green car. One was tall and thin, with long legs. Wearing a yellow shirt. I couldn't see his hair because it was hidden under the cap. He was very good-looking. He had light eyes, blue or green. He was wearing trousers with wide legs. I remember noticing that when he ran to the car, his trousers were flapping around his legs. And he had black shoes."

Sejer sat there agog. She had given the description with great confidence. That was how he looked.

"And the other one?" he asked. At the same time a clock began ticking in his mind.

"The other was shorter and more compact. Blond hair, tight jeans, running shoes. He tried to stop the pram," she added. "But he didn't reach it in time."

Something sounded so familiar. What was it about everything she had said? Something was niggling him. Something was ticking in the background, saying: here, here it is, for heaven's sake, can't you see it!

"Their age?" he whispered, as he struggled to decipher the peculiar signals buzzing in his mind. He thought: If I take too deep a breath, it will escape. So he sat there for a long time, hardly breathing.

"Maybe 18, maybe 20."

He wrote down key words. And began to have the satisfaction when the dots and lines, which had been whirling unpleasantly before his eyes for so long, started to form a pattern. Clear, distinct, almost beautiful. A warm feeling inside. This was what he loved.

"Can't you tell me anything more about the car?"

He strained to keep a calm tone to his voice, but it wasn't easy.

"I don't know much about cars," she murmured. "They all look alike to me."

"But it was a small car?"

"Yes. A small, oldish car."

He scribbled more notes. "This neighbourhood isn't very big. We'll find them," he added, "I'm positive we will."

"I'm sure that will make you happy," she said, smiling.

For a few seconds she hadn't been thinking about the dead child, and the first pang of guilt appeared, at the discovery that her child could be forgotten even for a few moments. What a betrayal!

"They're performing the autopsy now," she said bitterly. "And when they've finished, I won't have anything to say about it. What if they're wrong?"

"You mean as far as the cause of death is concerned? They're specialists," he said. "You can depend on them."

"People make mistakes all the time," she said. "I shouldn't have let go of the pram."

"You were being assaulted," he said forcefully.

"No," she said. "They stole my handbag, that's all. An old handbag, a thing of no importance. Four hundred kroner. And then I let go of the pram. Even though we were near the shore. I don't understand it."

"Why didn't you report it straightaway?"

He didn't like asking the question; it seemed to ask itself.

"It was such an insignificant business. I was worried about the boy, that's all. Because he kept crying. Besides," she said, looking up at him, "what would you have been able to do? File a report? Until such time as you could have dropped the case for lack of evidence?"

"Perhaps," he admitted. "But society is going to fall apart if we stop reporting crime. You shouldn't worry about how much work we have, you should always speak up if something happens. And the more reports we receive, the greater likelihood of increased resources. In fact, you have a responsibility to report an incident like that one."

She uttered a sound that might have been a laugh, he couldn't tell.

"I'm not laughing at you," she said. "I'm laughing at everything else. We can't do anything about the fact that we're here in this world. But why do we stay?"

She stood up. She didn't have a handbag. Her arms moved nervously, as if they were searching for the handle of a pram. At the door, she turned.

"Do you know what the worst thing is?"

He shook his head.

"He doesn't have a name."

She started down the corridor but turned round one last time. "I was never able to make up my mind. This is my punishment."

The lift doors closed behind her. He went into his office and slammed the door. Finally! Two men, one blond, one dark, in a green car. Zipp and Andreas.

*

Two officers left to pick up Sivert Skorpe. His mother stood in the doorway, regarding them with growing concern. "He always comes home at night," she insisted. They drove around town looking for him. Sejer wanted to be notified the second he was found. Then he went home, stopping at the Shell garage to put petrol in the car. Bought a CD at the till: Sarah Brightman. The traffic was at its peak, a steady roar that he hardly heard. As he drove, he went over his day's work. It had consisted of decisions he had made on the handling of various incidents, some major, some minor. Yet for others, the worst of all things had happened. They got at him, but at the same time he could deal with them, file them away. Was he made differently from other people? Plenty of people could not have handled the job he did. All he had to put up with, on the path to becoming chief inspector. Drunkenness and brawls, vomit all over his uniform. People with no willpower or strength or opportunities. And worse still, occasionally people with no scruples, no remorse and no fear. Even if he was confident that he had held on to most of his humanity, he was also capable of closing it off. To sit down and eat. Put it behind him, as Robert had said. Maybe sleep for half an hour on the sofa. He could usually sleep soundly through the night, though sometimes the itching on his elbows or his knees disturbed him. But his eczema had got better. When Sejer had reached home and Kollberg had finished greeting him, he caught sight of Sara. She wore only an undershirt and panties, and her hair was dishevelled, her cheeks red.

"What's up?" he asked.

"Yoga," she said, smiling. "I was doing some yoga exercises."

"Without any clothes on?"

She laughed as she pointed out how hard it was to do a headstand with a skirt falling over your head. He could surely see that. "You should learn some of the postures. I could help you."

"I don't have any ambition to stand on my head," he said.

"Are you afraid of acquiring a new perspective?"

He shrugged. Wasn't it too late for that? He was too old.

"Did anything exciting happen?" she asked, as she pulled on a skirt and blouse. He didn't want to stare at her while she got dressed so he went into the kitchen and turned on the oven. She came padding after him, barefoot.

"No," he said quietly. "Not what you'd call exciting."

Something about his voice made her uneasy.

"Robert," he said. "He's no longer alive."

"Anita's boyfriend?"

"They found him in his cell."

"How did he do it?" she asked. Professional interest. She had experienced similar things in her own work.

"He tore a shirt into strips and hanged himself. From the door handle of the wardrobe."

He went into the living room. Pulled the CD out of his jacket pocket and put it in the player. Found the track he liked best: "Who Wants To Live Forever?" He now had 537 CDs, all with female vocalists. He sat down heavily, thinking about what kind of determination it took to hang yourself from a kneeling position. All that willpower he could have used for a new life. Kollberg trotted over and lay at his feet. Sejer leaned down and took the dog's enormous head in his hands. He stared into the black eyes, touched his snout. It was as it was supposed to be, cool and moist. He lifted the silky soft ears and peered inside. His ears looked fine and didn't smell. He drew his fingers through the thick fur, which was longer and shinier than ever, reddish-yellow, with a few lighter patches; only his face was black, with hints of silver in places. His claws were long without being troublesome. In short, Kollberg was perfect. The only thing he lacked was the proper training.

"You may be huge," Sejer told him, "but you're

not especially smart." The dog wagged his tail expectantly, but seeing there were no dog biscuits, he let his head fall onto Sejer's feet with its full weight. Sara appeared in the doorway. She had a packet of spaghetti in her hand.

"So what do you do? In those situations?"

He sighed. "The usual things. The incident is investigated as what is called a suspicious death. Forensics take pictures of the cell. The prison staff are interviewed. Was the cell locked? Did anyone visit him? Was he depressed? And if so, had he seen a doctor? Forensics handle the case after that."

"Do you feel responsible?" she asked softly.

He shrugged. Did he?

"He was very cooperative," he said. "Almost too much so. He was eager to get through everything. He had plans. He had even managed to eat something, for the first time in days. I don't work at the prison. But I should have known."

"You're not a mind reader," she said.

He looked at her. "But you would have known, wouldn't you?"

She leaned against the doorframe. "I've lost a number of patients."

"Yes?"

"But it's true that I would have been on the alert. They often seem to liven up at the same time as they become suicidal. Because they've finally made a decision and can see an end to their despair. When patients come to us and want their medication decreased or ask to be allowed out, we're usually on the alert. But Robert was not a psychiatric patient. He was in prison."

"I've learned something, anyway."

"You're not a doctor," she said gently. "Have you told Anita's parents?"

"I talked to her father. He was very upset. Said he hoped it wasn't because of them. They didn't feel any resentment towards him. I don't think they had enough strength left for that."

Sara disappeared into the kitchen and he could hear the water starting to boil in a pan. Ten minutes later she called him. He washed his hands and sat at the table. It was lovely to sit quietly with Sara. She was capable of leading her own life, even though he was barely a metre away, capable of thinking her own thoughts without including him. Her face took on many amusing expressions as she followed her train of thoughts. He cast a swift glance at her every time he reached for the salt or pepper. He sprinkled a generous portion of Parmesan over his spaghetti.

"Sara. Your job is to make people talk. About themselves. About difficult subjects. How do you get them to talk?"

She smiled in surprise. "But you've conducted

hundreds of interviews and interrogations. Don't tell me that you don't know how to do your job."

"No, but sometimes I get stuck when I'm talking to someone. And I sit there and know that he knows! And I simply don't have the power to get anything out of him."

"That happens to me too."

"But still. What method do you use to get inside them?"

"Time."

"Ah. But I don't have time! An 18-year-old has disappeared without trace and his one close friend is so frightened that he practically faints on my desk. But then he purses his lips the way Ingrid used to when we tried to get her to take cod-liver oil."

"There's a gate to every garden," she said cryptically.

He had to smile in spite of himself.

"And if an exception shows up, then you have to jump over the fence."

"I'm a police officer. There are rules that I have to follow."

"Imagination is a good thing."

"Don't I have any imagination?"

"Of course you do. But you don't use it. How many times have you asked him to come in?"

"Twice."

"And where do you meet?"

"In my office. We need a backdrop of authority. So the suspects understand that it's serious."

She picked up the ketchup bottle and shook it vigorously over her spaghetti.

"Invite him out for a beer. Go to the bar where he went with Andreas. Find the same table. Wear some other clothes. Jeans and a leather jacket. Couldn't you let your hair grow a little longer, Konrad? I have a feeling that it would curl around your ears if you only gave it a chance."

He opened his eyes wide. "What is it with girls and curly hair? Just leave the dishes. I'll do them."

"I'm going over to see Pappa," she said. "I need to make sure he has food in the fridge."

There was that word again, that always made him feel embarrassed. Pappa. A familiar tiny pang.

"How is he taking it? That he's alone so much?"

"Do you have a guilty conscience?"

"Maybe he needs you more than I do."

"Don't you need me?" she said.

He looked at her in confusion. "Of course I do. I just meant because he's ill. I can take care of myself."

"Can you?"

He couldn't see what she was getting at. He looked at her face and then at the mound of spaghetti, searching for a clue. Of course he needed her. But he couldn't avoid thinking about her father, who had MS, sitting alone in his wheelchair. And the fact that he had taken Sara from him. Well, she wasn't always at his place, but increasingly often.

"I need you terribly," he said.

"More than my father," she said. "You need me more than my father does. Say it out loud!"

But he didn't say a word. He was trying to imagine what his life would be like if she were suddenly to disappear. Deep inside he was preparing for that. Would he survive it? Was he really expecting her to leave soon? Was he reluctant to give himself to her wholeheartedly? How much did *she* need *him*? She was so independent. Seemed as if she could handle anything. But could he be mistaken? He wasn't the one she needed, not really. He didn't want to play. Sooner or later she would find someone else, a younger man. Someone like Jacob, it crossed his mind. God help me, what am I thinking? I'm actually jealous. Of everyone who's younger and freer than I am.

"You have to forgive me," he said. "I'm a little slow."

He sat there, feeling puzzled, and looking at her. And in her eyes he saw something that took his breath away. An overwhelming tenderness. He had to bow his head. It was too much for him. They finished their meal in silence. But now he was inside her head, he could feel it. When they had finished, he washed the dishes. The phone rang. It was Jacob's eager voice, mixed with some kind of atonal ruckus. Sejer had to shout into the receiver.

"I can't hear you! Could you turn down that noise? Are you calling from home?"

"*Jazz from Hell!*" Jacob shouted back. "Frank Zappa. Is that what you call noise?"

Sejer could hear the receiver being put down on a hard surface. The noise vanished.

"I've been out to visit Mrs Winther's friend," Jacob said, breathing hard. "Konrad, there's something about that old lady! Excuse the expression, but I wonder if she's off her trolley, plain and simple, nuts."

"I see," Sejer said, waiting for Jacob to continue.

"You have to go and talk to her!"

"What?"

"She knows something. I could tell that something odd has been going on. I can't explain it. But as your mother used to say: I just know!"

"It's late," Sejer began. "I've got other things . . . Robert's parents . . ."

"I know. But she went to the station, and she called. She says cryptic things: that she knows where he is, that he won't live long and God knows what else. You've got to check her out!"

"She says that she knows where he is?"

"Without mentioning his name. But she knows. You have to talk to her. I don't have any real theory, but I just think the set-up is weird. What's more, she knows him, he's her friend's son."

"But you were there yourself, weren't you? Did you find anything, or didn't you?"

"I found out that you have to talk to her. You have to experience it for yourself."

Sejer quite simply couldn't ignore Skarre's kind of eagerness, his strong intuition. His dog gazed after him, and he thought for a second or two before he made up his mind and called to him. Kollberg raced through the room like a woolly bolt of lightning. Sejer caressed Sara on the cheek as he said goodbye and then walked down all 13 floors. Kollberg stopped on every step. Sejer paused to look at the dog's bulky body, and it dawned on him that old age was about to catch up with his dog. That he might have spared him all those steps. You're getting old too, he muttered. They stepped into the light. He stopped again. "You're old," he said out loud as the dog fixed his dark eyes on him. "Do you realise that?" Kollberg waited patiently as if expecting a treat. A piece of dried fish, for example.

"No," muttered Sejer. "Never mind."

CHAPTER 21

I had a horrible dream. I dreamed that I woke up in the cellar. On the floor, stretched full length, ice-cold and bruised. My head hurt, as if a dull hammer was pounding and pounding. I managed to get up and stagger out of the room. I headed for the stairs and caught sight of something lying on the floor under a tarpaulin. Someone had dumped their rubbish in my cellar! What a nerve! I had to step over it. That's when I looked through the plastic and saw two dead eyes and a gaping mouth with no teeth. I wanted to scream, but no sound came out of my mouth. When I woke up in my bed, my head was still pounding terribly. I woke up because the doorbell was ringing. I thought: It's Runi. I'm not opening it! But I went to the door anyway, my legs wobbling under me. My head felt so heavy that I had to hold it with my hand. Through the peephole in the door I looked straight at a man. He was very tall, with greying hair. He didn't look like a salesman or anything. I stood there for a moment, listening to the doorbell, that rang and rang. All this coming and going was getting on my nerves. No-one ever came to my house, so what was this all about?

The bell rang again, a long, determined peal. A voice in my head ordered me to open the door. Maybe he had peeked in the window and seen that I was home, as everyone kept on doing – I had again found a garden chair pulled over to the wall – and if I didn't open the door they would blast it open, and I couldn't let them do that. Everybody was after me, do you understand? And that hideous dream was still hanging on. If I opened the door it might go away. At the sound of a real voice. I opened the door a crack. Probably I had a fever. I could feel my cheeks burning.

"Irma Funder?"

The voice was very deep. Wrapped in that full, low voice, my name sounded beautiful. His eyes were dark and clear and unblinking. They held me fast. I didn't move, could only look at him. In the very back of my aching head something was buzzing, something important. Telling me that I had to get away! That I should fall down, surrender. It buzzed and buzzed. I strained to understand what I wanted. I wanted everything. To flee in panic, to collapse. To sleep for ever.

"Is everything all right?"

I didn't reply, just stared at him. Scrambled to

get out of my dream. I wanted to get out to that man. I nodded, without opening the door any wider, just kept on nodding. I've always been a yes man, I thought. And the thought made me angry. Not at this grey man, but at Irma.

"I'm from the police," he said as he continued to look at me with that serious expression. I thought he might be able to help. That he would understand. I put my hand to my head. And then he smiled. That made him look different, it lit up his furrowed face. A handsome man, it occurred to me, and so tall that he almost had to bend down to go into the kitchen. It's an old house. Nowadays they're probably built differently, but Henry wasn't a tall man, and I'm quite short myself. I creep around; I've told you that already. And now I crept after the man into the kitchen. I liked that, padding after that tall man. He looked around. Pointed to a chair. I gestured my permission.

"What's been going on?" he asked calmly. It looked as if he knew a great deal. But how could he? For a moment I considered telling him about my dream, but I changed my mind. It would just embarrass him. So I didn't answer. I was still standing there, holding my head with one hand. The other I put on my stomach. I was afraid the bag would get detached and fall to the floor under my dress. That was something this handsome man had to be spared at all costs.

"What happened to your head?"

For a moment I looked at him, confused, while I thought: How can he know about that? I held my hand in front of my eyes and saw that it was bloody. My fingers felt sticky. And then I realised that I was still dreaming, that the man at the table wasn't real, just a dream. I had to play along; every dream comes to an end. So I told him what happened, that a thief had broken in and hit me with something, down in the cellar. He left, and I went to bed and lay down. No, I hadn't had the strength to see if anything was missing from the house. And I didn't see his face. It was dark down there. The man listened patiently. Asked me whether I wanted to file a report.

Report? It hadn't even occurred to me. They wouldn't do anything about it, anyway. Then he stood up and walked around. Went to the window and looked out.

"You have a nice place," he said politely. "With a nice garden. And a lovely gazebo. I took the liberty of having a look around the back of your house."

There was a rumbling inside my chest, as if someone had lit a stove. The nightmare would soon be over, because I thought he was already starting to look a little hazy as he stood there with his back to me. But then he turned around, and some of his friendliness was gone. A commanding tone was clear in his voice.

"You should report this," he said. "Your cellar window is broken. The thief got in through the window. I'm going down to the cellar to take a look around. He may have left some tracks."

I leaned heavily on the table. At the same time I realised that the dream was over, because it always ends right before the big disaster. I tried to remember what the big disaster was, and happened to think of the body down in the cellar. That rubbish down there, or whatever it was. Of course he would see it and then come back up and say, "There's a dead man in your cellar, Irma. Do you know who he is?"

I strained to think clearly. Did I know? Andreas Winther. Runi's son. Apparently there were many nightmares. And a reality too, which I was trying to remember, but it was far away. Would he believe me if I told him what happened? What really happened? No, he wouldn't. He'd see me as someone who's very disturbed, which I wasn't. I'm not. I'm just so worn out.

"No," I said, surprised at how firm I sounded. "Don't bother. I'm not going to do anything about it. My son can fix the window. Ingemar. He'll come over if I call him."

"But you were assaulted," he said. "That's a serious matter to us. I urge you to file a report."

"I'm the one who decides," I said swiftly. "This is my house."

Then he looked at me, and his face filled with curiosity. There we stood, an old woman like me and this handsome man, right there in my own kitchen. Runi should have seen it!

"Where are the stairs to the cellar?" he asked. I didn't answer. He was standing on top of them in fact; he had both feet on top of the trap door. Those nice shoes of his. He peered out to the hall, maybe he thought the stairs were there.

"My head hurts," I said. "I need to lie down for a while. I'm not feeling very well."

"I'll take you to a doctor," he said. "You should have that cut looked at."

My eyes widened at the thought. "There's nothing wrong with me. I'm as strong as a horse. That's what my doctor says."

"No doubt," he said, "but you've suffered a blow to the head."

"I'll take a sleeping pill and lie down. I'm not some kind of weakling, either. I can put up with a lot." I said this with pride.

"I'm sure you can," he said. "And I can't force you, of course."

Silence. His eyes roved around the room, looking at the window and the trees outside, which were beginning to turn yellow. It wouldn't be long now.

"I'm looking for Andreas," he said softly. For a moment I pulled myself together and nodded.

"Andreas Winther. Runi's son. You know him. What do you think happened?"

I searched for a good answer. That thing under the plastic – that must be what he meant. They all talked about that young man with such reverent voices, as if society had mislaid something irreplaceable, and I had a strong desire to snort with contempt, but I restrained myself.

"Boys are always getting into trouble," I said. "And I don't suppose he was any different."

"He most certainly wasn't. Do you know his friend?"

"Do you mean Zipp?"

I searched a bit, through the pounding in my head. "Runi mentioned him. But I don't know him."

"I suspect, as you say, that they'd got into one thing or another." He looked me in the eye with eerie directness. "I'm sure I'll work it all out."

Yes. But by then I'll be long gone, where he won't find me. I was already on my way, I could feel the floor rocking beneath my feet, and then he stood up, and his face was very close. "I'll just take a quick look in the cellar."

I only came up to his chest. And I felt ridiculous, but I wanted that man out of my house at all costs, and they can't, for God's sake, use threats to get into somebody's house like that, so I said no, no, let's just drop the whole thing! I don't want to deal with this. And I assume that it's my decision. I haven't called anyone or filed a report, and if I needed help, I would have asked for it!

He just smiled and looked at me. "I think you might need help. Not everyone asks for it."

He bowed a little bow and went to the door. There he turned one last time, but he wasn't smiling any more, he looked serious and very determined when he said: "I'll send someone over. Goodbye, Mrs Funder."

But it was too late for that. I'm going now. You mustn't judge me, you weren't there! All my life I've measured people by what they ought to be, not by what they actually are. And now it's too late. I came into this world and I made nothing but mistakes. I'll soon be 60. I don't have the strength to start over again, it's too hard. When you know everything, what is there to live for? Something strange has seized hold of me right now, as I stand here, about to leave this house. Something that has kept me hidden for all these years. I shove the rug aside with my foot and open the trap door. Shout down the stairs: "I'm leaving now, Andreas. I'll leave the door unlocked!"

I walk through town wearing my brown coat. I feel a sort of peace as I walk. Not the way I usually feel, afraid that I forgot something important, a window left open, a candle burning. The wind starts blowing, a light drizzle billows towards my face. There's something dreary about everything. The crowns of the trees look weighted down. The rubbish in the streets, white paper smeared with ketchup. Stray dogs. I don't like dogs, especially scrawny ones. They look so cowardly and are always begging. Be brave, Irma! I don't feel despairing. I've been to the theatre and I feel the same emptiness you feel when it's a bad play. It was wasted time. Now you know everything. But I don't care whether you read this or not. But think about what I've said when you leaf through the newspapers: You shouldn't believe everything you read. You shouldn't trust anyone.

I think about Mother and Father. They're still standing in front of the yellow house. They're not waving now either. No, that would have been a confession. And then, finally, I think about Zipp. About whether he might wake up and make something of his life. Find something decent to do. I look at the pale September sun as it shines low through the treetops, the dry leaves that are slowly changing to pure gold. Well, not right now, because it's starting to rain, but maybe tomorrow. But no-one taught him, and no-one taught me. The house stands there, shining behind me. Henry said it was built on clay soil, and it was just a matter of time, and enough rain, before it would pull loose and slide down.

CHAPTER 22

The collision with his dog sent him reeling against the wall with a bang. He rubbed the tender spot on the back of his head. Listened for any sound in his flat. Was she still dressed? Was she smoking hash?

It was comforting to hear that she was talking to someone on the phone. To a female friend, no doubt. She was giggling like a girl. He tried to restrain the dancing dog and hung up his jacket. Went to the kitchen and washed his hands. Opened the refrigerator and looked inside. Kollberg came into the room and stood to attention. I'm standing perfectly still, said his dark canine eyes, I'm not whining or begging, I'm just slobbering like crazy. Sejer took out some food and set it on the counter. Two cold sausages covered with plastic. Hard-boiled eggs. A roll filled with something, maybe stewed fruit. He whispered "sit" to the dog and waved a sausage. I need to contact the district nurse, he thought. Irma Funder needs attention. Possibly she should even be hospitalised.

"No, are you mad?" he heard from the living

room. "Tell me more. All the details." And then she giggled again. He took the paw the dog offered him and handed over the sausage. Sliced some bread and cut up the eggs. Sprinkled them with salt.

"That's exactly what I don't like. I like to play," he heard.

He pricked up his ears. Who was she talking to?

"With the light on. Of course. Do you think I'm ashamed? No, I'm not 20 years old, I'm old enough to be your mother."

Sejer stood there with a jar of mayonnaise in his hand, as if frozen, and now he was listening in earnest. She must not have heard him come in. But of course she had, Kollberg always made such a racket that you could hear it several floors below. "But greed is exciting, I agree with you about that. But not always. Oh yes. Absolutely."

Sejer picked up the other sausage. His confusion prompted a trace of sadism. He started swinging the sausage out of Kollberg's reach. The dog tried to work out what the game was. Tried to stand up on his hind legs, but his body was too heavy. Seventy kilos and a low centre of gravity. So he fell back down, scraping his claws down his master's trouser legs. Sejer gave him the sausage. He spread mayonnaise over the eggs.

"Sometimes I need to be little. A little girl. It's the best thing I know."

He poured milk into a glass. A little girl? Wasn't she going to be finished soon? Was there a faint smell of hash? He suddenly felt so tired. But then it changed to something else. He thought: I need to go into the living room. I want to watch the news.

She was sitting at the table with the phone clamped under her chin. She heard him, and turned to give him a sly wink. He was caught completely off guard. His sandwich slid across the plate and threatened to go over the edge. Kollberg lay down next to him, his nostrils quivering. Sejer concentrated on his egg sandwich.

"I have to go to bed," said Sara suddenly. "I'll call back when I need you, okay?"

Then she smiled at the wall above the table, where he had hung up a calendar and an old certificate from the shooting range. He was an excellent marksman.

"What am I wearing?"

She looked down at herself, at the green corduroy trousers and the checked flannel shirt that she was wearing.

"A beautiful red, strapless dress made of pure silk. And I'm very tanned. I've just been to Israel. You're talking to a Jewish woman. Haven't you ever had a Jewish woman?"

Sejer had just taken a bite of his sandwich, and now he just about choked on it. He looked at his dog, grateful for the fact that he couldn't understand. Instead, he switched on the television and stared at the screen, at the face reading the news, which he couldn't hear, because he had turned down the sound. Out of sheer politeness he had turned down the sound. But now he decided to turn it up loud and make her hang up the phone. There was a war on the screen. Fighter planes taking off from a ship and flying like bolts of metallic lightning through the sky. He could feel the G-force as he sat in his chair.

"Good night, dear."

Sara hung up the phone. She walked across the room and perched on the arm of his chair.

"Didn't you see the roast beef in the fridge?" she asked.

Roast beef? No, he hadn't seen any delicacies like that, he had been listening to her, bewildered. Besides, eggs were fine. A little too much cholesterol, of course, but rich in protein, and that's what he needed to keep his muscles strong.

"Who were you talking to?" he asked.

"Phone sex," she said with a laugh as she brushed back her long fringe. Not the least embarrassed. He didn't say anything. He didn't feel hungry any more.

"I was bored, and you weren't here."

"Do you know how much it costs?" The words

flew out of his mouth, and then she laughed even more. She had a spontaneous, hearty laugh. He didn't understand why she was laughing. Actually, he would have preferred to be alone.

"So how do you know, my good man, that phone sex is so expensive?"

He didn't reply, just sat there feeling foolish. She kissed his rough, grey hair. "I've called them a lot, but I can afford it. I make more than you do." And then she laughed some more.

"But why?" he stammered.

"It's fun. There sits a real live man on the other end of the line." She leaned down and whispered in his ear. "You should try it sometime!"

He was still looking at his egg sandwich. It was only a matter of time before Kollberg snatched it away.

"Where did you get the number?" he asked, embarrassed.

"It was in the newspaper. There are lots to choose from. All depending on what your preference is. Aren't you curious?"

"No."

"They give you everything you want. Everything that's possible to send over a phone line, that is. And it's more than you might think!"

He picked up his sandwich, took a bite, and chewed carefully.

"You're freezing," Sara said. She put her hand on his cheek. She was hot as coals.

"Sometimes we just have to have a little fun in our lives, don't you think?"

Have fun? Was that important? The Devil rose up inside Konrad Sejer. He got up from his chair and towered over her with all of his 196 centimetres, and she sat there in surprise, like a little girl, looking up at him with concern. He thought: I'm stronger than she is. I could lift her up and carry her away. She could wriggle and squirm, but she wouldn't have a chance. He slipped his arm around her waist and held on tight, lifting her from the arm of the chair. She squealed with glee, but he noted with satisfaction the tiny hint of panic as he carried her across the room. He stopped in front of the old chest of drawers that had stood on Gamle Møllevej for all those years and weighed a ton. He bent his knees and with a groan set her firmly on the top of it. There was plenty of room. She shrieked with laughter.

"Sit still," he commanded, taking a few steps back. "If you move you'll fall off."

"I want to get down," she cried.

"You can't," he said. "Or the whole thing will topple over!"

"You can't leave me here," she said, laughing as she began to try to find a foothold to climb down, but stopped when she felt the chest start to topple under her weight.

"Don't move," he said gruffly. "I want to eat in peace. After that we'll go for a long walk."

He sat down again and started eating. Kollberg jumped around, barking and carrying on. He didn't recognise his master. Sara laughed so hard he had to tell her to hush, for fear the chest of drawers would pitch forward and crash to the floor. It was full of crystal. She ran a finger along the top. It was black with dust.

"I like dust," she teased him. "Dust contains a little of everything. A little of you and a little of me."

"Be quiet and let me eat!" he shouted.

Down by the river stood an elderly woman. She was standing to the right of the barge, which functioned as a café, but was closed now. She stood there a while, looking across at the railway station on the opposite bank. She stood erect, with an air of having finished something important. Then she took a few steps and stopped again, next to a stairway that led down to the water. She started down the steps. On the third step she stopped and raised her head to look at the bridge span, that long, slender line of concrete that connected the two parts of the town. People were walking back and forth across the bridge. The lights, thousands of them, glittered like broken reflections in the water. She went down another step. And then she did something odd that would have surprised anyone who might have noticed. She lifted up her coat, an old brown coat. Then she went down another step, and the water came up to her ankles. Now she was paralysed by the cold of the water. There were a lot of people in the square, but she was so unobtrusive, didn't make a sound when she finally fell forward into the water, with her arms spread out. She looked like a large child falling into a snowdrift.

"It's too bad she won't live. But then again, who does?"

It was spitting rain. Sara and Sejer were walking close together. Kollberg was on a short lead; the drizzle glittered in his rough coat. The few solitary souls still abroad started walking faster as they felt the rain come down harder. Sarah and Sejer cut across the square and headed over the bridge. Sejer wanted to go over to the other side and walk through the old neighbourhoods with the small shops. They walked at a brisk pace to stay warm. At the highest part of the bridge, they paused and leaned over the side. That's what people do at the top of a bridge. Enjoying the fact that they're still

347

alive. Sara looked at him. His distinctive face, strong and handsome. Especially his eyes and his thick hair. She buried her forehead in his coat sleeve and stared down at the eddies in the water.

"Are you tired, Konrad?"

"Yes," he said. "Sometimes I am."

"Too much going on at work?"

"Just the usual. But after all, I have been wandering around here on this earth for 440,000 hours."

"Good heavens! That's a lot!"

"Hm. You know Jacob. He's so playful. Whenever he's bored, he sits around with his pocket calculator."

Sara thought for a moment about that dizzying number. "You know," she said, "in a way it must be good to die in the water."

"Why's that?" he wanted to know. He didn't turn around, just kept looking down, and then over to the left towards the barge near the shore.

"To lie still and just float, to be licked clean by the water."

Licked clean. Perhaps. But the actual process of drowning wasn't like that. To hold your breath, feel your eyes bursting, and then your lungs, until you started to rise, swell up, and everything exploded inside your head. And finally, the fog. That's what he had heard. Red and warm.

"Just think of all the people who are dead under

that water," Sara said. "People we don't know about."

This is a dreary town, he thought, especially in the rain. So forsaken on the shore of this roaring river. But the bridges enchanted him whenever he saw them, all beautiful arched spans surrounded by glittering lights. Sejer looked back towards the square. Suddenly he let go of Sara's hand. She followed his gaze down towards the barge.

"A woman," he said, "she's standing on the steps. With water up to her knees!"

He let go of the dog's lead. Set off on his long legs, with Sara close behind. Sejer's shoes pounded the pavement and people started turning around to look at him. Kollberg raced along, his heavy body rippling as he ran. People who were coming towards them stepped aside at the sight of the big animal. Sejer reached the end of the bridge, hurtled round the edge, and raced for the stairs. For a moment he stopped to catch his breath. Something was floating in the water, something dark and compact. He ran down the steps, keeping his eyes on the heavy body rocking on the water. Slowly it sank. The ice-cold water spilled into his shoes, but he didn't feel it; he was trying to calculate the direction of his dive so that he could grab her.

"Don't do it," shouted Sara. "The current will take you!"

He turned part-way around, thinking: She's right. He wouldn't be able to do it, they would both go under. But he couldn't stand there without trying. Just stand there and watch her die. Sara ran down the steps, grabbed his arm, and shouted at his pounding head.

"Don't do it!"

She's afraid, he realised in surprise. Then the body disappeared. He followed a fleck of foam with his eyes. Saw the roaring speed of the river and thought: I was just about to drown, the way she drowned. He raised his hands and blew on them.

"It was a woman," he murmured.

He patted his hip and found his mobile phone. Kollberg was on the shore, barking. People came running from all directions. To stand here like this, he thought, just stand here and watch someone go under. It hardly seems possible.

The fire started in the kitchen. The coffee maker had been on for hours and was piping hot. The flames grew fast, and swiftly licked along the curtains. Soon they reached the red chair and the rug on the floor. The heat was now shimmering in the room; plastic melted, things fell apart and the blaze kept spreading, to the next room and the next. Outside, a great roaring sound came from the windows. A bicyclist noticed the flames.

The fire brigade arrived seven minutes later, and after them, the crime technicians. They fought their way inside, searching the rooms. The trap door to the cellar stood wide open. They looked down inside. Wiped the sweat and soot from their faces.

It was pitch dark. A policeman switched on his pocket torch, swung the beam of light around. Something greyish-white lay on the floor at the bottom of the stairs. More people arrived. They moved cautiously down the first steps and looked down as they shone their lights. They fell silent. They stared at the tarpaulin. At the bottom they had to step over it and stand on either side. The plastic had grown soft from the heat; it no longer rustled. They pulled it away. Stared in horror at what lay beneath. A tangled mass of plastic and hair and skin. It was, in a word, indescribable.

CHAPTER 23

September 10.

What Sejer remembered most clearly from his mother's funeral was the sound of dry sand striking the lid of the coffin. He couldn't get it out of his head. He opened the window to air the room, sat down and started again. More and more pieces of the great tragedy were piling up on his desk. A picture, however vague, was slowly taking shape. But he couldn't believe his eyes. How could this have happened? And why? Irma's body was fished out of the river the evening after she drowned. She was found floating against an old, rotting bridge foundation under the overpass. There she lay, rocking on the water, in the glittering lights. The bag had been rinsed clean in the river, but it was still in place under the tight vest. And then the fire. The discovery in the cellar. The circumstances in that dark room. What did it mean? To think that he had stood in her kitchen, only metres away from the boy. He remembered the feeling he had as he stood in front of her. The conclusion he drew at once, that she was not quite right in the head.

So what? That didn't give him the right to search her house.

He glanced up as Jacob Skarre came in, waving some papers.

"This is unbelievable," he muttered. It was the report from forensics. Skarre dropped into a chair. Sejer read aloud.

"'The boy, four months old, was found dead in his bed. The autopsy reveals that the cause of death was an epidural haematoma. A bleeding between the cranium and membrane of the brain. This is a result of a head injury. Such haematomas arise over time. They lead to increased pressure, and the swelling travels down the length of the spine, where it affects the respiratory system. Essentially, the child died because he stopped breathing. Immediately following the event, the child may seem perfectly normal, without visible symptoms. The doctor at the casualty department cannot be faulted for his evaluation. After a few hours, fatigue and lethargy set in. Lapsing in and out of consciousness. It is therefore reasonable to surmise that the child died as a direct result of his fall from the pram. The fall which, in turn, can be blamed on the assault perpetrated against the mother.'"

"Does this mean that we could have charged

Andreas with manslaughter?" Skarre wanted to know.

Sejer smiled bitterly. "Not even with the most ill-tempered judge in the land. They stole a handbag from her pram. They didn't touch her. That's simple theft, with a maximum sentence of three years. But it would never have happened. A young boy. First-time offence. He would have got off. With a severe fright and a warning."

"But the baby's mother – what about her?"

"Well. The mother is responsible for her own child, under any circumstances. She let go of the pram. And she didn't set the brake properly." He shook his head. "What does the report say about Andreas? What did they find out?"

"It looks like a nightmare. If they're correct in their assumptions."

"Which are?"

"That either he fell, or was pushed down the cellar steps. When he landed on the cellar floor, he broke his neck, or to be more precise, cervical vertebra number four. The injury would have caused significant paralysis from his neck down. So that's where he lay."

"And then she bashed in his head with a hammer," said Skarre.

"Yes. But not straightaway."

Sejer pushed the papers aside and stood up. He

leaned against the filing cabinet, tapping his fingers against the green metal.

"There are indications that he lay there for a while. All alone on the floor. With a broken neck."

"Define 'a while'."

"Several days. He disappeared on September 1, right? One of the wounds on his head, probably caused by his fall, was different from the rest. It wasn't deep enough to have caused a coma, maybe just occasional loss of consciousness. And it was severely infected. That kind of thing takes time. In addition, he had bedsores, on his back and elsewhere. And there was a blanket covering him. And a heater nearby. She was holding him prisoner. He must have taken in nourishment in some way, at least water. She gave him water," he concluded, sounding amazed.

"The baby bottle," Skarre said.

"What are you talking about?"

"She gave him water in a baby bottle. I stood behind her in a queue at the supermarket and she left it behind. It surprised me that she was buying such a thing. What do you think Andreas was doing there?"

"Money," Sejer said. "He had a knife with him. They found it under the workbench. A confirmation gift from his father."

"At the house of his mother's friend? Was that smart?"

"He may not have known who lived there. By the way, Irma Funder is in our files."

"Why's that?"

"She came here eleven years ago to report her husband missing. He disappeared without trace. Emptied his bank account and took his passport with him. Yet she claimed that something must have happened to him. Later her son showed up. Ingemar Funder. Quite embarrassed. He had found a letter in his father's office in which he explained that he couldn't stand things any more and was leaving the country. Some people can't handle that," he said. "Being abandoned that way. It must have been too much for her."

Neither of them spoke for a while. Skarre bit his lip. "You've talked to the son? What did he say?"

"Not much. He just sat and nodded gloomily. He already looked pretty gloomy, even before this. He looks like his mother."

"This is bloody awful – sorry," said Skarre, "but I'm thinking about that day when she stood in my office. I remember what she said. 'I know where he is. He probably won't live much longer.' And afterwards, when I asked her where she lived. And she gave me her address. Prins Oscars gate 17. Carefully enunciating the consonants as she looked into my eyes. She wanted to tell me where he was, but I didn't understand. He may still have been alive then," Skarre said.

"It torments me no end that we'll never get to hear Irma's version. And now it's too late. We can't charge anyone with anything. Can we?"

He had talked to everyone. Runi Winther and Ingemar Funder. Tried to explain. Did his best to find a version that they might be able to handle, but that seemed impossible. Zipp's mother had called, again and again. He didn't have much to tell her, just that they were doing everything they could. Then he went out to his car and drove through the streets, trying to take stock of things. Of what had happened and where he stood in his life. He was going home to Sara. Mother is dead and buried, he thought. And he felt the thin grooves of the steering wheel under his fingertips. His shoes were big enough for him to curl his toes. Am I living in the moment? No, he thought, because in my mind I'm already home. Without knowing what awaits me. Sara. With a hot meal. Or maybe she's left. This life is inhuman. One long descent, that ends in . . . well, what did he know? Lukewarm water? Shattered glass? That's more than enough, he concluded. Then he started making plans for the following day, as he always did. A few fixed points. For any eventuality. Even though anything might happen, and something important might turn up, he liked to itemise things, no matter how insignificant.

Kollberg was alone. He patted the dog to calm him and looked around. Caught sight of the note on the dining-room table. She's gone, he thought. He walked across the room and took a deep breath. Spread out the piece of paper. "Had to go see Pappa. Will be right back. Fish casserole in the oven. For you, you sugar dumpling."

Not what he had expected.

CHAPTER 24

September 11.

Ingemar Funder was driving an old Ford Sierra. He was a stout, dark-haired man with a heavy face and dark, deep-set eyes. He did everything with a quiet and modest manner, and he never drew attention to himself. He was known as a calm and meticulous man who never complained. But he lived alone. The company of others was too difficult for him. He stopped at the gate and got out. Looked up at the ruined house. He walked along the gravel and around the side of the house. It was dark, but he could see the gazebo that his father had built. A 40th wedding anniversary present for his mother. It was untouched by the fire and quite beautiful. He walked up the two steps and sat on the bench inside. He sat there for a long time. He thought about everything that had happened, and realised that he could go on as he had before. Then he stood up. He tested the floorboards with his foot. Some of the planks were loose and gave under his weight. He went out to the lawn. It had stopped raining. The clouds split open, and the light of a pale moon struck his powerful shoulders. For a moment he stood there, bathed in the bluish-white light. Eleven years had passed. Fifteen minus eleven is four, he thought. "Statute of limitations regarding penalties and other legal consequences: A deed is no longer punishable when the statute of limitations has occurred in accordance with clause 67–69." Four more years. At times, over the course of the past years it had occurred to him that his mother didn't remember. That she had simply repressed it all. They had never checked the handwriting on the letter. It had never occurred to them to do so. He was trustworthy. In a flash he remembered his mother's voice, her desperate scream and burning eyes. You have to help me, Ingemar!

*

As for the body of Andreas Winther and what took place in the cellar of the deceased, the police consider this a mystery. It is also unclear why he was in Funder's house. The only one who might be able to clarify matters is 18-year-old Sivert Skorpe, who spent September 1 with Andreas. However, this individual has disappeared. He is 1.70 metres tall, with blond hair, cut short. He is wearing tight black jeans and probably a leather jacket. He speaks with an eastern Norway accent. When he says anything at all, that is. Any information about this individual should be reported to the nearest police station.

Maybe you've seen him?